Searching for Patty Hearst

Roger D Rapoport

lexographic press

Advance praise for *Searching for Patty Hearst*

"Searching for Patty Hearst is the Catch 22 of the radical terrorist actions in the latter part of last century. It is an amazing, clever re-creation of those troubling times. The ultimate California love story."

Henry Massie
author of *The Boy Who Took Marilyn to the Prom* and *Lives Across Time.*

"The kidnapping of Patty Hearst was one of the most extraordinary stories of its time, and all of us who followed it imagined, many times, the conversations, inner struggles, and clandestine meetings that must have taken place out of our sight. How nice it is to now see the skilled Roger Rapoport weave such ingredients, and his own extensive knowledge of the case, into this gripping, evocative, and suspenseful novel."

Adam Hochschild, author *American Midnight* and *King Leopold's Ghost.*

"A very fine and revealing read."

Dr. Russ Ellis, Vice-Chancellor for Student Affairs Emeritus the
University of California at Berkeley.

"Award winning Journalist Roger Rapoport writes a timely reminder of the story of Patty Hearst's kidnapping in outstanding novel form. Rapoport goes over and beyond the original news stories and presents this narrative thanks to his extensive research, relentless interviews and personal ties, making Searching for Patty Hearst a must read 50 years later and beyond."

Shelley Irwin, host The Morning Show
WGVU/NPR West Michigan.

"Living on the West Coast during the Search for Patty Hearst fifty years ago, it was wonderful to retrace the essence of this singular piece of history, and to be given a new slant on it from someone who had been reporting on the events even as they occurred. This novelization of what may have happened, is thoroughly enjoyable, probably truer than other accounts, and certainly more entertaining."

Richard Riehle actor
Office Space, The Fugitive, Grounded For Life, Glory, Casino,
Fried Green Tomatoes

"What a joyous, mind-bending excursion to have the legendary Roger Rapoport doing up a novel on the legendary Patty Hearst. Always a world-class story teller, Roger's fiction is far more factual than today's plodding feature at the Times or Post....and way more fun to read. I mean.... who could resist this stranger-than-fiction true tall tale rendered even more luminous by a genius scribbler's freedom to tell the REAL truth? Thanks Roger. Thanks Patty. You make a great couple. See you both at San Simeon!!!"

Harvey "No Nukes" Wasserman, author,
The People's Spiral of US History and *Solartopia: Our Green-Powered Earth.*

"With all the skill and aplomb of the writer, editor, playwright, screen writer, journalist and movie producer that he is, Roger Rapoport tells the Patty Hearst story so that it is almost impossible to discern where fact gives way to fiction. Searching for Patty Hearst is both compelling and captivating, and it gives a whole new meaning to the term metafiction."

Peter Ferry, author of *Old Heart* and *The Travel Writer.*

"Roger Rapoport's tale about his 50 year-search for the truth about Patty Hearst's sensational kidnapping grabs your attention and holds you hostage until the very last page. A brilliant blend of dogged factual reporting and fiction."

Ronald G. Shafer
former *Wall Street Journal* Washington political features editor

Searching for Patty Hearst

Roger D Rapoport

cover design: James Sparling

book design: lexographic, typeset in Jubilat designed by Joshua Darden

Library of Congress LCCN: 2023943719

ISBN (paperback): 978-1-958156-02-5
ISBN (ebook): 978-1-958156-09-4
ISBN (audiobook): 978-1-958156-10-0

published by Lexographic Press LLC
5000 S Cornell Ave, Unit 6A, Chicago IL 606015

read@lexographicpress.com | lexographicpress.com

® Lexographic Press is a registered trademark in the US no. 6560471.

Distributed by Pathway Book Service
34 Production Ave, Keene, NH 03431, 1-800-345-6665

For James Sparling and Megan Trank,
friends, fellow travelers and partners in crime.

It is a trap of history that eyewitnesses remember accurately what they have lived through.

Theodore H. White

The difference between fiction and reality? Fiction has to make sense.

Tom Clancy

Searching for Patty Hearst

A Novel

Roger D Rapoport

Publisher's Note

Roger Rapoport has covered the Patty Hearst case as a journalist since 1974. Although this novel is inspired by that experience, it is a work of fiction. While some of the events described in this book, such as the kidnapping, the SLA communiques, the Hibernia bank robbery and the Mel's Sporting Goods shootout actually happened, this novel is a product of the writer's imagination. I'll let the author explain on the following page. Thanks for buying this book. It's an honor to have you with us.

James Sparling, Publisher, Lexographic Press

Author's Note

The 'facts' of the Patty Hearst case, especially her kidnapping and participation in a San Francisco bank robbery, have been the subject of both a legal and journalistic dispute for many decades. Today the "true" story as presented from many points of view continues to raise just as many questions as it answers. Rather than get bogged down by endless attempts to sort out the details that led to Patty Hearst's conviction in federal court, I have created a fictional narrative that attempts to make this often confusing story believable. This is what novelists do, going for what matters most to the narrative line. That means the actions of the characters, including myself, are not based on fact. The dialogue with very few exceptions (the SLA communiques and portions of the Bill Harris interview which actually appeared in the *Oakland Tribune*) did not actually happen. For example, people like Harry Harris exist, but he did not do the things attributed to him in this novel.

The actions attributed to these characters did not occur in the manner portrayed. In this book I am a storyteller, not a journalist attempting to tell the truth. What you are about to read is fiction.

Patty Hearst and Steven Weed, the central figures in this book, are dream characters for a novelist and I very much appreciate the way the two of them conducted themselves in the years since this case ended. Completely rewriting their journey, adding characters, inventing situations, creating dialogue and events in a novel that sheds light on one of the most important crime stories of the 20th century has been an honor.

Roger Rapoport, Author, Muskegon May 2023

Dramatis Personae

THE HEARSTS
Phoebe Apperson Hearst (her great grandmother)
William Randolph Hearst (her grandfather)
Millicent Hearst (her grandmother)
Catherine Hearst (her mother)
Randolph Hearst (her father)
William Randolph Hearst Jr. (her uncle Bill)
Patty Hearst
Will Hearst (her cousin)
Anne Hearst (her sister)

THE INNER CIRCLE
Marion Davies (her grandfather's long term mistress)
Anne Apperson Flint (Phoebe's niece)
Steve Weed (her fiancé)

TEACHERS & FRIENDS
Megan Walworth (Patty's classmate)
Cindy and Jeff Jensen (friends)
Sister Mary Catherine Francis (St. Jean's School for Girls San Francisco Director)
Edward Johnson (St. Jean's School for Girls San Francisco Art Professor)

THE SYMBIONESE LIBERATION ARMY MEMBERS, ASSOCIATES & VICTIMS
Donald DeFreeze (General Field Marshall)
Bill Harris (Comrade)
Emily Harris (Comrade)
Willie Wolfe (Comrade)
Angela Atwood (Comrade)
Camilla Hall (Comrade)
Patricia Soltysik (Comrade)
Nancy Ling Perry (Comrade)
Wendy Yoshimura (Patty's' Fellow Traveler)
Marcus Foster (Oakland Schools Superintendent)
Joseph Remiro and Russell Little (Defendants in Marcus Foster Murder Case)
Tom Matthews (SLA Kidnap Victim)
Jack and Micki Scott (Rented Poconos Hideout for SLA)
Eleanor DeFreeze (Donald Defreeze's Mother)

JUDGES, LAWYERS AND THE CORONER
Judge Oliver J. Carter (San Francisco Federal Court Trial Judge)
Vincent and Terrence Hallinan (Patty's First Attorneys)
F. Lee Bailey (Patty's Trial Attorney)
James Browning (San Francisco Federal Prosecutor)
Thomas Noguchi (Los Angeles Coroner)

ESTATE STAFF
Hank Nichols, (Wyntoon Manager)
Jim Carra (San Simeon Librarian)

FBI
Charles Bates (Agent in Charge San Francisco Office)
Cindy Winton (FBI Agent San Francisco)
Bobbie Winton (Cindy's Husband, a Police Officer)
J. Edgar Hoover (FBI Director)

UNIVERSITY OF MICHIGAN
Deborah Bacon (Dean of Women)
Peter Eckstein, Michigan Daily Editor

MEDIA
Harry Harris (*Oakland Tribune* Crime Reporter)
William Knowland (Publisher of the *Oakland Tribune*)
George Walsh (Ballantine Books Editor)
Marilyn Baker (San Francisco Reporter)
Baron Wolman (San Francisco Photojournalist)
Jonathan Larsen (Editor *New Times*)

THE ART WORLD
Massey (Angela Atwood's brother, an Art Appraiser)
Michael LeConte (Codirector)
Cari Sutcliffe (Codirector, Actress)
Tintoretto (Italian Master)
Elena Stromboli (Tintoretto Apprentice)

ROGER RAPOPORT'S FAMILY, REALTOR, ATTORNEY & AGENT
Judge Mark Brandler (Author's Great Uncle)
Estelle Brandler (Author's Great Aunt)
Arlene Slaughter (Author's Realtor)
David Pesonen (Author's Attorney)
Sterling Lord (Author's agent)

ACADEMICS, CLERGY, CIVIL RIGHTS LEADER
Sarah Anne Robinson (UC Santa Barbara Criminology Professor)
Rev. Cecil Williams (San Francisco Minister Glide Memorial Church)
Stokely Carmichael (Leader of Student Nonviolent Coordinating Committee)

Introduction

Sleeping With The Enemy

Will Hearst

Our marketing department at the Hearst Corporation tells me most readers skip introductions like this one. I appreciate your giving me a few minutes to celebrate the publication of this long-awaited book that offers breaking news in every chapter.

On the evening of February 4, 1974, I was a 27-year-old editor working late at Hearst headquarters in Manhattan. Tasked with helping my family's company create new magazines, my focus was on a cover piece about an aspiring Olympian battling multiple sclerosis. Millions of readers had come to expect this kind of human-interest story from our great company. Thanks to a team of top-notch writers and editors, our inspiring stories touched hearts from Nome to Key West. Faithful readers always looked forward to our features about courageous Americans equal to any challenge. They never tired of this kind of inspiring narrative inevitably ending on an optimistic note.

Trying to make a tight deadline, I was surprised to be interrupted by two company security officers who whisked me to a waiting sedan for the quick ride to New Jersey's Teterboro Airport. Five hours later the pilot of our company jet hung a right over San Jose and made his final approach to San Francisco International Airport runway.

When I arrived at the Pacific Heights home of my Uncle Randy and Aunt Catherine shortly after 3 a.m., a dramatic role reversal was underway. All of us in the extended Hearst family quickly discovered we were much better at covering the news than being the news. Suddenly the curtain was drawn back on the multi-billion dollar media dynasty my cousins and I were destined to inherit.

A mysterious enemy, the Symbionese Liberation Army, had taken one of our own. Kidnapped at the Berkeley duplex she shared with her 28-year-old fiancé Steve Weed, Patty Hearst would soon become the focus of one of the biggest people hunts in American history. Not since the Lindbergh baby kidnapping had there been anything comparable. Secrets that belonged only to us suddenly became staples in America's daily news diet. Within a couple of days our family was the focus of a worldwide media microscope. The whole world was watching how the Hearsts managed an unimaginable tragedy.

Until that terrible evening my 19-year-old cousin Patty was merely another heiress in waiting. We had grown up quietly in a bubble-wrapped world catered to by a coterie of nannies, drivers, tutors, tennis and golf pros, swim coaches and security teams, mostly moonlighting police officers. From Pebble Beach, to Cabo San Lucas, Lake Tahoe, Maui and Venice, we were citizens of the world. As global media influencers Patty's parents, Randy and Catherine, floated down the Potomac with the Kennedys on the White House yacht, dined at Buckingham Palace with Queen Elizabeth and Prince Phillip. They even enjoyed a private Vatican audience with Pope Paul. At the latter event his holiness invited Patty's parents to stay for dinner. Alas, they had to cut the visit off after 45 minutes to rush over to a visit with Italy's prime minister.

Leaders everywhere genuflected to my family–proprietors of one of the most effective media megaphones the world has ever known. Our influence, both domestic and foreign, was a given. When my father, chief editorial writer for the Hearst newspaper chain, spoke in his Sunday column, America listened. Our newspapers, syndicates and broadcast outlets held a firm grip on the nation's news coverage and quickly drowned out the opposition. From our standing ovation for the self-aggrandizing bigots running the House Un-American Activities Committee to our failure to denounce Ku Klux Klan lynchings in our southern newspaper towns, we had a dismal record on civil rights, voter rights, tax reform, national health care and McCarthyism. Our Washington bureau chief was, for many years, a favorite poker pal of J. Edgar Hoover.

Like me, Patty woke up every morning knowing that the solution to any problem was merely a phone call away. Someone who knew how to pull strings was quickly dispatched to keep us out of trouble. Smart, industrious, funny, beautiful, charming—these were some of the adjectives surrounding her each morning as she crossed Bancroft Way on her way to the University of California's verdant Berkeley campus laced by a stream flowing from Strawberry Canyon. This diminutive 19-year-old art history major loved flirting with my friends who envied her fiancé, Steve Weed, the leftist political firebrand and author she was set to marry at the end of her sophomore year. The fact that he had written a piece for *Ramparts* magazine calling our *San Francisco Examiner* one of America's ten worst newspapers was not being held against him. He and Patty had been in love since 1971 and there was no point in trying to talk her out of a Claremont Hotel wedding, where she would be too young to legally drink the Veuve Clicquot.

Settling in to my aunt and uncle's Pacific Heights guest bedroom with a view of Angel Island and Alcatraz, I recalled the last time I'd been with Patty, at a birthday celebration thrown for me at San Simeon. Now a California State Park, this grand coastal California estate, created by our grandfather William Randolph Hearst—'The Chief'—had been mocked in *Citizen Kane*, the drama perennially ranked number one on the American Film

Institute's list of best feature films. Fortunately our family had retained ownership of one of the ten room guest "cottages" where we all celebrated. That night, after gates were closed to tourists, the place was bedecked with piñatas stuffed with my mother's favorite Belgian chocolate. Patty's gift, a watercolor of my parents (Patty's aunt Bootsie and uncle Bill), was so beautiful I hung it above the fireplace in my New York living room.

Days after my sudden return to San Francisco, our company was being relentlessly demonized in a series of hateful communiques cranked out by the Symbionese Liberation Army. Around the country folks prayed for her and even sent donations to help cover the $4 million ransom demand. Weeks later this heartfelt sympathy collapsed when Patty joined her captors and dumped Steve in favor of a new lover, comrade Willie Wolfe. Now she was literally sleeping with the enemy, cranking out her own devastating communiques ridiculing our "corrupt" company's "feeble" efforts to pay her ransom as too little too late.

The *Examiner's* ace reporters had great difficulty covering this complex story. Dependable sources, normally happy to work with us on big crime coverage, refused to return our phone calls. It was challenging to write about tight-lipped federal and state authorities working behind the scenes with us to rescue Patty, particularly when she unexpectedly began releasing taped communiques on left wing talk radio KPFA denouncing her parents, Steve and our company as "fascist insects preying on the lives of the people."

With Patty crossing over to the dark side, any exposé we published on the tiny Symbionese Liberation Army could potentially compromise our attempt to ransom her. These new revolutionaries, who arrived with no introduction, mystified both the police and established leftist groups, such as the New World Liberation Front. At the same time they forced us to publish their outrageous lies on the *Examiner*'s front page as a precondition to further negotiations. We were ridiculed, humiliated and demonized. It was impossible to believe a word they or captive Patty said in their rambling diatribes attempting to portray the Hearst Corporation as the enemy of the people. This hostile takeover shook our credibility and left us impotent. Even worse, Patty, a private person who worked hard to preserve her anonymity, publicly accused my uncle and aunt of lying about their inability to afford a $4 million ransom demand.

Just three months after the kidnapping our family crisis took a terrible turn when my cousin became the Army's apparent partner in crime, robbing a San Francisco bank owned by the family of one of her close friends. Now no part of our far-flung empire was safe from these revolutionaries intent on upending our world of power and privilege.

As the story unfolded I imagined what might happen if each of the protagonists had an opportunity to tell their own side of this unique story. What did they see and hear? How had they responded to this crisis? More recently I wanted to know how this kidnapping and its aftermath impacted their lives.

Thanks to decades of persistence, Roger Rapoport has interviewed all surviving key players central to this historic American drama. By coincidence we were born on the same day in the same year: April 6, 1946. After graduating from the University of Michigan where he edited the *Michigan Daily*, Rapoport moved to San Francisco where he wrote for a magazine I published, *Outside*. An author of books on the student protest movement, nuclear power and Governors Pat and Jerry Brown, he also won awards for his Bay Area newspaper work. His coverage of Patty's kidnapping prompted other journalists covering the case to frequently interview him. His solid reporting landed him a six-figure contract with Ballantine Books.

Not only did he score the first interview with Bill Harris, the man who actually abducted Patty in a fireman's carry, he also managed to reach the coroner who autopsied six of her comrades. For this new book he spoke at length to many of the people who kept Patty one-step ahead of the law after she joined a San Francisco bank robbery. He also landed critical interviews with the young man present when she learned her revolutionary paramour, Willie Wolfe, had been killed. Another reportorial coup is the first interview with the FBI agent who busted her. Collectively these stories add up to a classic you will want to read and reread thanks to the persistence of a writer who doesn't understand the meaning of the word 'no'.

Details on what went wrong for the Symbionese Liberation Army during the night of the kidnapping will surprise you as much as they did me. Rapoport also pinned down facts about the Hearst Corporation that were news to insiders like myself. Key details on Patty's passion for Steve Weed offer a revealing portrait of their complicated love story.

If you are old enough to remember this kidnapping, you will appreciate these illuminating details news organizations like mine could never verify. Wading through a minefield of half-baked conspiracy theories, hearsay and utter nonsense, he offers first person accounts that provide unforgettable insights. Younger readers will discover that *Searching for Patty Hearst* is a not-to-be-missed time-traveling voyage into late-20th century America. I believe this book is the closest we will ever come to the true story of Patty's kidnapping, my family and these revolutionaries.

The reality of this case remains a moving target for all of us. Fortunately you are now in the capable hands of a gifted writer who has taken his time—half a century in fact—to tell the true story of the most remarkable kidnapping in American history. Ultimately it is up to you, the reader, to sort through conflicting accounts and reach your own conclusions about this landmark case. Although no eyewitness can offer the final word, this book is an indispensable journey through the labyrinth that is the taking of my cousin Patty Hearst, her time as a kidnapee, a revolutionary, a felon and eventually a free woman. I trust you will enjoy it as much as I have.

Publisher Will Hearst lives in San Francisco's Pacific Heights. He won the Pulitzer Prize for his coverage of the Zebra serial killings.

Roger D Rapoport

Oh No, I'm In Big Trouble

October 4, 1970

St. Jean's School For Girls, San Francisco

Steve Weed's fever was 102.4°. Three days earlier his doctor had diagnosed pneumonia and told him to cancel all appearances on the tour for *Is The Library Burning?*, his new book about the student power movement. Exhausted after a sleepless night, he had driven across the Bay Bridge on an Indian summer morning. Traffic was slow on this 80° day after a broken-down apple truck spilled crates of Granny Smiths across the roadway. By the time he arrived at St. Jean's, his audience had been chilling for 20 minutes. As he took his seat, Weed's fellow speaker Baron Wolman, the unofficial rock photographer of the '60s, surveyed the audience and whispered, "What a smorgasbord."

Weed spoke at many of these events and they all followed the same pattern. Students who had been in nursery school when Kennedy was inaugurated wanted to know how the counter culture had altered the nation's political currents. Sometimes the focus was on civil rights. On other days the New Left and what was left of the Old Left dominated the conversation. Vietnam War protests and draft card burnings were also popular topics. In some cases these events were hybrids, linking the music of the '60s to the political revolution that led to watersheds such as the Civil Rights and Voting Rights Acts. Everywhere you looked was the thought that this was the decade that transformed a nation and hopefully brought down the curtain on century-old Jim Crow laws, advanced women's rights and challenged religious orders like the Catholic Church to acknowledge its tepid response to the holocaust.

Everything about St. Jean's was perfect. The Greek pediments on the archway were a gift from the Crocker banking family. Descendants of one of the big transcontinental railroad pioneers, Collis P. Huntington, donated the stained-glass windows from the studio of Louis Comfort Tiffany. When the light was right the fountain in the St Jean's courtyard created impromptu rainbows.

An alumnus of Our Lady of Precious Blood on Detroit's Northwest side, Steve had enrolled in a Jesuit academy in 9th grade, before quitting to attend Cass Tech. Although he was a lapsed Catholic who avoided mass, the school was happy to welcome him and Wolman as part of a week-long high school history program featuring '60s icons. Steve never imagined he'd be teaching at Patty's school within a year.

Following introductions by the principal, Sister Mary Catherine Francis, Weed tuned in and out of Wolman's fascinating stories about immortalizing musical icons like the Grateful Dead, the Beatles, Joplin, Hendrix, Dylan and Morrison. Cynics said if you could remember the '60s you weren't really there, but Wolman had the photos to authenticate his presence, photos that had become an annuity. The students laughed at his funny backstage stories about icons that created the sound track for the new 'American Revolution'.

As Wolman segued to stories about Bill Graham and the

Fillmore rock music palace, Steve nearly dozed off. Only when his name was called at the end of an effusive introduction did he rise like a red-hot bagel popping out of a toaster.

"For me," he said after pausing for a sip of water to soothe his sore throat, "the '60's actually began in 1959 when I fell in love with the University of Michigan's Dean of Women."

While Steve continued, 16-year-old Patty Hearst, sitting in the back row with her best friend Megan Walworth, closed her eyes.

"You cool?" asked Megan.

Patty blinked, took a deep breath and whispered:

"Oh no, I'm in big trouble."

"He's so old," said unsmitten Megan.

"He's perfect," she said as Steve continued.

Megan shook her head and began replying until a nun shushed her.

"We'd better chill," said Patty.

Steve, who had been booked by St Jean's history teacher on a solemn promise to abide by the school's code of conduct, coughed, sipped water and continued.

"I was just head over heels for a woman in her late sixties. Smitten is the word that comes to mind."

By now two of the nuns were whispering to one another. Perhaps it was time to cut Steve short and introduce another speaker. They listened nervously as he reminisced about his campus heartthrob, Dean Deborah Bacon:

"For more than 30 years she ruled women on campus as if they were all her daughters. Dean Bacon was famous for her patented brand of *in loco parentis*—a phrase I assume you all know from your Latin class. If a young woman failed to make it home in time for a dorm curfew, this administrator made sure that she was locked out for the night. If a coed bounced a check at a store there was no possibility of graduation without restitution in full.

"She was famous for her lectures about the hidden dangers

of tight sweaters and short skirts, anything hemmed above the knee. You see the Dean believed this blatant form of self-promotion was actually a health hazard, the sort of thing that could tempt young men to misbehave. Unwittingly these inappropriately dressed "tarts" were like KGB moles undermining what was left of morality and decency in our great country.

"Dean Bacon's worst fears were validated in 1954 when Michigan became home of the nation's first panty raid. A mob assembled outside Stockwell Hall chanting: 'We want panties, we want them now.' "

That was the point at which Sister Mary Catherine Francis decided to pull the plug on Steve's appearance. As the lights were dimmed he was escorted from the stage, much to the students' dismay.

"That's so bogus," Megan told Patty as the students filed out.

In the hallway Steve loudly offered to continue his story at another venue:

"It's been brought to my attention that some of my comments are making your faculty uncomfortable. As it turns out I'm speaking tonight at City Lights bookstore in San Francisco. Feel free to join me there where we can resume our conversation."

By the time he arrived at the North Beach bookstore, Patty had already finished the first chapter of Steve's new book, the one with a photo of the California National Guard standing in front of the University of California's administration building.

The store was filled with rapt St. Jean's students eager to learn more about the '60s from this controversial author. His book was a kaleidoscope of campus protest from coast to coast. Steve continued his Dean Bacon story where he'd left off, in the upstairs reading room—a shrine to Kerouac, Ginsberg, Ferlinghetti and the rest of the Beats.

"The one thing I know for sure is that none of us have all the answers. The essence of a great bookstore like City Lights is that every time you step through the door you are going to find something you disagree with. This is a place where so many great ideas collide. Now where was I...? Panties, right?

"The ground-breaking panties raid began on a warm night beneath the windows of Stockwell Hall.

"When the first woman tossed her underwear from the fourth floor a roar went up that could be heard across campus. One by one others joined in as the men held up their treasure for the benefit of *Michigan Daily* photographers.

"Dean Bacon, on the scene before the first undergarment was airborne, quickly called the cops. She dispatched house-mothers who ran up and down the corridors banging on doors in a vain attempt to take control. Finally, when someone pulled a fire alarm, women emerged in their nightgowns, including several with their hair rolled up in curlers."

"'*Do something!*' Dean Bacon screamed at the police who didn't know if any laws were being violated."

One of the young women in her navy St. Jean's uniform, white blouse, gray blazer, blue skirt and penny loafers, raised her hand.

"Mr. Weed."

"Please, it's Steve."

"Steve, help us out. Were the cops enjoying this spectacle?"

"They were speechless. None of this was in their training manual. They could have arrested the chanting men for disorderly conduct but the charges might not have stuck."

"Far out," said the mesmerized student.

"Like the young men, Dean Bacon was frustrated. Her solution was to jump on the hood of an Ann Arbor police cruiser. She shook her fist angrily and demanded that the guys disperse. At first the menacing men tried ignoring her. The girls watched as the guys began to realize they were about to be upstaged by a 5 foot 2 inch administrator in a black dress and sensible shoes. A cop handed her a megaphone as she scanned the women looking out their dorm windows and began speaking about the moral issue at hand:

"'I am so ashamed of all of you. Tomorrow your parents, who have sacrificed everything, are going to be calling my office. And what exactly do you think I'm going to say?

"'Oh hello, Mrs Clink.... Susie threw her panties out the window. But they were wearing thin. She didn't part with any of her good panties. It's really all for the best and nothing to worry about. If she were in a car accident you wouldn't want her going to the hospital where a young resident would examine her in that kind of underwear.

"'And when the Governor calls perhaps I will say: Ah yes, I want to thank those taxpayers who have been so generous. Their benevolent support has helped us educate these fine young men destined to make a name for themselves in the lingerie business.'"

Another student raised her hand.

"What did you love about Dean Bacon?"

"Five years later I inherited a file from a previous *Michigan Daily* editor, Peter Eckstein. Paging through I found interview notes from women pinpointing how Dean Bacon had written letters to parents of white women dating inter-racially. Although we didn't have the actual letters, Eckstein knew that some of these women had been forced to withdraw from school by their racist parents.

"After many months of trial and error I found one of these victims. She sneaked into her mother's bureau drawer and discovered a letter from the Dean. I took it to the campus administration with the story we were ready to publish. The woman's mother explained how grateful she was to the Dean for protecting her daughter from the possibility of losing her virginity to a black boyfriend: 'If she had been pregnant, I'm not sure what we would have done with that love child.'

"Deborah Bacon resigned the very next day. Our story was picked up by the *New York Times* and for me it was the first step to a dream career."

"In other words," said one of the young women, "it was your first big story. Dean Bacon made you semi-famous."

"Her power grew from the fact that no one had the courage to challenge her authority. When you think about it, no one, not the Regents, the administration, or the alumni, gave her the right to impose her worldview on the rest of us. She assumed the kind of power that we see far too often in this country, power that flourishes secretly behind closed doors. She had no right to interfere in the private lives of independent women. This sort of bigotry was at odds with the very purpose of a university, teaching students how to think independently, to never let anyone steal your freedom."

"Or your panties," Patty's friend Megan Walworth said. "This must have been terrifying for the women, a sort of prelude to rape. Wasn't she right to battle that?"

"No question, it was a horrible situation, inexcusable. Those men were engaged in the worst kind of sexual harassment. The *Michigan Daily* editors deplored it. A faculty petition gathered over 1,000 signatures and the administration threatened to expel anyone who engaged in this kind of behavior again."

"The '50s were all about instant self gratification," said Megan. "Women were victimized in so many ways."

"You're right. During the Depression my mother was a journalism major who couldn't get a job in a male dominated profession. In the '60s we tried to change that, to make sure women were always able to realize their full potential."

"But wasn't it Student Nonviolent Coordinating Committee's Stokely Carmichael who said, 'the only position for women in the movement is prone?' "

"He couldn't have been more wrong. I know that some of you here tonight will become exemplary leaders. Let's face it, you come from a world of privilege and I know that most of you will join the struggle to help those who grew up without all the advantages you enjoy.

"What went wrong at your own school today was an example of what we are all fighting for. Never let anyone dictate what you should think or how you should handle your own lives."

"Not even you," said Megan.

"The one thing I know for sure is that none of us have all the answers. That's what I love about this bookstore. It's a place where so many great ideas collide and perhaps out of that synthesis we can teach ourselves how to avoid some of the mistakes leading to avoidable conflict and bloodshed. Together we need to revolutionize this country. Hopefully that can happen peacefully."

Waiting in line after the talk, Patty watched Steve greet each customer like an old friend.

When it was her turn he asked if the book was a gift:

"It's for my mother's birthday."

"Great."

"She's a University of California Regent. She'll absolutely hate it."

"What's her name?"

"Catherine."

Steve picked up a pen and looked up at Patty.

"May I inscribe this to her as Cathy?"

"No, it's Catherine."

Steve thought for a second and then wrote:

Dear Catherine,

Your wonderful daughter tells me that you are a UC Regent. That's great. I, for one, would like to see more women on the board. How about asking Governor Reagan to nominate Angela Davis? Hope to meet you soon.

Very Truly Yours,
Steve Weed.

As she picked up the book Patty left a note:

Steve thank you for not backing down this afternoon and inviting us all here tonight. I'd love to come to your next talk. Please give me a call and let me know when I'll have another chance to catch up with you. My number is 555-0001. I'm psyched about seeing you again.

Very Truly Yours,
Patty Hearst

Brilliant. Roger, you really captured how our love story began. Thank you. Can't wait to see the next chapter.
–SW

The Harrises

February 1, 1974

Chez Panisse, Berkeley

"You must be the Harrises?"

It was fourteen minutes past seven and every table was full. The hostess paused to examine her reservations as Emily Harris, smiling and out of breath, touched her hand like a sister. "Our car died on Shattuck Ave. We ran all the way. It's our anniversary."

Her husband Bill was in no mood to wait.

"We could eat at the bar."

Emily glanced at the bartender pouring more Zinfandel for a paunchy Berkeley psychology professor and his graduate assistant with cascading red hair touching the belt loop of her jeans. The professor sipped his wine while she chatted with the much younger bartender, a premed student from Dakar.

"That won't be necessary," said the hostess. "Why don't you help yourself to a glass of champagne. We gave away your table but one of our eight o'clock reservations canceled. Their flight was delayed by fog."

Forty-five minutes later, Bill and Emily Harris were studying the menu as the waitress dropped off a complimentary pâté. A 6 p.m. party lingered at the end of a birthday celebration and showed no sign of wrapping up their festive dinner. Bill was fading. He had slept only two hours the previous night. Emily rubbed her hand along his thigh to keep him awake.

"I can't believe my mother did this for us."

"Your mother is a class act."

"She tries."

"She knows we're broke. You can't afford to go to the dentist and she sends you a gift certificate to Chez Panisse."

"It's our anniversary."

The Shoplifter

February 1, 1974

Berkeley

Donald DeFreeze, wearing one of his favorite disguises and sunglasses, was standing in the philosophy section of Moe's Bookstore on Berkeley's Telegraph Avenue unsubtly cramming a copy of Herbert Marcuse's *Critique of Pure Tolerance* into his jacket.

As he turned toward the door he felt a tap on his shoulder.

"Can I help you?" said a small man with a big cigar and a bald pate gleaming under the florescent light.

"Yes, I was wondering if you could tell me where the men's room is?"

"Up those stairs and to the right."

"Thanks."

"And, if you'd like to check that book you're about to steal, I can ring it up at the counter. We'll have it waiting for you. Would you like it gift wrapped?"

Roger D Rapoport

Willie Wolfe

February 2, 1974

Berkeley

Willie Wolfe was standing in line at Kragen Automotive on University Avenue with three quarts of motor oil. After paying, he headed out into the lot and put the funnel into his van's radiator.

"Whoa my friend," shouted a young woman with a denim backpack. "You don't want to do that. The radiator is for water."

Wolfe slapped the side of his head. "Brain fart."

The woman moved closer and touched his beard lightly.

"Amigo, let me introduce you to a wonder drug called coffee. I'm buying."

A few minutes later the woman was sitting across from Wolfe at Dream Fluff Donuts on Ashby.

"Aren't you Willie Wolfe?"

"Guilty, and you're, uh..."

"Angela Atwood."

"I remember you, the woman who did a monologue from Mamet's *Sexual Perversity in Chicago* that stunned our prof. He was smitten."

"Didn't you do the one about the cod piece?"

"I'm trying to forget."

"No really, it was incredible."

"You really think so?"

"Watching you, I was convinced you could be the perfect Macbeth."

"Not my favorite play, his wife was such a bitch. Hard to imagine how two such hateful people found love."

"You look exhausted. How about another cup, I'd love to hear more about what you're up to."

"Right now I'm getting ready to take a little trip."

"Maybe you could use a second driver."

The Car Jackers

February 3, 1974

Berkeley

The following morning the Harrises, still high from their night at Chez Panisse, and Donald DeFreeze (wearing his latest disguise and nursing a $12.99 hole in his wallet), were at Cafe Méditerranée on Telegraph, just south of the University of California campus. Ten minutes later Wolfe, foggy from a night on Acapulco Gold pot, and Nancy Ling Perry, who arrived with photos of a Chevy Nova parked in front of a bungalow on Josephine Street, joined them. As the meeting started the SLA's two latest recruits, Camilla Hall and Patricia Soltysik—aka Mizmoon-rode up on their Schwinns. Angela Atwood, a Berkeley Repertory Theater stagehand who occasionally took on character roles (and rocked an awesome Mamet monologue), soon joined them.

"That Nova looks like he bought it for spare parts at a wrecking yard," DeFreeze told Wolfe. "It's too slow. We need to grab something with a stick shift for the hills. I ain't getting away in no hooptymobile that dies on the way up Grizzly Peak."

"Hey, I'm new at this, okay," said Wolfe.

"Listen," said DeFreeze in a low voice. "You all need to start considering our reputation. You think Che would have shaken up the world if he showed up for the revolution in a rusty Nova with bald tires? Goddamn Walter Cronkite is going to be leading the news with us. Your car makes a statement. It defines who you are. You can't start a revolution in a beater."

Bill Harris interrupted: "I think what DeFreeze means is that a Nova will make us look like amateurs. Let's carjack something a little classier."

Camilla Hall nodded. "For a week Angela and I have had our eye on the perfect steal. We've got the movements of the owner, a chemistry professor, down. It will be an easy grab."

"Let's get it done," said DeFreeze. "Now!"

Waiting For Massey

February 4, 1974

3033 Woolsey St., Berkeley

"I told you no anchovies!"

Patty Hearst grabbed the Piero's pizza box and headed out to the garage.

"I'll throw it out and do a shrimp pasta."

"We always order the 'everything but'," continued Steve.

"I already said I'm sorry."

As she raised the steel lid on the backyard garbage can a minute later, Steve grabbed the pizza and returned it to the dinner table. Flipping open the box he picked off the anchovies as if they were an endangered species. When Patty tried to help, he brushed her aside.

"Sorry I yelled but we always get everything but anchovies."

"I was spaced out," said Patty collapsing on a maroon couch strewn with pages from the fourth draft of her paper on Modigliani forgeries.

"My mother knows which buttons to push to launch me into orbit. I'm still re-entering earth's atmosphere after our North Beach walk last Sunday. The sun was out for the first time in weeks. She tried to behave. Then, as I was getting into the car, she gave me that look, probably the same one she got from her mother after announcing her decision to marry dad at 19."

"But he was a catch, a Hearst. She was set for life."

"Her mother was convinced Catherine was marrying the wrong Hearst. She preferred his twin brother David."

"Ah, Prince David."

"My grandmother guessed David was the heir apparent."

"I think Daddy grew up with an undiagnosed case of attention deficit disorder. Unfortunately that was before Ritalin was invented."

"What did your mother say?"

"'Patty, darling, I think you can do better.'"

"And?"

"I told her you were the smartest man I'd ever met and that the sex was fantastic. She cut me off when I started describing our orgasms."

"You did not."

"Just making sure you aren't tuning me out. I told her you were a lovely, sensitive man who would always look out for me."

"She adores you."

"Yes, we love each other in a strange way. Don't be too tough on her. It's not easy being the last Republican in San Francisco. She thinks Ronald Reagan should run for President. Ha!"

"No way. That's never gonna happen."

"A lot of people fondly remember Reagan playing that dying Notre Dame football star George Gipp in *Knute Rockne All American*. You know, telling the coach from his hospital bed that the team had to go out there and 'win one for the Gipper.'"

"Trust me, this time Reagan is going to lose one for the Gipper."

"What's your next move?"

"I'm going to add one more item to my Gump's registry: Acid for my mother to drop on the eve of our wedding."

After dinner Steve finished the dishes while Patty dried. He loved sloshing about in warm soapy water. A few months earlier he had disconnected their dishwasher, now only used for storage.

"Did I ever tell you how we all had to show up in our pajamas at family dinner parties?" said Patty.

"Back when you lived in the Frank Lloyd Wright place."

"...with the tree in the middle of the courtyard?"

"Yes."

"Didn't she fire Wright?"

"Nothing personal, mom fired all kinds of people, even Catholics. She was always having dinner parties where my sisters and I were brought downstairs to meet the guests. Once we'd finished saying good night she'd send us upstairs. One evening she welcomed a visiting Russian pianist who had played the third Rachmaninoff piano concerto at the War Memorial Opera House. It was weird parading in bright sunlight wearing our matching bunny jammies. I had the ones with the ears sticking up. It was so embarrassing.

"After we had all made nice my mother clapped her hands, a signal that it was time for us to magically disappear to our respective bedrooms as if we were members of the von Trapp brood in the *Sound of Music.*"

"I, of course, didn't take it well. I picked up my brown bear and began whining. 'But mom, it's only 5 p.m. It's not even dinner time.'"

"Our nanny, Francesca, swept us up and led the way to our rooms. I went on a sit down strike. Francesca had to drag me up the grand staircase on my butt to my room. I sat there looking out the window at all the neighbor kids having a ball on their bikes."

"Did you go down for dinner later?"

"No, that was our curtain call. The party went on for hours. The pianist played several encores. While my sisters read, I climbed into the attic and opened the door to the fire escape.

I waited until dark, headed down to the back lawn and snuck over to a friend's house. We spent the evening playing Clue. By the time I returned home the party was over. Francesca let me in through the kitchen door and I headed up the back stairs.

"Everything would have gone perfectly were it not for the fact that when I reached the second floor landing my dad was sitting in a big winged chair reading the Examiner. I started sobbing and gave him a big hug."

"'Patty,' he asked as I headed upstairs, "please don't tell your mother.'"

As Patty began pouring another glass of zin' for Steve the doorbell rang.

"Oh my God, I completely forgot about Massey."

As Patty rose, Steve motioned for her to stay put.

"Let me get it."

As he turned the lock Patty walked into their bedroom and grabbed her notes for their meeting with the art appraiser.

The Taking Of Patty Hearst

February 4, 1974

3033 Woolsey St., Berkeley

In the spring of 1929 Patty's grandfather, William Randolph Hearst went on another one of his legendary art buying sprees in Spain. Inspired by his boyhood grand tours of Europe with his mother, he prowled auctions across the continent like a big game hunter. Vast catalogs of upcoming shows across the continent were bedtime reading and auctioneers leapt when he entered the bidding. Many of the paintings and statues he'd purchased remained uncrated at Wyntoon, the family's crown jewel of an estate in the shadow of northern California's Mt. Shasta. In addition, favorite pieces from his San Simeon estate in central California were also moved there after his passing in 1951. Private treasures never displayed in public areas were part of the shipments from the central coast to the family's forest Valhalla.

During the winter of 1973-74 one of Patty's cousins presided over a fire sale limited to the old man's descendants. Bids for these fabulous antiques, rugs, and paintings were set at roughly 2 percent of decades old appraisals. Younger members of the family were even allowed to spend their anticipated inheritances to bid for these heirlooms on a layaway plan that would finish on their 21st birthdays. This was yet another one of the Hearst perks Steve struggled to reconcile with his political beliefs. After spending hours studying the private family catalog of what was on offer, he told Patty,

"Soon I'll own part of what I've been fighting against. I can't believe these treasures will be mine. "

"Ours," said Patty as she grabbed his hand, "ours."

One of Patty's UC Berkeley art professors recommended a San Francisco appraiser named Massey. He was dropping by to help Patty and Steve authenticate a painting of special interest. Even at bargain prices no buyer wanted to be stuck with a forgery.

Peering through the front door peephole Steve realized the caller wasn't their invited guest. In a city where 'No Soliciting' signs were often found on the doors of compassionate conservatives and liberals alike, Steve supported solicitors working for causes such as the Sierra Club, American Civil Liberties Union, Ralph Nader's Public Citizen and Greenpeace. His empathy was rooted in his years working his way through college soliciting in white Ann Arbor neighborhoods for the NAACP.

"It's a time-honored American tradition known as liberal guilt," he told friends. "It's the only progressive job many of these kids can get where they earn a little money and get some exercise."

This visitor, Angela Atwood, looked like she had just stepped out of a Pre-Raphaelite painting. She was missing the familiar solicitor's clipboard displaying checks from other donors. She did not have a lanyard with a photo I.D. verifying her employment. Her black scarf, necklace and curly back hair complemented makeup that easily qualified her for a job at a Macy's cosmetics counter. She looked upset.

"Sorry, but my car broke down," she told Steve. "I'm on my way to a performance. It's really important to me. I can't be late."

"Do you need a phone?"

"I'd appreciate it. I've got to call triple A."

The young woman advanced through the open door onto an heirloom Oriental rug that Steve and Patty received from her parents, a concession to their impending May nuptials. She paused to compliment Steve on the beautiful print hung by the hall tree.

"I just love Schiele. Where did you get this?"

"My fiancée picked it up at a gallery in Vienna last year."

"Did you know Schiele graduated from the same art college that rejected Hitler?"

"Fun fact," said Steve. "The phone's in the kitchen. Let me know if you need anything."

While she headed toward the kitchen two hooded men, Donald DeFreeze and Bill Harris, barged in waving carbines. The visitor with the 'car problem' bound, gagged and blindfolded Patty. When Steve began screaming DeFreeze stunned him with a rifle butt to his head. Meanwhile Harris rummaged about the house flinging belongings to the floor. Minutes later, he flung Patty up over his shoulder in a fireman's carry. He headed out the door for the trunk of a carjacked Chevrolet Impala. Because he had left the engine running for a quick getaway, the keys were still in the ignition. Realizing the lid was locked, Patty's kidnapper lowered his precious cargo to the driveway and ran around the side of the car to retrieve his keys.

Patty's getaway bunny hop across the driveway came to an abrupt end when she tumbled into a bed of ice plants. Seconds later she was retrieved and stowed in a trunk covered with several bags of potting soil. As the kidnappers backed down the driveway, an upstairs neighbor opened a sliding glass door. Gunfire from DeFreeze prompted them to close it again.

While the kidnappers sped off down College Avenue, Steve, dazed and bleeding, one eye bruised and shut, jumped up and ran out the back door of the house, sprinted through the garden and leaped a fence into a neighbor's yard. In just five minutes the daughter of a University of California Regent, sophomore art major Patty Hearst, had become the first captive of the new Symbionese Liberation Army: one of the smallest rebel groups in the American underground.

Roger, this is pretty good. It was a pretty brutal whack to my head. Lucky they didn't kill me or leave me with brain damage. —SW

Feeling Sorry For Her

February 4, 1974

The East Bay

With Patty Hearst safely tucked away in the trunk, the kidnappers headed up to Claremont Boulevard where Willie Wolfe was waiting in a carjacked van. The three kidnappers-Bill Harris, Angela Atwood and Donald DeFreeze-followed Wolfe in their Chevy Impala toward the Claremont Hotel, where couples on the deck watched the bay as they sipped their wine.

Suddenly a Berkeley Police squad car pulled alongside Wolfe's van. When an officer signaled for him to pull over, DeFreeze, riding shotgun in the car with Hearst, put his hand on the trigger of the bloody semiautomatic which had smashed Steve's head minutes earlier.

"Wait," whispered Atwood. After the policeman told Wolfe to turn on his headlights, the young SLA member politely thanked the alert officer for his help and headed up Claremont Canyon.

As the policeman sped off on a call to the crime scene at Steve and Patty's trashed home, the car and van proceeded up to the Tilden Park kids' steam train parking lot. There Harris and

DeFreeze quickly transferred Hearst onto the floor of Wolfe's van, abandoned the Chevy and headed south, down serpentine Grizzly Peak Boulevard, past lovers parked at turnouts overlooking San Francisco Bay with a view of the Golden Gate bridge on the horizon.

"The three men continued down the hill to the Caldecott Tunnel with bound and gagged Patty. After heading east to Walnut Creek, they turned south to San Jose and then north up the Peninsula. The rest of the SLA revolutionaries–Angela Atwood, Emily Harris, Camilla Hall, Patricia Soltysik and Nancy Ling Perry–followed in another car.

Determined to calm the woman he had just carried out of her apartment, Bill Harris held his victim's limp hand.

"We were supposed to be these big tough revolutionaries," he wrote that night in his diary. "But now, an hour after the kidnapping, I was starting to feel a little sorry for Patty. I held her hand for the next two hours as we headed for our first safe house.

"Intellectually, I saw that kind of sympathetic attitude could become a problem. It was just the sort of thing that could compromise my objectivity and lead to tactical mistakes that would interfere with bringing this action to a successful conclusion. This wasn't natural for me. But then I'd never done anything like this before. I wasn't like DeFreeze. I'd never served time. This was my first crime, my first action. No one becomes a revolutionary in a single day."

A Wake Up Call

February 5, 1974

Pacific Heights

A full moon lit up the hills of San Francisco as jets descended over San Francisco Bay like blinking stars. FBI Agent in Charge Charles Bates buzzed the intercom outside the Pacific Heights gate for a third time. This time he held the buzzer down until a man's faint voice came through the speaker.

"Who is it?" asked Patty's father.

"Mr. Hearst, this is Charles Bates with the FBI."

"Mr. Bates, it is after midnight. Could this wait until tomorrow? Perhaps you could drop by the office."

"Didn't you receive my voicemail?"

"I'm sorry. We turn off the ringer when we retire."

"Please, it's urgent."

"I'll buzz you in."

In the living room, Randy Hearst smoothed his bathrobe as Bates asked: "Is Mrs. Hearst able to join us?"

"She's still asleep. Shall I wake her?"

"Please, if you don't mind. We have an emergency situation."

A few minutes later Randy Hearst returned with his drowsy wife Catherine.

"My, my," she said while shaking the agent's hand. "I didn't know the FBI still made house calls."

Breaking The Blackout

February 4-5, 1974

The Bay Area

The first reporter on the scene at the recently 'remodeled' Hearst/Weed townhouse in Berkeley was the *Oakland Tribune's* Harry Harris. He had caught the news on his scanner while home watching white racist Archie Bunker make an ass out of himself on *All In the Family*.

Harry never missed an episode and his favorite TV dinner—Salisbury steak washed down with a beer—was the perfect coda to a long day on the police beat. Beloved, honored and admired by all, he had been drafted to lead the staff presentation at the *Tribune's* centennial set for February 21 at the Claremont. No expense was being spared for this gala where Publisher William F. Knowland, US Senate Majority Leader during the Eisenhower era, would be celebrating the longevity of the family publishing business with numerous celebrities including Governor Reagan and Supreme Court Chief Justice Earl Warren. He was set to announce a big suburban expansion plan for the paper, including a new printing plant.

As Harry headed for his little Dodge Dart, there was a call

from the city editor who had already dispatched a photographer to the scene.

"We're holding page one for you," he told Harry who was soon in the good company of reporters from the *Examiner*, the *Chronicle*, and the *Berkeley Gazette*, along with a bevy of radio and TV reporters. By the time the *Tribune*'s ace returned to the city room, Knowland was waiting impatiently at his desk.

"Damn, it's got to be the fucking Symbionese Liberation Army. That poor girl, those assholes wanna kill us all."

The previous fall, police arrested two SLA charter members, Joseph Remiro and Russell Little, on suspicion of murdering Oakland School Superintendent Marcus Foster. They were in custody at San Quentin awaiting trial. Donald DeFreeze was arrested as an accessory to the crime for transporting the suspects to a Central Valley hideout. After escaping from Soledad Prison he had become the SLA's general field marshal, recruiting former inmates and Bay Area prisoner rights activists, as well as fellow revolutionaries.

"You should know," Knowland told a nodding Harry, "that the Hearsts have blacked out this story tonight."

"That's impossible, reporters were jumping police lines to photograph the bloody apartment, interviewing witnesses and at the hospital trying to find out if her fiancée was going to survive. Hearst's own TV station was shooting every angle."

"The Hearsts believe the embargo will give the FBI, state and local police time to find Patty and bring her home safely overnight."

"That's crazy. The only reason these maniacs did this was to promote their cause. They won't deal until the family gives them front-page coverage. They're trying to launch a revolution on a shoestring."

By now the city editor, the photo editor, the managing editor and the editor-in-chief had joined the conversation.

"We've pushed back press time an hour to give you a bit of

breathing room," said the city editor who, like Harry, had joined the paper as a copy boy.

"Do the Hearsts know you're not caving on their blackout?" asked Harry.

Knowland looked down at his watch.

"Harry, sorry, I'm late for dinner with my wife. It's her birthday."

All eyes followed Knowland as he headed for the elevator. Finally the city editor broke the silence.

"Bill, is that a go for Harry?" asked the city editor.

Knowland gave the same thumbs up that had become his trademark every time the Senate passed another one of his bills.

"Circulation has doubled tomorrow's print run. I'm putting newsboys on the street tomorrow in front of the *Examiner* headquarters to make sure the Hearsts know what we think of their Mao style state censorship. We'll show 'em the meaning of freedom of the press."

Knowland stepped onto the elevator and, as the door closed, the city editor spun around and shouted at Harry.

"This better be good."

Harry's scoop ringing around the world helped make this the biggest day in Bay Area journalism since the 1906 earthquake.

By the time the *Tribune* landed on the desk of the AP night editor in San Francisco, I was asleep with my wife Margot at our cottage just north of the Berkeley campus in the El Cerrito hills. Except for the occasional sound of skunks lying on their backs scratching the underside of the floorboards, this small rental was a perfect refuge from the tumult and the shouting of the University of California.

As a 28-year-old refugee from daily journalism, I was writing books and magazine articles. At that moment I was on deadline for a book on America's super doctors. While Patty Hearst was being seized I was putting the finishing touches to a chapter on Dr. Norman Shumway, a pioneering Stanford heart transplant surgeon, provisional title: "I Left My Heart in Palo Alto."

The advance for that book had covered the down payment for a home Margot and I had just bought in South Berkeley for $44,000. All my spare time was spent stripping layers of wallpaper and fixing a hole in the dining room fireplace. Surveying this worksite, my new neighbor Karl offered his condolences.

"You shouldn't have paid a penny over $39,000."

I was in the middle of a bad dream about home repairs when the phone rang. My *New Times* editor Jonathan Larsen was calling from his Central Park West home in Manhattan: "Is there a chance you can get to Steve Weed?"

"Steve who?"

"Patty Hearst's fiancé Stephen Weed, a Cal PhD student in philosophy. Kidnappers took Patty and bashed him in the head while they were dragging her into a getaway car. The AP says he's under guard at a hospital in Berkeley. Go down there, interview him, and get us something by Monday. I'll hold the cover for you. We can pay $500, plus expenses."

"Who was that?" asked Margot as I climbed back into bed trying to figure out how on earth I was going to get past tight security and into Steve Weed's hospital room. My assignment was to ask him what it felt like to lose his beautiful 19-year-old fiancée while his skull was being smashed by a rifle butt.

The Right, The Left, They Are All Crazy

February 5, 1974

Daly City

"I fucking don't believe it," said Donald DeFreeze. "There hasn't been one single fucking word on Walter Cronkite."

Patty sat, tied up and gagged in a Daly City safe house closet on Northridge Drive, just a few miles from the epicenter of the great 1906 San Francisco earthquake. A portable radio turned up full blast made it impossible for her to follow the kidnapper's discussion.

While Hearst rolled from side to side, trying to work her bound hands free, DeFreeze's dismay was echoed by Camilla Hall: "There's nothing on NBC Huntley-Brinkley. The granddaughter of a legendary media baron is kidnapped and the networks black out the biggest story in the country. Her father won't cover the crime in his own newspapers. That's the kind of censorship you see in Beijing or Moscow. What ever happened to the first amendment? Even free speech radio has blacked us out. The right, the left, they're all crazy."

"The family is waiting for our ransom demand. For them this is just another business deal. Saving Patty is no different than buying or selling a magazine like *Squirrel Hunters Digest.*"

Nancy Ling Perry agreed: "They are worried that our price will escalate as soon as the public knows she's missing."

Patricia Soltysik saw it the same way: "The FBI, the Governor and the Attorney General are telling a company with virtually unlimited resources not to bargain. The shrinks and hostage negotiators want them to stay tough, to not get all weepy. We're being second guessed by the usual gang of idiots."

"I thought her mother was a friend of the Governor," said Bill Harris. "She was on Reagan's reelection committee, a major fund-raiser. Doesn't he care about saving Patty? He's got kids, right?"

The others listened as Emily Harris reviewed their ransom dilemma with Wolfe.

"Reagan plans to run for president as a political gunslinger. He can't cave now," said Camilla Hall. "Any sign of weakness would torpedo him."

"A heiress's life is at stake," Wolfe replied.

"We'd never hurt her," said Perry.

"They don't know that. Every day she is missing helps Reagan take his right wing platform to new heights. The longer she's missing the more money he can raise for his next campaign," said Wolfe.

"What matters is that they can't shoot because they might hit Patty. The FBI has already been badly hurt by the Watergate scandal. We have the perfect hostage. As long as she's with us we're safe."

Clunk!

"What was that?"

Patty's valiant attempt to wriggle free had ended in failure as she knocked herself unconscious hitting the side of the closet.

February 8, 1974
Pacific Heights

COMMUNIQUE No. 1
February 8, 1974

Subject: Prisoner of War

Target:
Patty Hearst, daughter of Randolph and Catherine Hearst corporate enemies of the people.

Warrant Order:
Arrest and protective custody; and if resistance, execution.

Warrant Issued By:
The Court of the People

On the aforestated date, combat elements of the Symbionese Liberation Army, armed with cyanide-loaded weapons served an arrest warrant upon Patty Hearst.

It is the order of this court that the subject be arrested by combat units and removed to

```
a protective area of safety and only upon
completion of this condition to notify Unit #4
to give communication of this action.

We also demand that the Hearst family
immediately begin a free food program.
```

After she finished reading the document, Patty's mother tearfully handed it back to her husband. Randy gave a quick snort of disgust. Fixing his eyes on his Catherine, he ripped the SLA communique into four pieces and wiping his hands clean of the scraps of paper, dismissed them into the waste-paper basket.

I'm Going To Call Security

February 9, 1974

Berkeley

"I've never heard of the Symbionese Liberation Army," an angry and heavily bandaged Steve told the FBI's Charles Bates, as armed guards patrolled the hallway outside the hospital room.

"No one in these photos ever came to one of your talks?"

Steve shook his head painfully as the Bates continued to lean against the hospital bed.

"Never met any of them when you worked on the Soledad Prison Project?"

"No."

"Never saw them at an antiwar rally?" Charles Bates repeated.

"NO!"

"Mr. Bates," said a nurse entering with a syringe, "if you'll please excuse me for a minute. The doctor is on his way down and we need to clear the room right now."

Agent Bates ignored her and continued hectoring Steve.

"You buy their communique, that they are holding her hostage in exchange for a multi-million dollar Hearst Corporation food program that will feed the poor?"

"Mr. Bates, I'm going to call security."

"That's OK, I'll be back tomorrow with a lie detector, Steven."

"I don't think the doctor will want that. Mr. Weed needs to rest."

Getting up to leave Bates asked: "Steve, is there anything you can tell us that will help us save Miss Hearst's life?"

"Please Mr. Bates, this is the third time we've asked you to leave. The patient is in no state for visitors."

As the nurse injected Steve with a sedative, Patty's fiancé looked up at the departing FBI agent. "Tell your agents to hold their fire. Killing her in a hostage situation would not look good on your resume after you're fired."

Kidnapping Makes Strange Bedfellows

February 10, 1974

Pacific Heights

"Anything wrong?" Randy Hearst asked his wife as their nephew Will lugged a pair of her matching Vuitton suitcases down the staircase.

"State Police in the pool house. Reporters are dozing on our lawn and others are leaving a mess in our bathroom. The neighbors are threatening to call an attorney. They can't back out of their own driveways. The house looks like it's been taken over by the Third Reich. I'm moving to a suite at the Claremont," Catherine yelled at him.

As she stormed out the front door, Catherine surveyed the nightmare that her front yard had become.

"Good morning Mrs. Hearst," said the *New York Times* bureau chief. "Do you have any comment?"

Right behind her were reporters from CBS, NBC, ABC and the Hearst's own television station. The *Washington Post*, the *Wall Street Journal*, *Time*, *Newsweek*, were all there hoping for something. Camping out in lawn chairs, calling in stories on phone lines hanging from trees, they had turned the quiet street into a tourist attraction.

Spinning around, she rushed back inside.

"Randy, I'm not coming back 'til you get rid of these creeps."

"Some of these creeps work for us."

"What does that have to do with finding our daughter?"

"We have to keep digging for leads. Any of these reporters or cops could wind up with a critical tip that would bring her home."

Realizing the futility of her line of questioning, she pivoted to the next item on the list of shit that was driving her to distraction.

"When are you evicting Steve? I can't believe you sent a driver to pick him up when he was discharged from the hospital. He's up roaming the halls all hours of the night."

"Agent Bates thinks this is where he needs to be for his safety and ours. He could help us find her. Steve's hurting right now but the sooner he recovers, the sooner he'll recall forgotten details that could help us track Patty down. He may have even crossed paths with some of the kidnappers earlier."

"When they were carrying our daughter out the front door he was fleeing out the back."

"He had been bashed in the head, he was in shock."

"He should have fought for her. Any man..."

"He lost his glasses. His vision was blurry. He didn't know where she was. If he had tried to rescue her they would have killed him."

"I know exactly how they feel. I could murder him."

"Catherine, please, right now he's our best hope. He loves her as much as we do."

"After the way he's attacked the FBI for years as part of the police state, why would they trust him?"

"Kidnapping makes strange bedfellows."

"I knew going to school in Berkeley was a mistake. This would have never happened in San Francisco. That place is a cesspool for the left. I knew they shouldn't have lived together until they were married."

"Like we didn't."

"That was different. You weren't writing articles in *Ramparts* attacking our company as America's worst media chain."

"My father launched his career trashing the big trusts. Populism sells a lot of papers and in Steve's case, magazines."

"Populist? Is that why *Ramparts* is going out of business, because it's so 'popular'? Who reads it? Lately he's been jumping on the socialized medicine bandwagon. Telling us that we're supposed to see Cuba as our role model. I wouldn't be surprised if he tries to talk Patty into a junior year abroad in North Korea."

"They're in love. Maybe you remember what that was like?"

"Yes, everything was perfect until it wasn't. I fear the same for Patty. When I look at Steve I see a white Jesse Johnson."

"Jackson."

"What?"

"It's Jesse Jackson."

"Johnson, Jackson, what difference does it make? All these leftists want is the front page and you're surrendering it to them every day."

"The kidnappers may have done us a favor, by giving her time to rethink that wedding. Many she'll dump him after she's freed. Please talk to him about going to church. I don't want my grandchildren to become atheists stuck in hell."

"I'll do my best. He seems to trust me."

"I don't trust him, not to mention the book he'll write about us while we're trying to save her."

"What book?"

"It's only a matter of time until he hooks up with some half ass Berkeley ghost writer with an agent in New York handling communists and socialists."

"You don't trust him?"

"Our girls tell me he's already taking notes. Randy, he's

spying on us."

"I'll talk to him about that."

"I'm moving out. Call me when he leaves. And for God's sake please keep him away from our remaining daughters."

Roger I think that this chapter needs another sweep. Not your best writing. You're getting a bit carried away. Watch your editorializing. Stick to the facts. I was the perfect guest. I always cleaned up after myself and did all of my own laundry. I even splurged on pizza for the whole family. -SW

Finding Us Would Be A Terrible Mistake

February 11, 1974

Daly City

"In addition to being a bad business deal, marriage is an institutionally misogynist construct. The worst form of capitalism, it gives a man the moral right to enslave women. Children add a terrifying dynamic. Not only do wives have to fetch and carry for their man, they are forced to provide nonstop childcare day and night hoping their husband might give them a few hours respite on the weekend. No wonder they are too exhausted for sex," wrote Patty.

"Patty we've read your statement," said Emily Harris. "I know you were up all night working on this but it doesn't work."

"People need to know I'm not some vague debutante. It has to be in my voice. People all over the world will be hearing what I think."

"No one cares about your views on men or marriage. Women don't need you to play Gloria Steinem and men will just tune you out."

"The way you are trying to twist my words isn't credible. Everyone will think that I'm reading from a script with a gun pointed at my tush."

"Look, I can't promise anything. Getting these guys to be open-minded is a bit like trying to turn Hamlet into Puck."

"I think they're starting to trust me."

"You were kidnapped because of who you are, not because of what you think. Our job is convincing the FBI that trying to find us would lead to many of their agents getting ambushed."

"They know you'll shoot. If they fire back I could be their first casualty. Maybe it's time to give me a gun. I'm a pretty good shot."

"I've been hinting about that at our security meetings."

"Why did you try to kill Steve?"

"We didn't. But we couldn't get him to stop screaming. DeFreeze and Bill went crazy."

"He did all that work for prisoners' rights."

"We had to shut him up. He was disturbing the entire neighborhood. The guy kept screaming, 'Not Me, Not Me.'"

"He was trying to rescue me."

"I'm sure he'll be breaking down the door any minute, waste all of us and get you out of this mess."

"Why did you tear up the house?"

"We were looking for money."

"A real cash and carry organization."

"You sound disappointed."

"The way you edited what I said is terrible. The worst thing you can do if you have me tape this is make it sound like it's scripted. It what they'd be expecting. It's the first rule of debate."

"You were a debater?"

"Our team came in second at State. Can we at least cut stuff that sounds obviously 'scripted' like 'fascist dogs' and 'bourgeois pigs?' That's not the sort of thing Patty Hearst would say. My family knows I'm more Johnny Carson than the Socialist Workers Party."

"How do you feel about 'political power grows out of the barrel of a gun?'"

"I'd rather go for something that will let my parents know I'm basically OK, that all they have to do is put a ton of money into the food giveaway program for the poor and I'll be back home for Mass on Sunday."

"They also have to trade you for prisoners Little and Remiro in San Quentin."

"Right, I forgot. Between us, did they kill that Oakland school superintendent?"

"I hope so. Right now we have to focus on your communique. Your approach sounds like you're stuck at an airport in the midst of a blizzard with hours to kill. There's no sense of urgency."

"How about:

> Mom, Dad, this is Patty. I'm OK and trying to make sense of what you are doing. I know you have a lot of so-called 'psychological experts' telling you how to bring me home. Right now I'm safe. No one is torturing me and you need to know you have zero bargaining power. Meet the demands of the Symbionese Liberation Army. If you listen to the FBI or your Governor buddy Ronald Ray Gun you may lose me. Borrow the money if you have to. I'll be a good return on investment. As dad always told me, some times you just have to climb out of the dugout and step up to the plate.

"I like it. Let me see if I can sell it to the boys."

"One more thing. Will you tell them I've burned out sleeping in this closet."

The Feeding Frenzy

February 12, 1974

Oakland

"This crap would get thrown out of a prison mess hall," a retired Richmond school aide from an impoverished neighborhood told an exhausted volunteer from upscale Sausalito.

For hours the school aide had stood in line with her shopping cart trying to get her fair share of the $2 million Hearst Free Food Give-A-Way Bonanza™.

Complying with the SLA's demand as part of a potential ransom deal, the volunteers had found it impossible to keep up with demand.

The disappointed woman, who had watched others walk off with large loads, was not going to leave the vast parking lot empty handed.

"Get back in that truck and give me some of the good stuff you're hiding, the food the Hearsts put on their table."

Eager to calm the woman, the reluctant volunteer turned to her supervisor.

"We're out, can anyone help this woman?"

"Here's a special card she can show tomorrow. Tell her she'll be at the head of the line. Ask her to get here by 8 a.m."

As the school aide walked angrily away a line of people continued confronting the volunteers with similar complaints.

They had come expecting to pick up tapioca pudding and Coke, fig newtons, lettuce, hamburger, pork chops, tater tots and pears. One by one they left with dubious produce and dented Campbell's bean (with bacon) soup cans.

Demand had clearly outstripped supply. 150,000 bags of groceries, at the vast Oakland Coliseum parking lot. Huge traffic jams on the Nimitz Freeway delayed the arrival of more than 20,000 people expecting to receive groceries paid for by the CEO of a multi-billion dollar media empire. Truck drivers trying to make their way to the improvised marshaling yard couldn't break through the bottleneck and a flat tire crippled one of the meat trucks.

The best laid plans of the Hearst Corporation and the city of Oakland unraveled for hours. After the first Safeway grocery truck finally arrived, the restless crowd cheered. Men flipped open the refrigerated trailer's rear door and began helping themselves to boxes of frozen chicken breasts perfect for a family barbecue, but the optimistic plan for an orderly handout at the poultry station was destroyed. Fist fights erupted as people began cutting in line to help themselves to everything they could carry.

When policemen tried to break up the mini-riot, some of the men began shouting and running toward a second truck filled with mozzarella cheese and Wonder Bread. Half an hour later police finally cordoned off the area and rerouted the rest of the trucks, creating a path to the food distribution area. Carefully lined up families who had come to the Hearst family sponsored giveaway stood in line for grocery bags loaded with fresh produce, milk, meat, strawberries, tapioca pudding and buttermilk biscuits.

As the older crowd waited their turn, young men ransacked trucks. By mid-afternoon volunteers ran out of pork chops. Then the milk disappeared. In frustration the woman in charge of Hawaiian Punch conceded to an *Examiner* reporter that her boxes were empty. As she spoke, a driver piloting a van for the Hearst family television station was confronted by a small mob. He was yanked out and put on a sidewalk as someone hijacked his vehicle.

Fed up, some of the frustrated families headed for a late arrival, a truck full of Valencia oranges just in from Fresno. Suddenly a young man wearing jeans and a hooded sweat-shirt vaulted up on the back of the truck and scaled the stack of Sunkist cartons. As he began tossing down boxes one slipped, hit the ground, broke open and sent oranges rolling across the parking lot.

Footage of people running around the lot scooping up spilled oranges became the perfect lead-in for evening news-casts. When one young man paused in the frenzy to take a bite from a peeled orange, Lonnie Wilson, a photographer from the *Oakland Tribune*, shot an image destined to win him a California Newspaper Association prize.

"At least they didn't try giving away watermelons," he told Harry Harris. "Hit someone with one of those babies and you could crack their head."

As police began dispersing the angry mob, someone no-ticed a refrigerated truck sitting in the rear of the parking lot. When they hoisted the rolling door, the men were nearly over-come by the stench of rotting meat.

One of them held up a bag of spoiled hamburger and shout-ed: "Even a rat wouldn't touch this shit."

The napping driver, woke up, jumped out and tried explain-ing that an air conditioning unit had broken down. All this meat was headed for the dumpster.

Many in the shouting crowd couldn't hear his explanation. Some of the men grabbed the rotting meat and headed off to dis-play it at an impromptu press conference.

"I'm so glad we discovered this meat before someone took it home," said an Oakland Food Pantry leader. "We are asking anyone who has received hamburger today to take it to the nearest dumpster."

People in line since dawn for free groceries picked over the remains of the day, rotting rutabagas, cauliflower and string cheese. Frustrated that so little was left, they began throwing the remaining food at volunteers. As police began to intervene, fistfights broke out and ambulances carried casualties to Highland Hospital. On television the free food program looked like a British soccer riot.

Speaking to reporters outside the family home in Pacific Heights. Randy promised that another, better organized food giveaway was set for the following week:

"I want to apologize to the people of the Bay Area. We will get this right next time."

At the Sacramento airport where he was boarding a plane to his ranch in the Santa Ynez Valley, Governor Reagan joked to reporters that with any luck some of the poor people at the giveaway would "come down with botulism."

Good one, Roger. I love the way you showed how the Hearsts were sabotaged.—SW

A Dynasty Double Parked On The Wrong Side Of History

Late February 1974

San Francisco/Oakland

As the *Tribune*'s presses rolled each night, messengers dispatched by competing papers waited outside the 13th and Franklin printing plant for the first delivery truck to head out to downtown Oakland news racks. They rushed the paper to the offices of other newspapers reporters and correspondents who quickly rewrote Harry Harris's work, sometimes with attribution.

After they finished digesting the Hearst Corporation and FBI press releases, reporters from national and local media waited night after night for Harry's next story to make sure their coverage was up to the minute. Like a first-rate weather person, the *Tribune*'s guy-on-the-ground knew how to decipher the isobars and forecast when the next deluge was going to hit.

In the aftermath of his one-day news blackout following the family kidnapping, young Will Hearst watched the competition humiliate his reporters. This kind of damsel in distress story was what readers expected from the *Examiner* and its sister papers across the US. His grandfather's editors were geniuses at peddling fear. Beginning with a "Chinese must go" campaign in the 19th century, the Examiner campaigned vigorously against the New Deal, school integration, liberating citizens from prisoner of war camps during Word War II, free speech at the University of California and the Vietnam antiwar movement. The Hearst empire, double parked on the wrong side of history, was trying its best for a makeover with the promotion of younger editors who thought the rabidly anti-Communist John Birch Society, was a bad joke. Randy understood that liberal San Francisco readers wanted a paper that was not a mere Nixonian mouthpiece spouting GOP cliches. Perhaps Patty had spelled out the problem best when she told her father over pizza one night, "Dad, no one under 80 reads the *Examiner*."

Desperate to improve the paper's reputation, Randy personally offered to hire the *Tribune* star away at double his current salary. Harry wouldn't even take a phone call, much less answer the *Examiner* publisher's special delivery letters promising a team of special assistants along with a private office where he could work on the kidnapping story. Catered meals would be included at all hours of the day and night.

"I'm allergic to San Francisco," he told one of his fellow reporters, as he headed out the door to track down yet another lead that would turn into copy sure to further humiliate the *Examiner*.

"Mr. Hearst should save his money for the Symbionese Liberation Army. He's going to need it."

When *Time* magazine arrived in Oakland to report a Harry Harris profile he refused to sit down for an interview.

"I'm not newsworthy," he told the inquiring reporter. "Jack London is the only Oakland writer worth profiling. Unfortunately he's unavailable for comment."

As the Hearst Corporation publicists struggled to deflate the SLA communiques, the poor little rich girl narrative began sinking like an overweight hot air balloon. Patty's own statements made it clear that she was losing faith in her family.

By the night of the *Oakland Tribune* centennial, the $2 million free food giveaway debacle led to late night TV show ridicule of the family business, especially when it was revealed that small mountains of cheese had turned out to be a gift from the Department of Agriculture's surplus food program.

"Can you believe it?" said reigning late night host Johnny Carson. "The Hearst family is now taking charitable donations."

In her latest communique Patty was outraged:

> I refuse to be a charity case. Please return all those donations. Dad, you need to tell your board of directors to take control now. Your slanted coverage is destroying your credibility. The people who kidnapped me only wanted to help hungry families. Your hand-picked surrogates created a riot. I'm having second thoughts about coming home. Maybe I should just stay with the SLA and join the revolution.

The schism between Randy and Catherine went public when she decamped at the Claremont Hotel with her twin Chihuahuas Zipolite and Tulum. After an AP photo of Patty's mother having a pedicure beside the hotel pool ran nationwide, the SLA was quick to up their ransom demand.

When Randy called his wife demanding an explanation she cut the conversation short.

"Sorry dear, I've got to run. Can't be late for my 2 p.m. doubles match."

All this was irresistible for competing *San Francisco Chronicle* columnist: Herb Caen.

> Fed up with being put down like the hysterical mom she is not, valiant Catherine Hearst has left the family's Pacific Heights nest in the capable hands of her husband Randy. Unable to cope with a bevy of hungry house guests, including her parched and ravenous future son-in-law Steve Weed, she has taken up residence in Oakland. As she confided to an old chum the other day from the balcony of her Bay view Claremont suite:
>
> "The whole thing has turned into a pathetic FBI-knows-best drama. It's ridiculous to think that a multi billion dollar company can't find a few million to rescue my little girl. I'm sick of all the misogyny. As usual the men are calling all the shots. I just hope one of them doesn't hit Patty."

While the Hearst kidnapping remained a lead story worldwide, death did not take a holiday on the streets of Oakland. Cub reporters covered Harry's police beat as their stories of gang-related shootings fell to the back pages in the wake of the biggest man and woman hunt in FBI history. Harry only stepped away from the dominant story for one day, February 18, to emcee the *Tribune*'s Centennial at the lily-white Claremont. Pickets protesting Governor Ronald Reagan's arrival lined Tunnel Road as VIP guests made their way to valet parking. A jazz band was playing in the hillside Tudor revival hotel's lobby as the guests ascended to the ballroom at sunset. Waiters served cocktails and caviar while everyone lined up for their chance to pose with publisher Knowland and his second wife who charmed everyone with her one liners.

"People like to say I'm a gold digger who married money," she said. "Obviously they don't know the first thing about the newspaper business."

After dinner Harry emceed the event with a slide show kicked off by a shot of young Bill launching his political career. The boy wonder, married at 20, a father at 22, skyrocketed through the California Assembly to become the youngest grandfather in the US Senate. Following a failed run for Governor in 1958, he returned home to manage the family business, making a goal line stand against the rising tide of the University of California Free Speech movement led by student firebrand Mario Savio.

Governor Reagan was quick to extol Knowland for courageously "standing up to these Stalinists trying to upend our democracy."

Knowland protégé Earl Warren, who wrote the Supreme Court Brown vs. Board of Education decision in 1954 that launched desegregation of American schools, skipped over the publisher's long record of tangling with African-American activists: "Bill has worked tirelessly to create lasting harmony between the races. No publisher in America can match his dedication to the less fortunate among us."

At the end it was Harry who brought down the house with a hilarious impersonation of the publisher struggling to ride an elephant. After the laughter died down he generously saluted his boss: "*New Yorker* media critic A.J. Libeling once wrote that freedom of the press belongs to the man who owns one. Fortunately, that's not our fate here. Thankfully we have a courageous leader who always puts his community ahead of himself, stands behind his reporters and insists that the truth be told. To him the news pages will always be sacred spaces where writers and editors educate and entertain readers seven days a week."

Four days later, for the first time since the kidnapping, the national search for Patty Hearst fell from the *Tribune*'s front page. As tearful colleagues consoled one another Harry Harris struggled for half an hour on his lead:

> MONTE RIO—In the Redwood-loving Russian River community of Monte Rio, 75 miles north of San Francisco, Oakland native son William F. Knowland, precocious politician and dedicated publisher, went to his Lord Saturday afternoon at the family vacation home. His sudden death shocked and saddened both friends and enemies of the controversial and outspoken community leader who liked being described as a man who "possessed the subtlety of a Sherman tank." Sonoma County undersheriff Robert Hayes said members of his family found Mr. Knowland's body. He said the death had apparently occurred a few hours earlier.
>
> An investigation by the sheriff's department disclosed evidence the victim died of a self-inflicted gunshot wound," Mr. Hayes said in a statement. "The weapon is in custody of the sheriffs department.
>
> His death comes just days after an ebullient Knowland hosted the paper's centennial at a lavish gala....

The Most Beautiful Woman I've Ever Seen

March 12, 1974

San Simeon

While I continued attempting to land an interview with Steve Weed, *New Times* dispatched me down the coast to visit 'the chief's' San Simeon. By now editors everywhere were scrambling for fresh meat on the famous case. Triggered by Patty's decision to enlist with the Symbionese Liberation Army and change her name to Tania (in honor of a Che Guevara comrade) her life underground was now a staple of the daily news cycle. The latest communique quickly sent out shock waves:

> It should come as no surprise that my parents have failed to meet any of the SLA demands. I no longer see any reason to hold out hope that my family's Hearsterical company will help anyone other than themselves. They have

> revealed the moral bankruptcy of a family willing to sacrifice me to safeguard their bottom line. In a few weeks my comrades have won the loyal support of revolutionaries everywhere. People are enlisting in our cause around the world. Thanks to SLA weapons training, I am now able to fight alongside them. We are prepared to battle anyone who stands in the way of a just society. Every night I sleep with my own gun gifted to me by my new comrades who have more faith in me than the capitalist pigs who were never serious about ransoming me.

Patty's defection was the latest chapter in the Hearst saga tracing back to her great grandfather's silver mines that funded her grandfather's newspaper empire and his mansion at San Simeon. Like Frank Lloyd Wright's Taliesin in Wisconsin, this 100 room Hispanic-Moorish palace overlooking the Pacific was a never-ending story. Construction under the guidance of the intrepid Berkeley architect Julia Morgan began in 1920 and continued until the chief's death in 1952.

"Welcome to San Simeon," said our witty guide Anabelle who clearly loved her job. A poised woman with a paisley scarf accenting her state park service uniform, she had an angelic voice:

"You are about to enjoy a rare experience, a walk through the kingdom of an American legend who left behind a special gift for the world to enjoy."

We paused for a minute while this veteran docent tap-danced across the mansion's life story. Hearst spent decades collecting marble floors, paintings, antiques, fireplaces, and ceilings pulled from monasteries, along with oak-paneled walls and gothic rooms. Then, he hired Morgan to create this landmark strategically placed above the coastal fog belt. She commuted down the coast by train each weekend to make progress on this capitalist cathedral. The Chief's heirs donated it to the state in 1958, after Frank Sinatra backed out of a proposed deal. The estate was surrounded by the 70,000 acre Hearst ranch. The family held on to just one cottage which was the private realm of Randy's brother Bill (William Randolph Hearst II) the empire's front page Sunday columnist and his wife, Bootsie. Among recent house guests were Patty and Steve who had come down for her cousin Will's birthday party.

Climbing staircases with my fellow guests, I walked through refectories, gazed at stained glass, looked at medieval tapestries and gawked at the bed where Cardinal Richelieu left this earth. When I asked her to put a value on a clock that once belonged to a Hapsburg emperor, a historic Medici chair or a Madonna and child portrait, Anabelle whispered, "priceless."

After admiring Spanish monastery ceilings, French gothic fireplaces, Flemish tapestries, Greek statues, and hundreds of other treasures, we climbed a tower to marvel at gilt Arabesque and a 360-degree view of the estate. Pausing to catch her breath, our guide continued:

"Can't you just imagine lovers Clark Gable and Carol Lombard here on their honeymoon closing these curtains and wrapping themselves in a cocoon of delight!"

At the end of our visit we walked out to San Simeon's crown jewel, the colonnaded Neptune pool surrounded with marble statuary, Roman mosaics, and terraces of roses, jasmine and acanthus.

"Close your eyes," she suggested, "and imagine a warm spring evening forty years ago with the Chief entertaining 250 of Hollywood's elite, political leaders and British royalty at a cost of $40,000 in present day dollars. Guests landing on his private strip were chauffeured to the San Simeon door in a Pierce Arrow convertible.

"Look over there in the corner of the pool. That's Greta Garbo surfacing, climbing out to eat a violet, and diving back in. Over on the right is Gregory Peck sipping a drink after a hike in the Santa Lucia foothills. Who's that on the balcony? Why it's Claudette Colbert watching ocean yachts sailing downwind on a broad reach. If only we could all travel back in time to that forgotten era."

In 1921 her grandfather abandoned Patty's grandmother Millicent to spend the remainder of his life living with actress Marion Davies who launched her career in a Buster Keaton comedy. Divorce was a nonstarter because Mrs. Hearst believed it was a mortal sin.

At his death 'the Chief' left behind a $260 million estate that included 27 newspapers, nine magazines, radio stations, a wire service, syndicate, three vast ranches, six big warehouses crammed full of art treasures shipped home from Europe and seven castles.

After her husband's passing on the Fourth of July 1952, Millicent took a portion of the $7.5 million left her and set up trusts for all her grandchildren. At 21 Patty was to receive a $500,000 trust fund and, after her father's death, voting shares in the Hearst Corporation.

Back at the visitor center I had been handed a handwritten note to call my old Berkeley librarian friend Jim Carra who had just responded to a message I'd left the night before.

"Ask the guard to show you my office."

A few minutes later we were on the balcony of the San Simeon library and archive that had once been the bungalow of Hearst's paramour.

"They brought me down on a two year contract to see if I could make sense of the chief's cluttered personal collection of journals, memorabilia, correspondence, photos and ephemera. His love letters are a testament to their affair that outlasted many marriages," Jim said.

"A true May-November romance."

"Yes, and as far as I can tell, she remained faithful to him all the way to the end. She adored the man. Even when he called off their Mexican wedding to avoid losing *Cosmopolitan* and other assets to his wife in a threatened divorce suit, she remained loyal."

"She wasn't a gold digger?"

"He certainly helped her land big roles but I'm pretty sure she would have made it without him. She also did a lot for him, especially when it came to repairing Hearst's relationship with his five sons.

"I understand Marion Davies and Patty's father were born on the same day in the same year," I asked the Hearst castle archivist.

"Correct, she was two hours older."

"She had a good relationship with your dad and all your uncles."

"Yes, although they were very protective of their mother who refused many invitations to visit San Simeon. Hearst's first wife worried that her husband's actress paramour was plundering their grandchildren's inheritance to pay for more overpriced Spanish antiques."

"Was that true?"

"Actually when the empire plummeted during the depression Marion Davies loaned him money and had enough influence over him to insist he bring in new managers who put him on a strict allowance. Parties were cut back and even the tennis pro who helped guests improve their game saw his salary slashed. She also made sure he swam every day, went for long walks and ate a healthy diet."

Over lunch brought in from the employee cafeteria, Jim Carra and I reminisced about mutual friends back in Berkeley. Finally, after more than an hour of catching up, he handed me a surprising document.

"Here's something you might enjoy reading. It's a transcript of Patty's interview with me for an art history class paper. She came down to see me just a few months before the kidnapping."

"She drove all the way down here to research a paper?"

"She wanted to know more about one of her grandfather's Italian paintings."

"Was that part of the San Simeon collection?"

"As far as I know he never exhibited this portrait of a beautiful bride waiting outside a church with her father."

"Did her grandfather ever write about this treasure?"

"Yes and that was why Patty came to see me."

Carra stepped inside to his desk and then returned with a copy of the document.

"Here's what William Randolph Hearst wrote:

'I spent the afternoon alone with an unforgettable woman. Looking at this hidden Tintoretto is like staring directly into the sun.'"

A few days after Knowland's death a big break came my way. My wife was shopping at the Telegraph Avenue Coop when she ran into her Mills College freshman roommate Cindy Jensen. They headed over to Peets for coffee where she learned Cindy had actually taught with Steve at St. Jean's High School.

In 1971 Cindy was the first faculty member to discover the affair between the 25-year-old history teacher and the student heiress. It happened one Saturday morning when Cindy stopped at Steve's apartment to drop off a well-worn copy of the Kama Sutra that had done wonders for her marriage. As she pulled in to Weed's driveway, Cindy spotted Patty and Steve necking on his doorstep.

After Weed and Hearst moved to Berkeley in the fall of 1973 the couple met every Sunday night with Cindy and her husband Jeff for pizza and *Colombo* on TV. Cindy also told Margot that after Steve was kicked out of the Hearst family home, Patty's man for all seasons was couch surfing at Cindy's Berkeley place several nights a week. Margot subsequently learned Cindy had helped Patty plan her Claremont wedding, and had hand sewn her own bridesmaid's dress. Cindy also tipped Margot off that Steve was on the tennis court every Monday with Jeff, the son of a famous Hollywood agent who lived down the street from Charlton Heston. The picture was taking shape.

Roger I have a big problem with this chapter. As I explained to you many times there was nothing "clandestine" about our affair. Would you please stop trying to make me look like a predator. Thanks very much.—SW

The Ghostwriter

April 5, 1974

Berkeley

My struggle to land Steve Weed for a *New Times* interview got a bounce when Margot received an invitation from her old roommate. Would we be free to join her and Jeff for their regular Sunday night dinner with Steve?

A couple of days later, Cindy, Jeff, Margot and I sat down in the living room to watch *Colombo,* having feasted on Jeff's lasagna followed by apple crumble. As the last pre-show commercial for Camels came on there was a knock on the door. It was lanky Steve carrying a backpack, tennis racket and a bottle of Zinfandel.

After a quick introduction, Cindy heated up the leftovers and we sat down to watch Colombo star Peter Falk gumshoe his way to a murderer, barbecuing ribs on the backyard grill. As the credits rolled Cindy brought out sheets and made a bed for Steve from the couch Margot and I had been sitting on. On our way out I invited him to stop by our house to discuss the possibility of an interview.

The following afternoon Steve showed up at our place unannounced. We headed out to the backyard and sat down to talk. Unlike the calm, soft spoken Steve I'd seen on television outside the Hearst home in Pacific Heights, he was animated, self-deprecating, even droll. The media's hit job over the past several months had, in some ways, been as damaging as the Cinque's blow to his head.

Steve was shockingly portrayed in the news as a shady teacher who had an affair with a student just past the age of consent, a cross-country Princeton marijuana dealer, as well as a potential conspirator in the taking of his fiancé. In the media he had the aura of a paranoid Pinter character struggling to figure out who was trying to put him away and why.

Margot invited him to join us for wine, mac and cheese, broccoli and a cherry cobbler. At the end of the evening he asked for a look at the back unit of our Berkeley brown-shingle we had spent months restoring.

The following day I began tagging along with Steve on his daily rounds.

'On the Tania Trail', the *New Times* story I published several weeks later, began thus:

> The night Patty Hearst was kidnapped wearing only a bathrobe from her Berkeley apartment the Symbionese Liberation Army left her fiancé Steve Weed, punched, beaten, and bleeding. It was just the beginning of the punishment the 30-year-old philosophy graduate student was about to take. He recovered from his beating only to be wounded much more deeply – by the April 3rd tape in which Patty announced she was dropping him and her family to join the SLA.
>
> Weed felt he could no longer sit by and watch the antics of the Hearst parents or the FBI. He had to do something himself. And so he began a desperate round of

negotiations with different radical leaders on the West Coast.

After the story was published, George Walsh, an editor I had written for at Hearst's *Cosmopolitan*, called to invite me to New York: "I just joined Ballantine Books and we'd like to talk to you about your Steve Weed piece. Great job in *New Times*. I think there could be a bestseller here. Come over to New York," George said over the phone.

On Ballantine's tab, I jumped on a helicopter at the Berkeley Marina, connected to a five-hour flight, first class, to JFK, and checked in to New York's Algonquin hotel. However, the hotel was oversold and I spent the night on a roll-away bed in the manager's office entertaining myself with the latest restaurant report the city health department had given the Algonquin.

The following morning I joined Walsh for breakfast where he asked me to ghost write a book with Steve on his life with Patty Hearst.

"What happens if she gets killed?" I asked.

"That seems unlikely," the Ballantine editor told me. "In any case we don't see how Steve, given his present situation, can do this himself. He doesn't have time and he's a pretty stodgy writer. His books don't sell. His *Is The Library Burning?* was a disaster in stores."

Unlike fiction, memoirs, poetry or short story collections, celebrity autobiographies reside in publishing's Never Never Land. They begin with a curious editor or an agent convinced readers want to know what lives inside the beating heart of a tech billionaire, an Oscar winner, or a President. Their subjects are smarter, better looking, raise kids who make Phi Beta Kappa at Brown, vacation on yachts in the Aegean and, above all, are more important than you or me.

There is also another category for people like Steve: The accidental celebrity.

Steve's story "worked" because he was the innocent victim at the heart of an irresistible true crime mystery.

Steve had gained a certain amount of fame in the civil rights and anti-Vietnam war movement at a time when most undergraduates were trying to figure how to conjugate French verbs or understand DNA. He was there in 1965 when the Reverend Martin Luther King Jr. led civil rights activists across the Edmund Pettis Bridge in Selma, Alabama. He was there in '68, helping overwhelmed paramedics load the injured into ambulances, after Mayor Daley's police storm troopers attacked innocent protesters in Chicago's Grant Park during the Democratic convention. When hundreds of thousands marched on Washington to end the Vietnam War, Steve spoke with such eloquence that some of what he had to say brought tears to the eyes of network television anchors. For a time he was a brand name for the left and his progressive ideology inspired many young people. Publishers were proud to release his books and schedule *Today* show interviews, even though sales were lukewarm.

Patty's own infatuation was piqued by Steve's remarkable ability to bring his personal history to life in a compelling way. He was a first for her in many ways.

Then, in a single day, Steve Weed ran aground.

He was the only available eyewitness to the kidnapping of Patty Hearst, himself a victim of that terrible night. Steve's vulnerability was a critical selling point. George Walsh, his publicity department, his sales force and, ultimately, the bookstores and libraries, were all eager to capitalize on Steve's new fame. They wanted him to share his unique point of view on a story that had captured the public's imagination.

Patty's decision to join the Symbionese Liberation Army and dump her fiancé for Willie Wolfe, personalized the drama even more. An 'as told to' book needed to explain this surprising twist that appeared to defy Patty's past. A week after my New York meeting with George Walsh, a letter arrived from agent

Sterling Lord confirming Ballantine's $125,000 offer. I sprung it on Steve as Margot served pineapple upside down cake following a spaghetti dinner washed down with a great French Burgundy he and Patty had liberated from the Wyntoon cellars.

After finishing the letter he gave Margot a wink: "Well I guess that means you and Roger are finally off food stamps. "

We repaired to my office and agreed that after the agent's commission Weed would get a two-thirds share, roughly $75,000 —worth about $450,000 in today's money.

After I typed out a collaboration agreement, Steve hand wrote an addendum: "Both parties agree that all interviewing for the book will be done by Steve Weed."

"Interviewing is what I do. Let's be a team," I interjected.

"The Hearsts were pretty angry with what you said about them in *New Times*."

The following day I began writing a profound and troubling human-interest story. There was no time to lose. The catch, Sterling Lord had reminded me, was this drama's evanescence. Our opportunity could vanish the moment Patty miraculously emerged from captivity to publish her own tell all book that might torch Steve's. Any chance of success meant sticking to a seven day a week writing schedule.

The publisher believed I could help Steve write a touching love story. Girl meets boy. Boy loses girl. Girl goes off deep end. Boy tries to rescue girl after she joins her captors who trust her with a gun. Above all he had met the litmus test of most successful tell-all books. George Walsh wanted a writer he could depend on to make Steve lovable in the face of Patty's nationally publicized insults attacking his manhood.

One only had to glance at the names of successful ghostwriters behind celebrity biographies on the bestseller list to appreciate this publishing fact of life. Like a good lion tamer, a ghostwriter's job was anonymously insuring his subject's obedience to the publisher. Ballantine believed I could deliver Steve's book in good order. The key was sidestepping celebrity angst that might delay publication, leaving this title behind in bookstore purgatory–the remainder table.

Alas, not every author is comfortable putting their life in the hands of a ghostwriter trying to make a buck. My collaboration with Steve was hurriedly born out of necessity. Both of us wanted to write a book. Eager to earn his trust, I agreed to his request that he do all the interviewing of Patty's friends, family and teachers. Their stories would be supplemented by my own long interviews with Steve, along with historical research on the Hearst dynasty.

To take some of the pressure off Steve, Margot and I invited him to move into a spare room in our back unit that came with a shower. He helped himself to breakfast every morning around noon, and then lit out for interviews. In the evening he met with friends, often returning to our place around midnight. His new digs were duly noted by matching pairs of FBI agents regularly parking cars on our street to keep an eye on everyone coming and going from our house.

As our collaboration progressed I learned Steve had been grooming Patty for a larger goal. He believed she was destined to take command of the Hearst Empire upon her father's retirement. Her prominence would be an impressive asset, a woman's voice everyone in the room would honor.

"She would abandon the family's realpolitik and turn the Hearst empire into a progressive media organization," he explained. "No window dressing, a real commitment to all the righteous causes they had persistently ignored or denigrated."

He dreamed that post-kidnapping Patty would become an articulate spokesperson for the rights of those abandoned on the margins of American society. Perhaps one day she would lend a hand to achieve the hopeful vision of our founding mothers and fathers.

"Boring from within," he told me as I barbecued burgers one evening, "is the kind of thing Patty knows how to do. Look how she landed a lefty like me."

At dinner one night be didn't flinch when Patty's latest communique led the evening news:

> Where are the men? Will, you were the cousin that always looked out for me. Steve, what do you have to say?

Steve's response in an interview on local television was pure Randy:

> The SLA needs to stop pretending that Patty is writing this pathetic propaganda.

Patty was outraged. In another communique she fought back on behalf of her comrades:

> As for my ex-fiancé, Steve Weed, it's clear that he will never get why I've freely decided to stay and fight with the SLA. Instead of giving paid interviews to People Magazine he should join our revolution. Giving lip service to my safety is worthless. For years he has portrayed himself as a dedicated humanitarian. If you can stand to read one of his stupid books you'll realize why they don't sell. Those weeks he spent sitting by the pool in my parents' backyard, raiding their refrigerator, pretending that I have been brainwashed – it's all so nauseating. I am so glad to have the love of comrade Willie Wolfe who does not lie awake dreaming of becoming a Hearst. Steve, try to grow a pair before it's too late.

As my interviews with Steve continued a pattern emerged, one best described as the ghostwriter's dilemma. Some of what Steve told me was useful but much of it failed to give readers what they deserved to know. He was now staying out late night after night, a fact that made my wife worry: "What if he got mugged? Or worse? There goes your book."

While Steve continued giving way too many interviews in which he carelessly leaked valuable parts of our story, I was struggling to make sure our book had a long and happy publishing life.

Aside from the kidnapping drama, there was little about the couple's story that "worked" *prima facie*. Going beyond published accounts of their lives together was my biggest challenge. Steve completed a few interesting interviews with Patty's old friends and came up with funny stories about living with the overwhelmed Hearst family after his release from the hospital.

Unfortunately much of what he told me sidestepped key questions being asked by my Ballantine editor. George Walsh wanted to know stuff that had not already appeared in the *New York Times*. I shared his premise that the international newspaper, magazine and television story of the kidnapping was a middling first draft of history. I was tasked with uncovering secrets that would make our book a best selling page-turner.

Increasingly frustrated by the slow pace of Steve's interviews and his refusal to let me talk to any of the key players, such as Patty's parents, I reached out to the always-one-step-ahead-of-the-FBI Harry Harris. Within days Harry began helping me piece together a book that could potentially turn Steve and Patty's origin story into a bestseller. I decided to quietly hire him as a part-time investigator, making sure he wouldn't let Steve know about our deal.

Thanks to Harry's terrific leads I was finally able to write new chapters our editor wanted. Week after week I convincingly documented why the ransom effort failed and created what my editor told me were "compelling profiles" of the key Army members. As the book progressed Steve appeared to be having more difficulty putting steam on his reportorial mirror. Abandoned by the Hearst family and his fiancée, he was increasingly on the defensive.

"The one thing everyone seems to agree on in the Hearst case," wrote one acerbic New York journalist, "is how much they dislike Steve Weed."

Typing on my Olympia Electric, I dreamed of writing in the grand tradition of the film classic *Citizen Kane* and W.K. Swanberg's family biography *Citizen Hearst*. Building on a great legacy, Patty's story would give readers unforgettable insights into this powerful media empire destined to one day be worth $35 billion. Instead of gliding in and out of magazine assignments I would have a chance to chronicle this important family's younger generations. If she lived, I had a hunch the drama surrounding her rebellion would continue for years.

Although I was billed as the "as told to" coauthor, editors I cared about would know that the writing was mine. Solving the book's central problem would help me finally pole vault from writing $500 *New Times* articles to the publishing stratosphere. With luck, the Book of the Month Club might choose our work for a main selection. An American Tragedy would suddenly free me from worry about paying my $260 a month mortgage and the $60 a month and rising health insurance bill.

Thanks for sticking up for me. I was in an impossible situation. Have you given any thought to trying to reach out to Patty after all this time. It sure would be great if she pitches in. She would be a great interview. I really think she has been holding back a lot to protect her parents. Now that they are both dead she may finally open up.—SW

The Silent Investor

April 16, 1974

Berkeley

Hummingbirds were busy dining on the feeder hanging from a magnolia branch in my backyard as Berkeley legend Arlene Slaughter arrived. The agent who sold my wife and I our brown-shingle Craftsman house on Woolsey Street a few months earlier was surprised to return so soon.

"You've done a great job on the renovations," she said, after a quick walk through. "These craftsmen homes are in very high demand. I just love the new fireplace. Who did your tile work?"

A local legend for recruiting white buyers to front for black families purchasing North Oakland homes in the segregated '50s, Slaughter had led many a picket line protesting *Oakland Tribune* publisher William Knowland's disgraceful record on segregation and racial justice. With her help we purchased our Berkeley home for $44,000, $1,000 below the asking price. Skeptical neighbors told us the real estate agent and the seller had fleeced us. Despite their qualms, we were thrilled to move in to the charming Bateman neighborhood.

For 25 years Slaughter had been the left's favorite Berkeley realtor. A generous donor to political campaigns for minority candidates, she was also active in the prison reform movement. Famous for loaning down payments to first time buyers, she was also a fixture in our new neighborhood, eagerly supporting residential permit parking to block hospital workers from clogging neighborhood streets all day long.

Slaughter had been a reliable source for a number of local stories I'd written. After the Oakland School Superintendent Marcus Foster was murdered over his installation of metal detectors at school entrances, she was quick to post a reward for information leading to the arrest of his killers.

"The Symbionese Liberation Army," she told me, "gives Reagan and the right exactly what they need to crack down on the black community. Donald DeFreeze is going to get all of them killed. The warden at Soledad said he escaped after threatening to execute some of the guards. He needs to be back behind bars yesterday."

While we waited for Steve Weed, I filled her in on our book deal with Ballantine and the advance that had made me the envy of journalists covering the story.

"So I guess that means you won't need to scrape by anymore writing about the hidden dangers of nuclear power plants for *Ramparts.* What's the title of your book with Steve going to be, *Jilted?*"

"*Patty Hearst: A Symbionese Love Story.*"

"I love it. Do you really believe the communique where she claims to have dumped Steve for Willie Wolfe?"

"She called him 'the sweetest, most gentle man I've ever met.'"

"Steve believes it's pure propaganda aimed at extracting more money from her family."

"She sounded credible to me. I've read she and Steve were having a lot of problems."

When Steve arrived half an hour late, he was quick to hug Arlene as if she was an old family friend.

"I am so sorry," he told her. "The *Life* magazine photographer took like 200 shots. Apparently I'm going to be a cover story.

I guess that makes me a sellout. At least I was able to get in a little about some of my causes."

"Glad you could make it. I've heard a lot about you."

Our meeting focused on my idea to invest our big book advance in Berkeley real estate. The book advance was $125,000. The agent got $12,500 leaving $112,500, of which Steve got about $75,000 and I, the rest. It was not an insignificant amount of money at the time for either of us.

"Are you thinking of buying a personal residence?"

Steve, who was living with us rent free, hesitated.

"When Patty comes back, Berkeley won't be her first choice."

"Then you and Roger will be buying and selling jointly?"

"I was kind of thinking of being a silent investor."

"From my perspective it's good to buy the worst house in the best neighborhood," said Slaughter. "Once you fix the place up you should be able to make a nice profit. I can help you find the workers you need."

"Can we do this in a way that won't let people know I've started dabbling in real estate?" asked Steve. "I don't want people to think I'm cashing in on Patty's tragedy."

"What could possibly give them that idea?" asked Arlene.

"I just think it will be easier if I'm a silent investor."

"You okay with that?" Arlene asked me.

"Sure, I'll make a bundle and be able to go off and write my true crime novel."

After helping himself to a glass of ice tea, Steve suggested the perfect way to stage open houses.

"I've got some pretty great furnishings, rugs, paintings and antiques sitting in storage, Patty's family stuff that will create a classy look."

"As long as it's insured, that's fine," said Arlene. "Just be sure there aren't any bedbugs."

After he left to get a haircut, Slaughter asked if coauthoring a book, while being Steve's landlord and potential business partner in the real estate business might have a downside.

"I trust him."

"Have you considered the possibility that Patty is not just some dumb broad brainwashed by the Symbionese Liberation Army?"

"Definitely, we're both skeptical. He wants some kind of proof that she joined of her own free will."

"Nothing he's saying makes any sense. His ex-fiancée hates him, the parents hate him, and the SLA hates him. You heard what she said about the cowardly men in her family failing to come to her rescue."

"She's outraged that they destroyed any possibility of a ransom deal they can easily afford."

"The only people on his side are his friends and your publisher who thinks he will make a killing."

"Do you think publishing the truth about their lives pretty much destroys any chance of them living happily ever after."

"Any book written from one point of view, even Patty's, would be suspect. Steve could be accused of shading the truth. There is no way you can tell when he's lying."

"He's done a few decent interviews with her friends and family."

"That might help, but it seems weird that he agreed with our plan to become a real estate speculator while his fiancée is still missing? Do you really want to go into business with this guy?"

Three weeks later Steve and I were at Northern Title on Solano Avenue closing the deal on our very first property, a two-story fixer upper on Claremont Avenue. After Slaughter looked over the sale documents, I began signing page after page of paperwork. Finally it was Steve's turn to sign his check that would become part of the down payment. As he finished, a broker walked into the office and shouted to a secretary:

"Did you hear about the latest on Patty Hearst? The FBI

has security camera images showing she was one of the five San Francisco bank robbers yesterday at the Hibernia Bank! She has just put out a communique boasting about her role in the crime."

Steve quickly grabbed his check, stood up and left. As I began to run after him, Slaughter grabbed my shoulder.

"I hope you are writing the book on more than a handshake."

"No problem, I've got the whole deal with him in writing."

Roger, please cut this chapter. I'm a much-loved realtor in Cupertino and this could hurt me with my clients. Thanks for understanding.—SW

The Sex Will Always Be Fantastic

Late May, 1974

Berkeley

Trying to keep up with the explosive SLA story was my biggest challenge. Breaking news kept interrupting my writing schedule as the revolutionaries made mistake after mistake. A terrifying May police shootout and fire at their makeshift South Central hideout led to the deaths of six of Patty's comrades including commander in chief Donald DeFreeze, her new lover Willie Wolfe, Angela Atwood, Patricia Soltysik, Camilla Hall and Nancy Ling Perry. Steve was convinced that Patty, a wanted bank robber, was left with no choice and would now have to turn herself in.

His optimism was hopelessly naive. Even if Patty did return home there was little chance that she and Steve would reboot their Claremont wedding plans following their trial separation.

I was also beginning to weary of Steve's presence, especially the humiliating way he treated Margot. He spoke to her as if she was a domestic servant. His condescension was appalling and I could never understand his lack of gratitude. When we broke the good news that Margot and I were expecting our first child he snickered.

During those months Steve spent much of his time trying to ignore Patty's potential vulnerability in a court of law. He was convinced any attempt to prosecute her for the San Francisco bank robbery or her role in the Los Angeles carjacking/kidnapping of a teenager following a sporting good store shootout would collapse. Given the facts of her kidnapping and incarceration, he believed no judge would move forward on such a case. After she had a chance to recover with professional help there would be a quiet wedding and a new life together outside the Bay Area spotlight. Steve had every right to his opinion, even if he was dead wrong.

I finished Chapter Nine on Thanksgiving weekend and presented it to Steve first thing Monday. For months I had done my best to reassure him that I could seamlessly channel his voice into a *New York Times* bestseller. The fact that his latest book, *Is The Library Burning?*, had sold just 537 copies and been hit with big bookstore returns was a sore point for him: "I told Random House I was willing to fly anywhere, speak to any audience, do whatever it took to get the book going. The only big interview they got for me was on Firing Line with William F. Buckley. His producer flew me down to Los Angeles, put me up in the Bel Air Hotel and then that jerk proceeded to destroy me in front of a national audience with his patented cynicism."

Although the political movement he championed was big on self-criticism, he did not take well to reviews that trashed his idealism. As one Chicago critic put it: "Sadly, this is not the book Weed was born to write."

This hard knock underscored why Ballantine hired me to ghost write Steve's new book. Chapter 9 was critical. My editors wanted to know if Steve had second thoughts about the way he'd treated Patty in the difficult months prior to her kidnapping. Was it possible that she had remained with the two SLA survivors, Bill and Emily Harris, to give herself time to reconsider the path she had been on with Steve?

I also studied the possibility that she had adroitly brainwashed the Harrises into trusting her. This was a considerable distance from the original Symbionese Liberation Army communique portraying her as a class enemy.

There was one other key point. The Harrises believed that in her presence they were less vulnerable to police or FBI agents opening fire. I suspected they needed her as much as she needed them.

Writing this critical part of the story depended on getting Steve to focus on the book. Margot and I had invited him to live with us in our home because we believed this would help him avoid distractions standing in the way of making our deadline at Ballantine.

While I was at my desk trying to meet my thousand word a day quota Steve hung out with his friends on our patio dining on chili cheeseburgers, orange whip and fries from the Smokehouse. After they finished eating, he and his entourage headed over to the Fillmore for a Grateful Dead concert. Questions I had about his lame interview with Patty's St. Jean's girlfriend Megan Walworth would have to wait another day. I couldn't figure out why she didn't tell him anything we didn't already know.

Megan Walworth: The Virgin Challenge

June 1974

Palo Alto

While Steve flew off to interview one of Patty's closest childhood friends studying theater at Trinity College Dublin, I plunged into transcripts of recorded interviews he left behind.

Instead of focusing on the true story of his life with Patty, he had strategically omitted key details about himself and his lover. Even worse, his own biographical narrative was hopelessly self congratulatory. By sugarcoating his story he was making it impossible for me to do my job. Luckily, I had good sources of my own.

I knew from my agent back in New York that Steve had, during his heyday as a left wing political acolyte, taken a good advance for a book on the black power movement. He had easy access to leaders in the Southern Christian Leadership Council and many other key organizations in the battle for Lyndon Johnson's

Civil Rights Act of 1964.

With his Nation coverage of the 1966 Watts and 1967 Detroit riots added alongside his touching profile of Angela Davis, he was a good choice for a New York publisher. His proposal for a book tentatively called *Colorblind: Segregation's End,* was a work of art. After a bidding war Steve received a sizable advance for a book he never delivered. By the time he went to St. Jean's to teach American history, his lawyer had worked out a plan to repay the advance for the never-delivered book that stretched out over six years.

His decision to ban me from interviewing Patty's closest friends, even my wife's Mills College roommate Cindy, created a major roadblock, leaving out much of the material that our publisher and the reading public wanted. Uncovering what he had left out was a challenge. At the same time I knew that after I uncovered what he didn't write he would try to abandon the good stuff on the cutting room floor.

Fortunately, Megan Walworth called one afternoon when I was fighting my way through yet another worthless Weed interview with Patty's former art teacher. Megan welcomed me to her Palo Alto apartment where she was now a Stanford junior majoring in comparative literature, as well as the arts editor of the Stanford Daily. We sat out on her terrace watching hummingbirds dart in and out of her azaleas. Megan, her red hair tied back in a pony tail, was wearing a Yosemite t-shirt, shorts and sandals. She served me Chablis and cookies.

Before I could begin our interview she launched into an unexpected monologue, that began by confirming many of my worst fears about the future of my collaboration with Steve.

"The quicker you repay Ballantine the better. He is going to destroy you Roger."

"But now that he's off the Patty Hearst expense account he needs the money."

"After all the time you've spent with Steve you don't seem to grasp the fact that he has been lying to you."

"But, why would he want to undermine his own book?"

As I helped myself to her oatmeal raisin cookies Megan made it clear that I failed to properly understand the history of these Berkeley lovebirds.

"To know Patty you have to understand St. Jean's," she told me against the background growl of a 747 banking en route to San Francisco airport.

"Patty was a sophomore transfer student, driving to school every day in her MG, happy to have escaped that Monterey boarding school that ran like a prison. Her first affair with a groundskeeper there was an utter disaster and her grades plummeted. She begged her parents to let her move to St. Jean's. Lucky for her, the nuns thought it was a good idea."

"How did Steve get a job at St. Jean's? I thought they kicked him out when he gave that talk about the student power movement."

"Right, we had to trek over to City Lights in San Francisco for the rest of his talk on his book *Is The Library Burning?*"

"That was his last book right?"

"Correct. When writer's block paralyzed his work he shifted over to teaching."

"But if the school booted him out that day, how did he wind up getting hired?"

"Chill. I'm getting to it. Sister Mary Catherine Francis, the nun who stopped his talk, took a medical leave the following week and just disappeared. Her interim successor was one of the younger more progressive teachers at the school who liked what Steve had to say. She was a big fan of Catholic radicals like Jesuit Priest Daniel Berrigan, an anti-Vietnam war pacifist who broke into a Pennsylvania draft board and burned records."

"Huh?"

"Remember this was San Francisco, not the Vatican. There was a progressive wing of the Catholic Church in the Bay Area, people who had marched in the South with Martin Luther King and against the Vietnam War. Some of them even got arrested. This interim had heard Steve give the Ida B. Tarbell memorial lecture advocating for a national anti-lynching law at an Asilomar Urban League Conference down in Pacific Grove."

"You must have been thrilled when he showed up on the St. Jean's campus."

"Sure, we all were. Of course this was the 60s, women had the pill, free love flourished and as young Catholic girls we had a ..."

"Conflict of interest."

"Sure. At St. Jean's Patty and I decided to form our private after-school virginity club."

"How come Steve never told me this?"

"Membership required keeping a diary of your secret fantasies. There was a prize for the best story read at each monthly meeting, usually a book like *Lady Chatterley's Lover*, *The Story of O* or something by Henry Miller."

"Were these fantasies about guys at Catholic Boys Schools?"

"Oh no, we focused on the male faculty."

"Priests?"

"Never, they were obsessed with choir boys. We dreamed of the young men. And that was when several of us came up with the Virginity Club challenge.

"Patty and I kicked it off. There was a tall gorgeous funny chemistry teacher and Steve. We flipped a coin. She got Steve and I got the other guy. The first one of us to get laid by either of these teachers won a trip to Tahoe.

"Patty lost. The chem teacher was a quickie. Steve turned out to be a challenge. He didn't want anything to do with her."

"Why?"

"The night she showed up unannounced Steve was in bed with me."

Roger, I'm gonna need some time to think about this one. Thanks.—SW

[Two weeks later]...

This is great, just what we needed!—SW

Me & Patty: Steve Weed
Chapter 9
OCTOBER 1974

One night I came home late and discovered Patty had locked the bedroom door. She'd been doing this a lot over the past few weeks and I respected her privacy, spending the night on our living room futon. The following morning I suggested heading out to a place we both dearly loved. We drove across the Richmond/San Rafael Bridge, went north on 101, exited at Lucas Valley Road and headed west to one of our favorite places: Heart's Desire Beach on the Point Reyes Peninsula. Besides being one of the most beautiful places in California, it was also home to two things she adored: an Elk herd and Dale Polisar, an amazing clarinetist who played jazz every Saturday night in Point Reyes Station with pianist Bart Hopkins.

On the beach she launched into an hour-long monologue. Clearly she wasn't ready to marry anyone. After all those months of hinting about a ring she now realized it was too late to undo our wedding. As kids splashed in the water and their parents did yoga, Patty told me: "A society wedding with some priest I've never met is something I'm doing for my mom. I don't believe in the Catholic doctrine. It's a religion that treats women like chattel.

"I keep having these suicidal dreams. The campus clinic doc cautioned me against making any major decisions right now or signing any documents. Do you think people would forgive us if we told them we are postponing the wedding?

"I know, all the deposits have been made, the caterer has been hired, people are flying in from all over and gifts are pouring in. It's so strange that after worrying about us for so long my parents have begun seeing you as a 'fait accompli', someone who will be my guardian angel.

"When you went back to the Midwest for that speaking tour I drove out here and overdosed on some painkillers. The police took me to Marin General where they called my cousin Will, who rushed out and drove me home. I made him promise not to tell you or anyone. The psychologist suggested we might want to consider a smaller wedding.

"I preferred marrying at Wyntoon. After the ceremony with family and friends on the McCloud riverbank we'd honeymoon in the little fairytale village."

It was a stream of consciousness monologue. When she was finished, Patty broke into tears and told me that when she was 12 a cousin tried to rape her during a walk along that river. After she smashed him with a rock he was rushed to a Redding hospital.

"I was afraid he was going to die, " she said. "But luckily I only broke his forearm. Since that day I've never been afraid of anyone. I don't live in fear. But now I'm really worried.

"I'm worried about trapping you in our weird family. I can see how hard it's going to be for you to give up on all these women you've been with since we met. How will you tell them you are no longer available because your bitchy wife is going to haul out a shotgun if you don't stop cheating on her? Steve, I'm frightened that you want to have kids and I don't."

The sun was setting over the Pacific as Patty and I walked back to the car. We drove across Marin and San Pablo Bay into Berkeley without words. By the time we reached our apartment I realized she was expecting me to reach out to her, to find a way to calm her fears and let her know that she could believe in our future. Patty wanted me to touch her heart with words that should have come out spontaneously: I should have said that I wanted to spend our lives together more than anything else. That's she'd be able to trust me and never have second thoughts about our marriage. Our kids will be brilliant and care for us perfectly in our old age, and the sex will always be fantastic.

That is what the moment called for. Instead I poured both of us a glass of wine and turned on the television, sat down and watched 'Colombo'. When I looked up at the end of the show Patty was at her desk, studying for an art history exam.

Roger this is lovely writing. I appreciate the fact that you presented our doubts, the kind every couple faces before heading to the altar, with tenderness and compassion. If you don't mind I would like to do a bit of editing on this one. It brought tears to my eyes as I thought about what life with Patty might have been like. I'll try to get you my thoughts quickly as I know you are on deadline for the 50th anniversary of the kidnapping in 2024. Hard to believe we're both grandparents. –SW

Cindy Jensen

November 19, 1974

Berkeley

As we walked past Tilden Park's little Lake Anza, Margot's Mills College roommate Cindy Jensen was catching the eye of passing joggers. In her tan shorts, low cut blouse and sandals, she was one of those bright young women who seemed to define Berkeley. Protected from the sun by a straw hat and 50 SPF sunblock, Cindy was, as Margot liked to say, "drop dead gorgeous." A confirmed vegetarian, she walked with the grace of a ballerina and spoke with the self confidence of a speech major.

Thanks to her surprise invitation I had a chance to see Cindy beyond the shadow cast by her husband Jeff and their good friend Steve. Now it was her turn to vent on a perfect Berkeley day with a light breeze coming in through the Golden Gate. Her bedside manner toward me would have done credit to any oncologist summarizing the latest blood work for a dying patient.

"I've been worrying about you for months. There's a tsunami headed your way and I want you and Margot to be prepared."

"Have you been talking to Patty?"

"If only."

"Did Weed get arrested?"

"No but he's decided to dump you. He doesn't think he needs a ghost writer, just a yes man like my husband who will simply edit and proofread. Your beautiful book about him and Patty, which I've been reading, is on life support. It's only a matter of weeks until Steve lets you go."

The daughter of a Princeton physicist who did pioneering nuclear bomb research work with Oppenheimer and Lawrence during the World War II Manhattan Project, Cindy grew up in the peaceful 50s. During this placid Berkeley era many people didn't lock their doors and crime was pretty much about shoplifting lingerie at a shop like Hink's Department Store on Shattuck.

After graduating from Mills she had followed her father's lead and gone to work at the Lawrence Lab atop Strawberry Canyon. From her hillside office she had a panoramic view of the campus, the bay, the Golden Gate bridge, San Francisco and down the Peninsula. She calmly seemed to take everything that was going on in her stride.

After visiting the lake we headed over to the Little Farm.

"Patty liked to come up here and feed the goats," Cindy told me as we headed past the barnyard. Pausing to sit down at a picnic table she handed over one of the sandwiches packed for our Tilden outing.

"I should have warned both of you about Steven. Thanks to Patty's allowance which covered their rent, her car and much of their living expenses he didn't have to work. As his writing career declined and he was no longer in demand for political speech making, Steve was essentially unemployed."

"I thought he had a graduate school scholarship."

"Yes, but he didn't need to do any teaching or any other kind of work generating supplemental income. He worked slowly on his thesis with no immediate prospect of getting his PhD."

"Now you're saying that he thinks he can make 100 percent of the book income by dumping me."

"Yes and now that he's no longer a beneficiary of the Hearst empire, he wants to write a book that will put him back on the speaking circuit and give him a chance to pick up awe struck students eager to score with the former lover of Patty Hearst."

"It's a good book," I said.

"That's the problem. It's too good. Instead of thanking you for making him rich he is trying to destroy you. I wish you could hear him and my husband reading your chapters out loud over a few beers."

"They are ridiculing the book?"

"It's worse than that. At night they are tossing some of your pages into a backyard bonfire, roasting marshmallows in the flames."

As we began hiking up a eucalyptus lined trail Cindy voiced her concern for Steve's well being.

"I've tried to tell Steve that my Jeff is not the kind of writer who will stand up to his worst instincts."

"Every writer needs a great editor."

"I liked what you wrote, the way you described how Steve completely mishandled the kidnapping. His screaming forced the SLA to knock him out. Moving in with the Hearsts was guaranteed to destroy his future with Patty."

"Big mistake. Would you move in with your in laws if you knew they couldn't stand you?"

"I'm sure Patty felt that Steve had moved over to the wrong side. Sadly you are working with a man Patty no longer really likes."

"What was the point of the wedding?"

"She believed marrying Steve would help him recover."

"Recover from what?"

"At her insistence he was being treated for depression. As far as I could tell the drugs were making him worse. Perhaps the problem was mixing them with alcohol."

"Did you try to talk her out of getting married?"

"Oh yes. We took a trip during spring break last year to

Oaxaca. Patty wanted to see the ruins at Monte Alban and try some of the famous Mezcal. The whole tourist area is a world heritage site. We spent a lot of time on the Zocalo exploring the folk art scene. Great markets and the best chocolate in the world. Amazing music, not just Mariachi."

"It must have been perfect for her."

"Yes. The Zapotec and Mixtec ruins were amazing. Away from Steve she was thriving, even talking about moving to Mexico."

"Why did she come back?"

"In Oaxaca weddings come with parades of marching bands led by costumed actors on stilts. One night there were four weddings at the central cathedral, all with their own parades. Patty thought it would be very cool to try this in Berkeley."

"Sounds like she had some faith left in Steve."

"She believed fixing Steve was only a matter of finding the right doctor who could prescribe the right medicine."

"Where do you think she is now?"

"I don't know, but I hope for her sake she doesn't come home."

"Is there a chance Patty might talk to me?"

Cindy stopped at a clearing with a commanding view of the Orinda hills. She grabbed my hand and began shaking her head.

"You're not thinking of trying to collaborate with her?" she asked.

"I'm sure Ballantine would be interested," I told her.

Two days after my talk with Cindy, Steve showed up unexpectedly in my birch-shaded back yard. I put down my editing pen on the picnic table as he glanced up at my next door neighbor Joyce working in her adjacent second story home office:

"Let's go inside."

Sitting down on the couch he quickly explained that I was fired.

"That's impossible. We have an agreement."

There was a knock at the door. Steve jumped up to usher in his lawyer Ed Bernhardt, immaculately timed to witness my firing.

About half an hour later, after they'd gone, I walked down the street in a state of semi-shock to share the summons and complaint with neighbor David Pesonen, an attorney who had fought and won a battle to stop a nuclear power plant planned for Bodega Head on the Sonoma County Coast.

"What do you think?" I asked after he'd finished reading the last page of Steve's Alameda County Superior Court filing demanding a permanent injunction on our book and anything else I might write about the Hearst case.

"Do you have $450,000?"

I Think I Know Why She Isn't Coming Back.

January 2, 1975

Alameda County Superior Court

Patty's Fiancé Wants To Throttle Berkeley Writer

Steve's demand that the Alameda County Superior Court block publication of the book we'd been working on made the evening news. Harry's *Oakland Tribune* story on the preliminary hearing with Judge Scott Henderson sported this colorful headline. I loved the pull quote from Steve in boldface:

"Working on a book with Roger was harder on me than getting assaulted by the SLA."

Convinced that all publicity was good publicity, some of my friends insisted that with or without Steve my ghostwritten book would become a bestseller. Just do it and hang the consequences, they seemed to say. Who could resist the untold story as told to the ghostwriter who was sued trying to tell it?

By contrast, after flying to New York and failing to persuade Ballantine to publish his secret rewrite of my work, Steve prayed the judge would ban the book we had been collaborating on for nine months.

His case wasn't helped by the fact that my neighbor and lawyer, David Pesonen, discovered Steve had plagiarized my writing for his 'new' manuscript. The first three chapters of his rewrite had 150 examples of lines he had copied from my work verbatim. In his deposition Weed attacked me for writing faster than he could rewrite. He needed an injunction against me to give him time to finish his revision and sell his sanitized book to another publisher. "Roger's finished Chapter Nine and I'm still working on Chapter Three," he told the judge.

As his claim and my counterclaim moved ahead in court, I wrote about our failed collaboration for *New Times*. The story ended with a call from Marilyn Baker, the KQED TV reporter who was now writing her own book on the kidnapping. She wanted to know if I had any ideas on how to locate Patty.

"Sorry I can't help," I told her, "but I think I know why she isn't coming back."

Steve's lawyer made a courtroom scene before the judge, waving my *New Times* cover story that spilled the beans on our falling out. He demanded that I be held in contempt.

"This article is filled with lies attributed to my client," the lawyer yelled. "Mr. Weed denies that Ms. Hearst ever told him she wished her parents would die in a plane crash. It's simply not true that her mother delighted in reading the racist Little Black Sambo series to her daughters. Steve never referred to Ms. Hearst as a 'little bitch' after she made negative comments about him on a taped SLA communique."

The judge, who had read the article prior to the hearing, challenged the lawyer's story.

"Counsel, are you also saying that he never drank some of the vintage Bordeaux he and Ms. Hearst took from the San Simeon wine cellar."

"That's a lie," yelled Steve, as his lawyer tried to restrain him. "I didn't touch their precious fucking wine."

The judge pounded his gavel.

"Mr. Weed, you're out of order."

Turning back to the article, the judge resumed his inquiry.

"What about the assertion that your client flipped through one of Ms. Hearst's checkbooks saying to Mr. Rapoport, 'Wouldn't it freak the FBI out if we tore off some of these checks and just started dropping them off on various street corners.'"

"Another lie," yelled Steve.

"Plantiff's motion for an injunction on this work is denied," said the judge.

On the way out of the courtroom Harry invited me to lunch at Rattos in Old Oakland, determined to find out how an old friend could have possibly been so hopelessly blindsided.

"Steve was living under your roof, eating your food, pretending to collaborate with you all those months and you never realized he was lying to you all that time. Didn't you cross check any of the nonsense he was peddling."

"Actually I did."

"Then why didn't you fire the little fucker, give back your

part of the advance and go back to the other book you were supposed to be writing about those super doctors down in Houston?"

"After Patty dumped him I thought he'd reach a point where I could convince him to tell the truth."

"What gave you that idea. I thought you were an investigative reporter."

"I made a mistake."

"Roger," said Harry digging into his pesto pasta, "a mistake can get you killed."

Patty Hearst Came Home Last Night

September/October, 1975

San Francisco Federal Court

Failure to promptly repay your advance will force us to take legal action against you.

Our editor at Ballantine had written Steve a demand letter reiterating his decision to reject Steve's pathetic rewrite of my chapters.

While the lawyers worked on a settlement I stepped away from the Hearst kidnapping case. I returned to the world of the super doctors, interviewing celebrity physicians including dueling Houston heart surgeons Denton Cooley and Michael DeBakey.

In the spring of 1975, shortly after the fall of Saigon and the end of the Vietnam war that neither Steve nor I had fought in, he finally dropped his lawsuit. My former collaborator took back his rights to our book after paying me $15,000. He repaid our advance to Ballantine, as demanded, and continued working on his own book with another publisher who paid him a smaller advance.

On September 18, 1975 the FBI arrested the Harrises while they were jogging in the Golden Gate. Hours later Patty was apprehended in her San Francisco apartment and the 'kidnapping of Patty Hearst' came to an end.

I was assigned by the Los Angeles *Herald-Examiner* to cover the arraignment on the 19th floor of the San Francisco Federal Building. After clearing security I ran into Jack and Micki Scott, the couple that hid Patty and the Harrises for six months at their rented Poconos farmhouse in Pennsylvania.

"What do we do now?" Jack asked Micki as he reclaimed his wallet and looped his belt back around his jeans. Jack had just followed his wife through the tight security check on the 19th floor of the San Francisco Federal Building. Now, shortly after 1 p.m., the Scotts were faced with a difficult decision in a hallway packed with lawyers, journalists, and worried relatives of the celebrity defendants *du jour*. In just one day the FBI had taken the last remnants of the Symbionese Liberation Army into custody without incident. This was a badly needed boost for the agency being pilloried by the media for its inability to find another missing kidnap victim in Michigan, Teamsters leader Jimmy Hoffa.

In the courtroom to the left of where Jack and Micki were sitting, the Harrises faced a 2 p.m. bond hearing. In the courtroom to the of right of them Patty Hearst was scheduled for a bond hearing an hour later. Because Patty was being arraigned separately from the Harrises, everyone had to make a difficult choice. This was especially hard for the Scotts, now under investigation for hiding all three SLA fugitives in rural Pennsylvania.

"I'll go watch the Harrises," said Micki Scott. "You go see Patty's hearing since you were the one who was romantically involved with her."

Jack laughed at his wife's little joke and then headed for

a seat in the second row with his friend, the Reverend Cecil Williams, Minister of Involvement at Glide Memorial Church, the only Methodist sanctuary in the world boasting a rabbi-in-residence.

In the early days of the Symbionese Liberation Army offensive, two of their communiques were routed through Williams. Because his church was the focal point of the San Francisco counter-culture, he also chaired a coalition of community groups attempting to ransom Hearst through the abortive food distribution program.

With Glide serving as a neutral party, Williams was hard at work on a plan to guarantee the Symbionese Liberation Army safe passage out of the country in return for Patty's release. Alas, Randy bailed when the SLA insisted on taking him along for the ride to political asylum.

"I'm not going unless you come along, Cecil," Patty's father said when the Reverend dropped by the family home to submit the SLA's latest non-negotiable offer.

Rev. Williams and Jack Scott told the media they were surprised by the arrests. Why had the Harrises been out jogging together in Golden Gate Park without disguises?

"Jack and I warned them to jog separately back at our farmhouse," said Micki Scott. "They were careless."

She was also surprised that the three of the most wanted bank robbers in America came home to a city flooded with FBI agents tracking them down.

"The only place that could have been worse for them would have been Berkeley."

A minute later a young man came over to Cecil Williams and stuck out his hand.

"Just wanted to say hello to you, Reverend. I lived next to DeFreeze at Vacaville Prison for nine months before he was transferred to Soledad and escaped. He was one heavy dude, always in the room typing and taking care of business. If he got mad he'd really let you know it. He never scared me. I mean we shared books and records and chowed down every Friday with Charlie Manson.

"I also met some of those guys who came to see DeFreeze, like Willie Wolfe. He helped out with the Vacaville inmate tutoring program. You know Willie was just like Patty said he was. I can see why they fell for each other."

I took my seat in the front row of the press gallery as word filtered in that a judge in the courtroom across the hall had set bail for the Harrises at $500,000. Minutes later Patty's parents, cousin Will and sister Anne arrived with her attorney F. Lee Bailey who had taken over the case from the leftist father and son team Vincent and Terrence Hallinan. After the prosecution was seated, a security guard plugged into an earphone marched in. The court rose for Judge Oliver Carter, who was confused by the unfamiliar guard's presence in the gallery.

"Get that man out of here. I don't want him in my courtroom."

After a clerk explained this intruder was part of a special security team, Judge Carter called for a recess.

By the time the judge returned to the bench, half a dozen new guards were sprinkled across the courtroom. Thirty minutes later Patty was ushered into the courtroom sporting a 'PARDON ME' t-shirt and unbelted brown corduroys. Her hair was a mess. Her lawyer said nothing in his motion for Patty's bail about the zeal she had expressed for the SLA in her communiques. There was, her lawyer said, no danger in releasing her to the custody of parents. Nor did he deem it relevant to mention that Patty had quite recently described said parents as "swine."

After listening to F. Lee Bailey's argument for pre-trial release for Patty on bail, Judge Carter, however, refused to turn her over to the family she had denounced as "pig Hearsts." Instead of spending the night in her childhood bedroom filled with stuffed animals, she went back to jail.

As the bailiffs took a handcuffed Patty away, Jack Scott and Cecil Williams left the hearing. On the courthouse steps Micki Scott, carrying an afternoon edition of the Hearst's *Examiner*, joined them. They glanced at a front-page headline:

Patty Hearst Came Home Last Night

Across the bay, Harry Harris had wisely taken a different tack with the *Oakland Tribune*.

PATTY HEARST BUSTED WITH HER KIDNAPPERS

> SAN FRANCISCO—After 19 months of killings, gun battles, kidnappings, police standoffs, bank robberies, and food riots, California and the Bay Area breathed easier last night with the arrest of the last three surviving members of the Symbionese Liberation Army.
>
> Among them was heiress, UC Berkeley art major and self-described "urban guerrilla" Patty Hearst. She was denied bail in a federal courtroom as her mother and sisters wept.
>
> "I am not going to be responsible for the lives that could be lost," said Judge Oliver Carter, as the nonchalant young defendant sat in silence with her counsel.
>
> "Six people have already died in this case. This defendant is a serious flight risk and I will not put her family or this city in jeopardy for another minute."

Patty's October bank robbery trial was perfect timing for Steve's publisher who decided to move up the publication date of *My Search for Patty Hearst.*

Weed was booked for 22 radio and TV interviews during the first ten days of the trial. Just four hours before his own scheduled turn as Patty's first defense witness he told a TV reporter that Patty was a "sarcastic" young women who has "always been a bit of a rebel."

The implication that she may not have been brainwashed by the SLA prompted F. Lee Bailey's defense team to reverse course and drop Weed from their witness list.

Although Steve's advance for his book was a fraction of

the deal he and I had with Ballantine, his publisher made sure it was in book store windows on the day Patty took the stand. Unfortunately for him, other competing works were already out and trial coverage superseded Steve's so-called "shocking" revelations about their private lives.

The critics at papers like the *San Diego Union* were no help: "Say what you will about Patty Hearst's ex-fiancé, he is clearly no threat to F. Scott Fitzgerald."

Another take on Steve's book appeared in a *Oui* magazine piece, 'The Selling of Steven Weed: Patty-Cake, Patty-Cake, Agent Man, Make Me Some Bread As Fast As You Can'. This story, featured an illustration of Steve posing as a cigar store Native American holding out a copy of his new book in his outstretched left hand.

The author, Robert S. Weider, began: "'One of the most controversial, bizarre and terrifying tales of the century, and he tells it all, in his new book.' Merv Griffin holds up the book and talks, as only he can.

"Now he'll tell it to us, in his first TV appearance, since the FBI captured Patty....'"

"And Steven Weed comes blinking into the lights—author raconteur, ex-fiancé near-miss-Hearst-in-law, turned celebrity and victim of the year, 1974. He is here to cash in on the longest-running box-office news event of the seventies by hyping the long-awaited personal account of his ordeal, *My Search for Patty Hearst.*"

Dear Roger: My lawyer told me
you need to cut all the Weider
stuff. He thinks it's libelous.
—SW

It's Too Soon To Tell

December 3, 1975

Goleta, California

While the Patty Hearst bank robbery trial dragged on amidst a San Francisco media frenzy, I headed south on US 101 for a reality check at the University of California Santa Barbara's Institute of Behavioral Psychology. Dr. Sarah Anne Robinson, the institute director, chaired the White House Urban Crime Task Force task force. This research center was nationally known for its pioneering work in criminology. While well-paid mental health consultants presented their opposing theories in court on Patty's state of mind when she participated with the SLA in the Hibernia bank robbery, I sought an independent point of view. Was it possible their testimony at the trial was less than the whole truth?

The institute's studies focused on the reliability of eyewitness accounts, a subject of considerable interest to me. I had recently read an article on Lyndon B. Johnson's presidency summarizing competing accounts of the battle over John F. Kennedy's decision to choose Senate Majority Leader Johnson as his 1960 vice-presidential nominee. A bevy of parties to this decision, including the President's brother Bobby, had all written fascinating memoirs on the period. They all disagreed on many of the key details of Kennedy's pick, a choice that would lead to passage of the Civil Rights Act, The Voting Rights Act, Medicare, and the War on Poverty. Aides in the same room at the same time watching Bobby's heavy-handed attempts to block Johnson's nomination, contradicted one another on the key facts.

Dr. Robinson poured a steaming cup of percolated Folgers coffee and sat down in an easy chair next to her slumbering labradoodle. She spoke with the kind of authority and objectivity that would capture the hearts and minds of any jury.

"Our staff frequently serves as expert witnesses at criminal trials," she told me. "In court cases it inevitably comes down to who can tell the best story. The challenge is inevitably the same. You can never credibly tell your own story unless you are willing to expose others."

"This gets complicated when you realize there are essentially five parties to a criminal case: the defendant, the prosecution, the defense, judge and jury.

"Roger, it sounds like you have covered some great trials. The challenge in every case is that our senses limit what we observe. Uncertainty can complicate a jury's decision. It all comes down to deciding if they can trust the person presenting evidence.

"For example, medical professionals have a documented bias toward diagnosing a problem differently, depending on their specialty. This is the result of confirmation bias - why did the person come to see me if they did not have that illness."

"To a hammer everything looks like a nail."

"More or less. Patients who have self-diagnosed and seek confirmation compound the physician's dilemma. They may emphasize certain symptoms and not mention others, leading the doctor to a certain conclusion."

"That sounds dangerous."

"I read your *New Times* cover story last night and it's possible you're another victim of confirmation bias. That story on the Ku Klux Klan at Camp Pendleton was riveting. But did you ever stop to consider why the Klan has been incredibly successful infiltrating the Marines?"

"I assumed base leaders turned a blind eye to the Klan."

"You argued that point convincingly. If I didn't know better I would have believed you."

"Did I miss something?"

"What you left out is that some Marine recruiters are actually Klansmen themselves."

"You're kidding."

"They turn out the kind of numbers prized by Marine leadership. It's simply a matter of getting members of a private cult to quit and go to work for a government cult that gives them a better tailored uniform and pays a living wage. In the process racists became patriots."

"And they don't have to wash their own sheets."

"A company laundry is a nice perk."

"Makes sense."

"Of course they aren't going to tell you they enlisted after being recruited by a Marine who happens to be a card carrying Klansman. My father was a Marine and I can tell you he's more horrified by this breach of ethics than we are. Unfortunately some recruiters will do anything to exceed their quotas and win a bonus big enough for an inside passage Alaskan cruise."

"Do you think Patty was brainwashed?"

"If she loses in court her lawyers will use that excuse to build momentum for a Presidential commutation."

"She's exploiting the media to peddle that story."

"That's pretty ironic when you consider her family history. The point is you are paid to give readers exclusive information. It's tough to go to your editors and tell them there's no story. You are forced to report some version of what someone says about people you'll never talk to, including her alleged rebel lover and the criminal mastermind leading the Symbionese Liberation Army."

"So, by reporting suspect information I'm meeting the expectations of my editors and my readers."

"Yes, and there is something else you are missing. Most people who have been following the case have a built-in bias against the SLA."

"I get that. They are inclined to take her word for it."

"Even if she loses and goes to jail I guarantee you she'll get early parole. No matter what the judge and jury decide she is a privileged white heiress, the daughter of a family with one hell of a megaphone, great lobbyists and plenty of money to contribute to political campaigns on both sides of the aisle.

"That's why I'm thinking about writing a book on the case."

"You already did that with her ex-fiancé."

"It didn't work out."

"And now you want to try again?"

"That's a definite maybe."

"How do you expect to get to all the people you need to see? Why would kidnappers like the Harrises want to talk to you when they are standing trial? Anything they say could be used against them. Patty, of course, would never want to see you after your time with Steve, who she despises."

"Where did I go wrong?"

"Look, like all of us you have to make a living. Steve was a quick sale, an easy way for you to get a foothold in Berkeley real estate."

"People think it's funny that he and I were going to buy houses together."

"Bad judgment tends to compound itself. Why do you want to write another book that will probably take decades to report and complete? By the time you're done you'll end up doing author talks at assisted living centers in Petaluma."

"What about libraries. Don't you think they'll want it?"

"Sure but your book will be buried behind dozens of other books."

"I'm going to find a way to get to all the people who never talked to the media."

"That's going to take a very long time. And even if you do get to kidnapper Bill Harris, he's going to give you a bill of goods. Same thing for the FBI, Patty's family, the lawyers, that kid Tom Matthews they kidnapped in Inglewood, Wendy Yoshimura ... they are all going to be hopelessly biased.

"Look what happened to the six members of the Symbionese Liberation Army who died. Buoyed by their successful kidnapping, they naively believed they could remain a step ahead of the law in urban California. Their instant success upending the Hearst media made them think they could succeed with more guerrilla actions. Suddenly the whole world was riveted by their demands. The Hearsts were willing to give them their $4 million as long as they set Patty free. They couldn't take yes for an answer."

"Perhaps, but by the time that happened, Patty had cooled on the idea of being a Hearst. She had a new lover."

"You failed to understand that under these circumstances it was impossible to collaborate with the now-jilted Steve. His emotional bias distorts reality. It interferes with perception in a way that blocks or filters out what is actually happening. These biases can be exacerbated by physiological issues, as well as external influences."

"That also applies to me, a so-called investigative reporter trusting Steve Weed for six months on a co-written book missing the inevitability that he would kill it with a lawsuit."

"I'm delighted you haven't lost your sense of humor."

"Are you working on the court case?"

"The prosecution and the defense both wanted me to serve as an expert witness in the SLA/Patty Hearst San Francisco bank robbery case. I turned them both down for the same reason."

"That's part of why I'm here."

"As you know, consultant prostitution pays great in academia. But that's not what we do at the institute."

"The money's good."

"As you've learned, Roger, what matters most is your reputation. Besides, it doesn't matter who wins this high profile case. Patty's worst-case scenario is that she will serve a few years and probably have her sentence commuted. That will, of course, lead to a big book and movie deal. I don't want to be pilloried or praised by this woman. We try keeping it in neutral around here. Twisting the truth to serve a dubious client, and getting paid for it, could put the entire institute in jeopardy. Look at it this way. What's going to happen when your agent goes out to pitch your next 'big book'?

"I've been tainted."

"My advice is to slow down and take the long view."

"Like China's Zhou Enlai who, when asked through an interpreter, what he thought about the impact of the French Revolution said...."

"It's too soon to tell."

"The irony is that Zhou misunderstood the question. He thought the reference was to the French student revolt in 1968."

"As long as you believe the interpreter."

"In this case, the interpreter would be a credible source."

"Because he had no incentive to lie?"

"Bingo. Unfortunately there are a number of common ways our brains can "trick" us into a misconception. A University of Wisconsin study shows these biases serve as filters, hindering our ability to make accurate decisions based on the truth. In most cases this obstacle won't be a matter of life or death."

"You're worried about high-risk situations where a decision improperly filtered due to cognitive bias can be fatal."

"All journalists are trained to believe that the eye of the

beholder is the *sine qua non* of a great story. You think that by simply finding eyewitnesses your stories will write themselves."

"What their brains have recorded is inevitably the closest we will ever get to the truth."

"Every defendant can explain why he or she should have never been arrested. Every lawyer tells the best story possible in defense of their supposedly innocent client. Every FBI agent and police officer swears to tell a straight story based on training teaching them how to properly handle supposedly perfect evidence. A carefully chosen eyewitness offers judges and juries what lawyers, in their closing arguments, call 'indisputable evidence.' Our studies suggest that anyone who takes the stand can be misleading in many important ways. There really is no such thing as pure objectivity."

"We the media try to tell our readers and viewers what happened, based on unimpeachable sources we relentlessly cross check."

"Think about it Roger. Patty will testify under oath that she was forced by her kidnappers to rob a bank or cover them with gunfire while one of her comrades was stealing a bandolier. The defense will reinforce her view day after day."

"When opinions are repeated over and over they may be accepted as fact. This approach, repeating a lie over and over, is the essence of many legal arguments. Now in the other courtrooms across the hall the defense representing revolutionaries Patty ran with will present the opposite point of view. The Harrises are going to claim that all of the crimes Patty committed were free will acts. After the bank robbery they even trusted her with a gun. These revolutionaries will demolish the idea that she was forced to do anything against her will. They'll point out that for over a year she could have easily walked away and turned herself in. She wasn't even living with the Harrises when she was finally arrested."

"That doesn't sound like coercion."

"Now you understand why none of us here at the institute want anything to do with this show trial. The prosecutors and the FBI are fighting to save their reputations. The defense is being paid a fortune to set her free, including a share of her potential book rights. There is no way to independently confirm who is telling the truth."

"How do you avoid these traps?"

Dr. Robinson handed me a paper she had just published in a British journal.

"Don't overestimate your intelligence or the quality of your judgments. Once you think you're on the right track you could be subject to the kind of confirmation bias that led you to trust her fiancé as he was secretly rewriting all the stuff he told you."

"And leaving out so much of what I needed to know... I never suspected..."

"Why would you mistrust the guy who was making you rich? He lied to you twice, first when he convinced you that he was giving you the straight story for *New Times* and again when he pretended to let you become his ghost writer for a great deal of money."

"I believed him because I had to."

"He wanted to marry Patty and become a Hearst."

"I wanted to write a profitable book."

"That meant your book was destined to be dead on arrival. I'm sure some of what he was telling you was actually true. He needed you to write his first draft. At the same time he gave you enough good stuff to pacify your publisher and hold them off. Then he dumped you, cut out what he didn't like and published his own book. He wanted a book that would help him win back the woman he'd dearly loved. You were in his way."

"Which is why he waited until the book was nearly finished to fire me. He slept in my cottage, ate my food, entertained his friends, and did yoga in my backyard for six months and I never caught on.

"It was similar to your Klan story for *New Times*. Did you ever consider how those stupid racists you interviewed at Camp Pendleton managed to qualify for the Marines?"

"I just assumed..."

"It never occurred to you that those recruiters also had a network of stand-ins taking the Marine qualifying exam for hopeless Klan applicants who previously flunked the test?"

"I was focused on their persistent attacks against black Marines."

"In their minds, vicious attacks they committed against blacks never happened."

"I guess all of us can be victims of emotionally triggered misconceptions."

"I was an expert witness in a case where a female doctoral student accused a male psychology professor of propositioning her. He denied it. My job was to help a faculty committee decide who was telling the truth. There were no other eyewitnesses to the incident that triggered the student's accusation."

"What did you do?"

"In separate sessions I asked each of them to repeat verbatim what was said. Then I brought them together and asked them to repeat their stories in front of each other."

"The second time would be a lot more stressful."

"Because we had recorded both sessions, the committee was able to review all the discrepancies between the first and second versions. After we reached 20 changes each in their respective stories the committee asked for an explanation.

"That was easy. I gave both of them a brilliant neuroscience study demonstrating that stronger encoding and storage of emotional memories is driven by engagement of a specialized system of stress hormones—glucocorticoids. Arousing content can dramatically impact neuronal processes underlying memory consolidation and storage."

"Memory isn't always a faithful record of what was

perceived through sight and sound?"

"Its contents can be forgotten or contaminated at multiple stages. As neuroscientists and research psychologists explained in a book you should read, *The Invisible Gorilla*, our intuitions can easily deceive us. These experts believe details are heavily swayed by emotional states associated with witnessed events and their recall."

"What did the committee do?"

"They called back both parties to report their findings. The professor and student apologized to each other."

"You don't hear that kind of thing very often."

"If I were you I'd let go of your past experience, abandon all deadlines, work on the book when it makes sense and avoid taking anyone's word as gospel, even mine. Ultimately you need to let the reader reach their own conclusions about Patty Hearst and her supporting cast."

"What do you think about the idea of my fictionalizing the book?"

"A true crime novel! Now that's perfect. Roger, I just love it."

"Any suggestions/recommendations?"

"Around here we have something called a longitudinal study, where you follow the same group of people for decades. It's one way to avoid snap judgments. The results are endlessly fascinating."

"Are you suggesting I create my own longitudinal study?"

"Only if you want to."

"What happens when stories people tell me don't always square up on the plumb line of history?"

"At best they will help you create a first draft. The final word is left to historians who spend years pinning down key facts others may have missed. Alas, their job is often complicated by the fact that eyewitnesses may have left this earth. It's not like you can just send John Wilkes Booth a letter to double check a detail about his gun barrel. That's why your idea of fictionalizing the story makes sense."

"You think I'm the right person to take all this on?"

"Sounds like you've already started."

"How long is this going to take?"

"How long do you have?"

As I walked out the door I turned back to Dr. Robinson with one final question.

"What happened to that professor and graduate student who went before the committee?"

"The professor took a new position at Cornell where he just won a big multi-year research award from the National Science Foundation. After receiving her PhD here, the student was hired for a psychology faculty position and just won tenure. We moved in together last month and are adopting our first child in August, a boy. His name is Cody and it looks like he is on his way to becoming a soccer star."

"I'll look forward to watching him play in the World Cup."

This is a good one and I think you're on the right track. I just wish you could find a way to understand why I had to do what I did. Not sure about brain damage from the SLA attack but I was clearly off base in the way I treated you and Margot.—SW

Part ii

My Own Search For Patty

Where Secrets Come To Die

June 3, 1979

Wyntoon, CA

When Amtrak's Coast Starlight rolled in to Dunsmuir at the foot of Mt. Shasta at 3 a.m. there was only one vehicle in the parking lot. The owner, a bearded man in jeans and a Golden Bear sweatshirt, was sleeping in the cab of a pickup with a bumper sticker that read: *When Guns Are Outlawed, Only Outlaws Will Kill Their Kids Accidentally.*

As we rolled north on a warm summer night I was beginning my own search for Patty Hearst. Just a few months earlier she had won early release from federal custody in Pleasanton, California. My four years working on other books, newspaper and magazine articles had been a welcome break from the case. Now the proud father of two young children—my beautiful daughter Elizabeth had been born a year earlier—I was happy to be working on stories that had a beginning, middle and end. Reading Steve's book, as well as many competing works by celebrity journalists, convinced me that all the prize-winning coverage, exclusive TV interviews, and inside accounts of the kidnapping set up more questions than they answered.

After Patty was convicted on bank robbery charges, she was sentenced to seven years in Pleasanton federal prison. Celebrities like John Wayne and government officials such as FBI Agent In Charge Charles Bates enlisted in the well-funded Committee To Free Patty Hearst. After President Gerald Ford freed Patty in 1978, she went to work on a book herself with a well respected journalist.

Bill and Emily Harris had another three years to go on their sentence for the Los Angeles kidnapping, carjacking and robbery case that centered around Mel's Sporting Goods and Tom Matthews, the carjacked bystander. Catherine and Randy were living separately in San Diego and New York as their divorce lawyers negotiated a settlement. Steve had disappeared from public life, fired two screenwriters and was working solo on the thirteenth draft of a screenplay based on his book. Variety reported Jodie Foster and Sean Penn were the first choices of potential director Steven Spielberg, who had yet to commit. Steve's new agent insisted on hiring a script doctor as soon as his client could line up enough campus speaking events to cover the cost.

After winning a Pulitzer Prize for his coverage of the Hearst case, Harry Harris, settled back into his beloved crime beat in Oakland.

"Since Knowland died it's become harder and harder to find time for investigative reporting. Every time I make a few calls there's yet another murder to cover," he told me at breakfast the day before I headed north on the night train.

"You think there is more to the story?"

"Yes, without a doubt, and you are the perfect reporter to find the truth."

Every time I looked at the Patty Hearst case I saw open ends. Was Harry right? Could the "official" story of the kidnapping be a media myth? How could I get people to break their silence and tell me what really happened?

Finally I was back on the case, riding shotgun as Hank

Nichols, eased his truck out of the station lot and climbed northeast across a moonlit landscape carpeted with pine and oak. This is what I loved about California. Every time you gained 1,000 feet of elevation you were in another country.

"So glad your train was on time," he said as Barbara Mandell came over the truck radio crooning '(If Loving You Is Wrong) I Don't Want to Be Right'. "Often it's hours late due to freight traffic."

We were on our way to Wyntoon, the Hearst family estate Nichols had managed for 40 years.

"I came here as a summer worker and never left," said the UC Berkeley grad. Unless you were willing to brave the McCloud River's class 4 and 5 rapids via kayak or canoe, it is impossible to see this hidden estate without an invitation. And even if you did paddle down to this Hearst aerie, you would quickly be asked to leave.

Ancestral home of the Wintun Indians, these lands in the shadow of the Siskiyou range had escaped the logger's ax, the roar of the interstate, a myriad of RV parks and their dump stations. Unlike San Simeon, this retreat had not become a state park blowing the minds of a million visitors annually. Wyntoon was the family's private refuge, the place where secrets came to die a slow and painful death.

Patty's great grandfather, silver magnate George Hearst, paid cash for this 10,000 acre sanctuary in 1904. Never one to think small, he built a seven-story replica of a German Rhineland castle with a Gothic dining hall and monumental fireplaces. After the scion's death in 1914, his widow Phoebe turned the place into a family summer camp where her five sons played with the workers' children as well as friends who drove up from San Francisco. A tireless philanthropist and suffragist, she was also a highly regarded nature writer and close friend of conservationist John Muir.

Phoebe died during the great flu pandemic of 1918, leaving the Wyntoon estate to her niece, Anne Apperson Flint. One of George's sons, Patty's grandfather William Randolph ("The Chief"), was depressed for months after learning that his consolation prize, the Wyntoon art collection, was on loan to the San Francisco Palace of the Legion of Honor for an exhibition. Now operating a flourishing newspaper empire, he quickly retaliated. With an assist from family security, he seized the paintings before they could be returned to storage up north. A bitter family feud finally came to an end when The Chief purchased the entire Wyntoon estate from cousin Anne.

In 1929, a year after The Chief became lord of the manor, the grand mansion burned to the ground. He promptly hired Berkeley architects Bernard Maybeck and Julia Morgan, to design a new mansion fashioned from a recently-purchased 12th century Spanish monastery. While that treasure cost only $90,000, he paid $1 million to ship the structure across the Atlantic to New York stone by stone.

It took a trainload of freight cars to move the monastery to Dunsmuir where a fleet of trucks spent days ferrying it on to Wyntoon, complete with artwork The Chief had reclaimed from his cousin in San Francisco.

As the country collapsed into a depression, Hearst campaigned vigorously for the reelection of Republican Herbert Hoover in 1932.

"Nobody's perfect but we believe Herbert Hoover has earned a second term," proclaimed the company's editorial pages coast to coast.

Hearst fought tirelessly against Roosevelt's New Deal as his company drifted into bankruptcy in 1937. Now on a strict allowance, his edifice complex was cut short. Among the casualties was the proposed Wyntoon mansion.

As the company slowly recovered from receivership, Julia Morgan designed a downsized Bavarian village with three whimsically decorated homes, Hansel, Gretel and Rapunzel. Proving that we're all still kids, muralists painted the exteriors of these turreted homes in fairy tale fashion. Wandering doves, snuggly bunnies and rainbow feathered turkeys brought Morgan's alpine vision to life on the banks of the McCloud.

After unlocking the gate to a private access road, Hank drove eight miles to this alpine sanctuary. I rested for a few hours in a guest cottage and rose for a walk to the riverside gazebo. Here Hank and I were served blueberry waffles. An amateur history buff, the estate manager offered me a nuanced overview of this Hearst sanctuary.

Following the Japanese sneak attack on Pearl Harbor, The Chief worried that San Simeon could become a future Japanese coastal target. He retreated to Wyntoon with Marion Davies who despised the place nicknaming it 'Spittoon'. While The Chief stayed safe in the mountains, his editorial writers campaigned for the internment of more than 100,000 Japanese-Americans he believed were a security risk.

Given his passion for the movies, especially films featuring his paramour Marion Davies, there was one important exception to his racist outlook on life. Friends with many of Hollywood's Jewish elite such as Louis B. Mayer, he had zero tolerance for American anti-semitism.

This led to a showdown with visiting businessman and former British ambassador Joseph Kennedy who arrived with his teenage son Jack.

Nichols told me that on the first night of the Kennedy visit Hearst had recoiled at his famous guest's attacks on the "Hollywood Jews."

According to reports from the serving staff, the elder Kennedy insisted Jews were "a bunch of con artists busy robbing him blind when they weren't busy grooming actresses for their personal pleasure."

The old man replied that he had many close Jewish friends around the world.

"And how would you feel if one of your sons married a

Jew?" the ambassador asked.

"Actually one already has."

With celebrity visitors like Charles Lindbergh, Spencer Tracy, and Claudette Colbert, the lord of the manor was never bored. When I inquired about Hearst's vast art collection my host led me to a brightly painted steel building. Inside were a series of climate-controlled vaults.

"We've stored some of the artwork shipped here for the castle he was too broke to rebuild. Over the years much of it was sold to the family at a deep discount."

"A kind of private fire sale."

"A public auction was unthinkable. The Chief's heirs always respected a clause in his will stipulating that the art could only be sold to descendants."

"Harry Harris told me you knew Patty well," I probed.

"Yes, and he mentioned you were trying to write some kind of book about her. Don't you think she's a bit young for a biography? Patty was just getting started."

"Do any of us know who we are at 19?"

"She's actually 25. I see her life as a panorama that touches the heart of every parent. It's ironic that these self-proclaimed freedom fighters chose to imprison an innocent young woman."

"She loved it here?" I asked.

"This place was her second home. Patty adored riding our horses. I was so looking forward to that wedding. My wife and I had booked a junior suite at the Claremont. We don't get out of this place much. Keeping it alive is a high wire act. Julia Morgan was a great architect but the mechanical side of this place is out of the 17th century. Her plumbers must have all been on parole."

"How do you know Harry?"

"Our dads roomed together at UC Berkeley. They visited from time to time and loved fishing."

"Harry's dad actually knew Patty's family?"

"He and my dad always made their visits when the Hearsts

weren't around. Both of them were allergic to the rich and famous."

"And you?"

"They've paid me generously for over 40 years. I realize they were badly damaged by the kidnapping but there's so much you don't know."

"That's why I'm here."

As we walked the property I was impressed by Hank's vitality and self-deprecating wit. A youthful 70, he joyfully choreographed our visit as if this was his first tour.

"Patty visited every summer with cousins who never tired of Wyntoon. As a girl she loved sitting by the river watching the mallards splash about as her uncles fished these waters. This estate was her chance to connect with siblings and extended family away from the oversight of parents off on Mediterranean cruises, Botswana safaris or golfing vacations in Scotland. By the time Steve began joining her at Wyntoon, she had developed a keen interest in the warehouses where her grandfather's art was stored."

"Was Steve her first love?"

"Oh no, at 14 she fell for one of the summer cooks, a physics major at Humboldt State. When they were caught *in flagrante delicto* up in an attic he was instantly banished. Her mother even mailed him a pack of condoms he left behind in the ruckus COD."

"Patty's dream had been to build a retreat here, a place where she could become a visual artist. While Steve was less interested in the possibility of leaving the Bay Area, he shared Patty's passion for art, especially pieces carefully stored in our climate controlled vault. Not sure what to bid on at the family auction, she recruited a San Francisco art appraiser named Massey for guidance."

"No first name?"

"He always went by his last name. Patty didn't bid on anything without his counsel."

"What was he like?"

"He was here several times before the kidnapping, looking over items Patty and Steve wanted. They weren't the kind of pieces you'd normally pay much attention to, court paintings, royal portraits, what my professors back at Berkeley referred to as dynastic art."

"The kind of thing Tintoretto was famous for."

"Yes, and Patty, based on her own research, was convinced some of this work was seriously undervalued."

"Was she right?"

"That's hard to say, but one day I walked into the barn and found her exploring a small side vault I didn't even know existed."

"How did she get in?"

"I'm not sure, but if you're serious about this book there's one thing you need to know about Patty. She was an escape artist, par excellence."

"How did you handle it?"

"At first I thought she was pulling rank. I was pretty good at getting the rest of the family to do what I wanted. Alas Patty was beyond words. She only heard what she agreed with. She is probably the most single-minded person I've ever met. The way she ran around with Steve when she was only 16 was astonishing. They took trips to Hawaii, drove about California for weeks, and came up here whenever they felt like it. For her it was always spring break."

"What about her parents?"

"When she was younger the nannies handled it. By the time she was a teenager her parents were on the road half the time, holding court all over the world. Patty existed as an emancipated minor."

"Perfect for her."

"She and Steve made love everywhere imaginable. One time I walked into the barn to do some repair work and there they were stretched out together on a blanket. I'm sure they heard me and just kept right on going for an hour."

"Did he help on her treasure hunts?"

"Yes, particularly when she found this one vault that no one else paid attention to. She took a liking to this one painting and asked if she could borrow it for show and tell at one of her classes."

"Did you ever get it back?"

"No, Patty gave this piece of art to Massey for an appraisal. Several weeks after the kidnapping Steve called with an update."

"When he was recovering at the Hearsts from the SLA beating?"

"Yes, he told me he had just met with one of Patty's cousins who accepted his $1,000 offer for the painting."

"Doesn't that sound a bit low?"

"Roger, in this job there are some questions you never ask."

Some damn good reporting here. So well done I almost believed it. As fiction this works nicely. BTW I just heard back from my libel lawyer and he says there's no problem with that section I was worried about. Whew.—SW

A Guy Like Steve Isn't Going To Settle For Years Of Conjugal Visits

December 5, 1983

Berkeley

As we walked through busy Ho Chi Minh Park, Artistic Director Michael LeConte kept his eye on the juggling marathon entering its third hour. Like so many events that captured the imagination of the People's Republic of Berkeley, this one was a political statement, a fundraiser for a women's shelter that meant so much to the East Bay. I loved this town, perched at the edge of the future.

As a Berkeley homeowner it was great to belong to a city that had long been in the forefront of civil rights, voluntary school desegregation, domestic partner benefits and the arts. From the first police radios, to the lie detector and the farm-to-table movement, Berkeley nurtured great ideas. Landmarks such as nuclear pioneer J. Robert Oppenheimer's lab and Alice Waters' kitchen at Chez Panisse, made this city of just over 100,000 a shrine to America's innovative genius.

"Any time you're cutting edge, there are times when you're going to cut yourself," said mayor Tom Bates. "Eighty percent of our ideas don't go anywhere, but 20 percent have some real wisdom and vision. What works in Berkeley happens elsewhere in three to five years."

Like Julia Morgan, LeConte was an exciting member of that 20 percent club. He was founder of the user friendly Berkeley Players Theater, walking distance from my family's home on Woolsey Street. With my son and daughter at Emerson School, just blocks from the University of California campus, Margot and I were busy fighting the proposed Alta Bates Hospital expansion into our neighborhood. My latest book *California Dreaming* on Governors Pat and Jerry Brown, was in bookstore windows and I was commuting each day to my job at the San Jose Mercury. One benefit of that job was a 20% discount on my first computer, an $1,800 Apple IIE (with a dot matrix printer) perfect for my son who loved playing 'Where In The World is Carmen San Diego?' on it.

I loved Michael's plays. Now he and I were on our way to meet one of my favorite actresses, Cari Sutcliffe, who also happened to be his wife and co-director.

Everyone knew that after the May 1974 incineration of six members of Symbionese Liberation Army, Patty and the Harrises fled to Pennsylvania. There Jack and Micki Scott hid them in the Poconos. Jack, a sports sociologist and former sports editor at *Ramparts*, and Micki, a teacher, introduced them to a New York author. His interviews were conducted for a book aimed at financing the SLA revolution. The writer was certain there would be a bidding war for this exclusive story coauthored by the Harrises and Patty. Alas, this project fell apart when the writer was unable to find a publisher willing to take him seriously.

Sometimes things are just too cutting edge.

There was an important gap in the story, one that began on the warm May 1975 night Patty and the Harrises were forced to flee the Pennsylvania refuge where they had lived for many months. Convinced security had been breached after a neighbor kid saw them doing paramilitary training in the woods, they disappeared hours later. It would be another five months before they returned home to California. What happened to them during that hiatus was a major hole in my research.

I stumbled on the answer in the *Oakland Tribune* tower with a tip from my colleague Harry Harris. He discovered that San Francisco State theater arts major Emily Harris, had been the Berkeley Players' costumer during the company's first season.

At the San Francisco bank robbery trial the prosecution established that she had stayed in touch with LeConte via a network of pay phones. In her testimony Emily admitted that the theater kept the Symbionese Liberation Army well stocked with wigs, outfits and makeup including special touches necessary for Patty's freckles. While there were many serious debates among the comrades about kidnapping, carjacking and potential assassinations, no one challenged the effectiveness of Emily's disguises.

Patty's vague testimony claiming they had stayed with a series of friends added to the mystery of this "lost year" between the South Central shootout and Patty's capture. I hoped Michael and Cari, would help me piece together the missing story of the '75 gap in her movements before her return to California and the Sacramento bank robbery.

Cari opened the door to greet me with the kind of warmth a major patron might expect at a Berkeley Players' champagne fundraiser. A star in many LeConte directed plays, she had interned with the company after dropping out of the Pacific School for the Performing Arts in Solvang. Together they had played Beatrice and Benedick in Shakespeare's *Much Ado About*

Nothing--favorite roles they periodically reprised on tour to great acclaim.

As we sat down in their living room, I was surprised to discover she was familiar with my *Oakland Tribune* work.

"When you phoned, I reminded Michael that you had been crushed by Steve. We wanted to help you out. Both of us love your stuff, especially that story on the woman battling Korean sex tourism. It's nice to read travel pieces with a political edge. Those predators should all be in jail."

"We heard a rumor that you are having trouble with your new solo book on the Hearst case," said Michael.

"That's why I am here. My theory is that without your help Patty and the Harrises would have probably have been killed."

Cari agreed. "Our disguises were to die for."

"They were really short of cash and the smugglers who took them back east wouldn't let them carry their guns. Without firepower there was no way they could keep body and soul together robbing banks."

Thanks to the help of a river freight line owned by Cari's uncle, their floating barge theater, *Bard on the Big Muddy*, was a highlight of the Mississippi tourist season. Their series of one-night stands were a big hit in small towns that lacked live theater. With umbrellas and mosquito repellent on hand for all their fans, shows happened rain or shine.

Everything was going great for our little company until we got that call from Wendy Yoshimura," said Cari. "They were on the run again."

While Cari took a break to head into the kitchen, Michael brought out a photo album with a montage of scenes from their floating repertory company: "That's Emily helping set up the stage for our first *Hannibal* production," said Michael. "She was also great on sound and lighting. I welcomed her as an understudy although we never actually used her."

"Had she studied acting?"

"She tried but was too stiff and always had trouble with memorization. Her real strength was backstage."

"What about Bill?"

"We talked for hours and he was opaque when it came to economics. I could never bring him around to my view that capitalism and communism were in danger of collapsing on the same day."

"What did Emily see in him?"

"She thought he was the smartest man she'd ever met and loved the way he put his ideas into action. Or as she liked to put it, 'he'd rather build another bomb than go out for pizza.'"

Cari returned with her quiche and Caesar salad as she doubled down on Michael's assessment.

"Did you have any second thoughts about helping them out when they were broke?"

"Not really," said Cari. "Patty and Wendy Yoshimura needed to find a way to get back to California. Patty and I spent many nights sipping Chablis on the stern as we steamed down the Mississippi. There was this one magical moonlight evening, just south of Prairie du Chien, Wisconsin, where she told me about a showdown with her mother over the wedding menu:

'There were days when I honestly considered the possibility that there was some kind of a mix-up at the hospital. My mom and I were so different. The big influences on my life were nannies, my sisters, friends and some of my teachers, especially my art professor Edward Johnson who took us on a month long tour of he great museums of Europe. He was the first gay man I ever met, a gifted painter and confidant of many of the St. Jean's girls. We all loved his one-liners ridiculing the school administrators.

My mother pretty much opted out. Arguing with her about anything was impossible. Unlike my parents, Steve was just not a steak and potatoes kind of guy. His parents were vegetarians. Mom's solution to that was fried tofu as the main entree.'"

I asked if Patty felt differently about her new family after the

South Central firefight wiped out two-thirds of the Symbionese Liberation Army.

"Obviously she'd been much closer to the four women comrades who died than the two men."

"I thought she was head over heels for Willie Wolfe."

"She said everything changed after he announced it would be better for both of them to consider an open relationship."

"Willie was rethinking their future."

"The women, especially Angela Atwood, accused her of being a bit of a Calvinist. Patty also didn't know Willie's backstory."

"Was he married?"

"Yes, and his wife was expecting at the time of his death."

"Did she talk about Steve?"

"Not much. After the bungled ransom attempt she concluded he was unable to outmaneuver her family. Patty was certain that if the police didn't shoot her, a bank robbery trial would lead to a long prison sentence. She told me:

'A guy like Steve isn't going to settle for years of conjugal visits. My being in jail would mean an end to private planes, luxury condos in Hawaii and Lake Tahoe, and especially the fine art that had become an obsession. There were days when I believed he was more interested in our family's oriental rugs than writing another book.

'He loved the unheated pool at San Simeon. After I was in for two minutes I had to jump out to escape hypothermia. Steve swam for hours, sometimes going underwater from end to end. One time he was below so long I thought he'd drowned.

'He did his best to fit in. I didn't have the heart to explain that the only way to become a Hearst is to be born one.'"

As we finished lunch Michael showed me photos of the company's *Twelfth Night* production that drew big crowds to their well-lit barge.

"As you can see, we were a hit everywhere. One of my favorite moments was going through the lock system above Dubuque,

Iowa. It was a holiday weekend and an entire flotilla of boats followed us in to town to see our show. One family arrived on their vintage float-plane and sat on the wings."

Sipping my coffee I continued paging through the scrapbook, stopping when I saw the freckled face of ....

"You didn't..."

Over the next two hours Cari and Michael explained how they looped the remnants of the Symbionese Liberation Army into their little traveling company.

"We were always short of crew," said Cari, "and it was easy enough to put Bill to work as our chef, while Emily helped out on set decorating. They needed the money."

"What about Patty?"

"We felt it was important to keep her sub-rosa," said Michael. "She got bored and offered to understudy multiple roles. You understand there were no understudies in our company. Actors went on even if they had a 104° fever and a raging headache. Then one night it happened. After the actress playing Cesario fell and broke her leg, Patty stepped in."

"And no one suspected..."

"Of course not. She was a woman playing a male character. It was perfect casting and she was luminous. The last place in the world anyone would have expected to find her was a floating performance of *Twelfth Night*, 1,500 miles from San Francisco.."

"Did any of the other actors realize who they were working with?"

"Nada," said Cari. "Patty was such a natural actor that no one even considered the possibility that she was one of America's most wanted fugitives. Critics at the local papers singled her out for praise and she loved going on stage."

"What about the Harrises?"

"They continued working backstage and did a great job. Because we provided room and board, they were able to replenish their diminished coffers with our low pay."

"Everything went perfectly," said Michael, "until we hit Alton, Illinois. It was the strangest thing. There was a rave review and, as is our custom, we called the reporter the following morning to thank him for his kindness. These notices meant a lot to the cast who used them in their pursuit of future roles. During our call he mentioned that he had done a background search on the actor playing Cesario and couldn't find anything about her. Then he mentioned something eerie:

"'I was really struck by her voice. She sounded exactly like the Patty Hearst we all heard in the communiques broadcast on the nightly news.'"

"That brought down the curtain on Patty's acting career," said Cari as she served a lemon meringue pie. "We quickly loaned them an old beater and Patty was on her way back to California."

"Wasn't it risky for her to be driving? What if she got pulled over?"

"Wendy Yoshimura did the driving. That's how she wound up in Sacramento. The Harrises went separately by bus. There were new wardrobes and disguises waiting for all of them at Post Office general delivery when they arrived. We even added a makeup kit."

"How did the rest of the summer barge tour work out?"

"The secret leaked out that Patty Hearst was playing Cesario. By the time we returned to Red Wing our audiences had more than doubled. For the first time our show began turning a profit."

"The FBI arrived quickly to ask questions," said Michael. "They'd picked up the rumor about Patty. From that moment on undercover agents were front row center every night."

"Did they enjoy the show?"

"One of them was so badly bitten by the theater bug he wound up studying drama at the University of Missouri. He just became our new stage manager."

A Revolution Upended By A Parking Ticket

October 1986

Oakland, CA

A brisk wind cooled San Francisco's Market Street as Bill Harris and I walked out of the *Patty Hearst* screening. For an hour and a half we watched the Symbionese Liberation Army kidnap, beat, rape, rob, torture and shoot its way into infamy. Harris, who abducted Patty Hearst thrown over his shoulder on that February 1974 night, was now back in the limelight, this time as a cinematic mad dog revolutionary.

"It's a revival movement," said Harris as we headed for his Nissan after the screening.

"She's a brand on billboards, talk shows, the papers, magazines, and the paperback racks, compliments of the Hearst organization. I sure hope she has a great agent who landed her a good contract. I suppose no one portrayed in a film ever felt their story was told the way it really happened."

Twelve years after the Symbionese Liberation Army crisis,

43-year-old Harris still exhibited the energy that made him and his comrades the centerpiece of one of 20th century America's greatest manhunts. But that evening he was just another member of the preview audience, my date for the evening. A small man with flecks of gray in his beard, his hair was cropped shorter than it looked on his wanted poster. Taking a little time off from my job as the *Oakland Tribune*'s travel writer, I had been assigned to interview him for an exclusive three-part feature.

"You covered this case when it happened," said my editor LeRoy Aarons, the first openly gay editor of a mainstream American newspaper. "Maybe you can finally get the kidnapper to talk."

Bill and his wife Emily had come to the Bay Area from Indiana in 1972 and were active in Bay Area revolutionary politics through Venceremos, a revolutionary organization big on armed self-defense. Heavily infiltrated and investigated by the police, Venceremos collapsed. They never had a chance to get beyond a blueprint for civil insurrection.

"In the aftermath," he said, "we were active in the prison reform movement and looking hard for a new organization with a broader revolutionary perspective. We discovered it on the front page of the *Oakland Tribune* in November 1973. Harry Harris's astonishing account of the Symbionese Liberation Army's assassination of Oakland's school superintendent represented a bold approach to radical politics.

"Although we were well connected in radical circles neither of us had heard of these wild and crazy guys. We bought a stack of *Tribunes* and sent clippings of Harris's story to friends appalled by this breach of revolutionary etiquette. Cyanide-tipped bullets were simply not the way to halt an Oakland Public Schools anti-crime program that included armed hallway patrols, a computerized system to remove suspected troublemakers and a mandatory student photo ID program. Nonetheless, we saw the Symbionese Liberation Army as a worthy successor to Venceremos.

"Like the other recruits I was filled with so much rage I didn't care if I got killed trying to liberate victims of a fascist state. I admit that murdering that school superintendent was a mistake, but we supported their goals.

"They believed that the pacifist ideals of MLK or Gandhi would only lead to defeat. As a Vietnam vet turned anti-war activist and prison rights worker, I was tired of trying to fight oppressive institutions by working within the system.

"Unfortunately we made errors. One of those was identifying with the spontaneous uprisings that were taking place in Europe and Asia. We thought we were on the cusp of a worldwide revolutionary experience when we really weren't."

Topic A after the Harrises enlisted in the Symbionese Liberation Army was the liberation of Little and Remiro now awaiting trial for murdering Oakland's school superintendent.

"By the time we arrived," Harris said, "the Symbionese Liberation Army already had a file of potential kidnap victims who could be exchanged for Little and Remiro. I mean these people were organized. They had information on the heads of companies like Bechtel, Exxon and Fairchild, but the prime candidate, a young woman they had learned about through her engagement announcement in the San Francisco Examiner, was Patty Hearst. She was ideal; an heiress, and a perfect symbol of the ruling class. What plutocrat wouldn't want to quickly ransom their daughter from a gang of revolutionaries on the eve of her society wedding?"

Bill spent weeks with escaped Soledad prisoner Donald DeFreeze converting rifles into automatic weapons. All eight kidnappers had trained for weeks. There was just one problem: the Symbionese Liberation Army did not have enough cars. They decided to "borrow" a vehicle in the style of the Uruguayan Tupamaros portrayed in the film *State of Siege*, and then return it to the rightful owner.

"After we forced our way into Hearst's apartment, she was

cool. Patty didn't resist as we tied her up and gagged her. Our problem was Steve Weed. He was screaming his head off and DeFreeze shut him up by smacking his head with a rifle butt.

"Our quick trip up Claremont Boulevard led to Tilden Park where we transferred Patty to a second vehicle at the steam train parking lot. My greatest fear was that she would freak out and start screaming, giving us away to another driver at a stoplight. The best way to reassure her was to reach down and hold her hand, to let her know that we weren't going to kill her.

"After pulling into the garage at our 1,150 square foot safe house, we took Patty, still blindfolded, up to our new hideout. Shaken, scratched and bruised from the kidnapping ordeal she calmed a little when Emily untied her wrists. Nancy Perry helped her clean up and then gave her some water and a little bit of food which she refused to touch."

"Weren't you afraid she was going to start screaming?"

"Mizmoon stood watch on her that first night and on following days the other women took turns guarding her. She didn't say much, mostly just asking for drinks, bathroom breaks and clothes to replace the little bit she had on when we took her, a bathrobe and some underwear. The women took care of that for her. Fortunately Mizmoon wore the same sizes.

"Because we didn't have much money, our safe house was packed. The only way she could have privacy was to sleep in the closet. She could read there and listened to the radio. Except for the periods where we were having private discussions, she was able to come out and join us, in the living area where we slept, ate, and worked on strategy. As we ate, she talked and asked about the ransom effort. At first she was blindfolded and later we wore masks in her presence.

"At the beginning we called her 'Tiny' fearing we might be overheard. Later she took "Deborah" as her new name, after Deborah Samson who became the first woman to fight with the American revolutionary Army by disguising herself as a man."

"Did you talk about releasing her?"

"We did. After the Hearsts rejected our offer we discussed it at length. We just couldn't figure out a way to do it without all of us getting killed. The only thing we knew for sure at that point was that Patty didn't want to go home. She was sick of her family, sick of the Hearst Corporation and sick of Steve."

"If you accept the movie's thesis that she was brainwashed," I said as we walked toward my car on Mission Street, "that doesn't explain why you would have wanted to keep her, much less trust her with firearms she could have easily used to blow you away."

Bill, pausing to give some chips to a hungry panhandler, didn't have a pat answer: "That decision was unanimous. As she learned more from us about the size of the Hearst family fortune, the billions they had at their disposal, it was clear that our ransom demand was not the problem. Same thing with Steve. She could not understand why he would move in with her parents who hated him. Then there were all these crazy conspiracy theories that implicated Patty in her own kidnapping.

"As we waited to hear from the Hearsts, Patty started having these long talks with Willie Wolfe. This connection surprised us, especially when they would stay up late at night trying to figure out a good way to let the world know that she was abandoning a life of privilege and Weed.

"Is that when she asked the SLA to arm her for their next action?"

"She wanted to join our revolution. Willie Wolfe advanced the idea that Patty would give us more bargaining power, not just with her parents but also with the authorities who would arrange safe passage to Cuba.

"Obviously the explanation her lawyers dreamed up—that she'd been tortured into running with us—didn't impress the jury that convicted her in the Hibernia bank robbery case. The fact that we chose a bank owned by a close girlfriend's family hurt her defense. To get my perspective you have to know a little more about her.

"We assumed we were kidnapping this rich heiress, a kind of empty-headed daughter of the ruling class. We quickly discovered that she was an extremely intelligent, worldly young woman, who was tough, self-reliant, full of initiative and, as we later found out, bravado. Also, thanks to her dad's training, she was a hell of a shooter.

"Patty was a master at getting what she wanted. She knew exactly how to nail Steve Weed as part of her exit strategy from the family. Thanks to his research for a *Ramparts* exposé she understood the darker side of the Hearst empire and was in the midst of a period of intense struggle. As an independent woman she was also having doubts about her impending marriage to Weed, and, of course, there were parental conflicts characteristic of 19-year-olds.

"Without an acceptable offer from her family we struggled to find new ways to advance our mission. As a gesture of good faith we asked her father to create a multi-million dollar free food giveaway, no big deal for his well-connected company. Then everything blew up. There wasn't enough food to go around and people began rioting. The California Attorney General suggested that anyone who accepted the donated food could be considered an accessory to the kidnapping. The U.S. Attorney General demanded that the Hearsts refuse to negotiate for her release."

In a talk days later at a coffee shop on Oakland's Piedmont Avenue Harris told me how the new revolutionary Patty tried to look under the hood of this radical cadre.

"All of a sudden she began showing keen interest in some of the Symbionese Liberation Army's causes. She studied books such as *Soledad Brothers: The Prison Letters of George Jackson* and *Tania,* the story of Bolivian revolutionary Che Guevara's comrade and lover. As her revolutionary crash course continued, we all worried continually about our ability to defend ourselves against a police onslaught. Of course Patty knew she could potentially be caught in a crossfire. She couldn't understand why her family would not just meet our demands.

"More than any other factor, their indecisiveness convinced her she could no longer depend on Randy and Catherine to send in the cavalry."

Harris sipped his Americano as he explained that the kidnappers were very well armed with carbines bought at places all over the Bay Area, including the San Jose flea market.

"As I said, DeFreeze and I had converted these weapons into machine guns. Although neither of us knew how to do this, Donald was a mechanical genius. We set up our own welding shop in the kitchen, complete with oxygen tanks, acetylene torches and lots of buckets of water in case of fire.

"Of course we wanted Patty to be able to defend herself if we were attacked. As you can imagine some of the cell members were reluctant to arm the prisoner lest she turn on us. We compromised by giving her a shotgun but holding on to the shells until she needed them. They were tipped with cyanide Nancy Ling Perry had stolen from a University of California lab while she was working on her English degree."

A young woman seeking Harris's autograph, which he gladly gave her on a coffee cup, briefly interrupted our conversation.

"Thank you so much," she said, "I'm glad that you got out. Any chance you'll ever publish a book on what really happened? I read Patty's version and she raised as many questions as she answered. If, as she said, all of you were raping her why did she decide to go with you to rob a bank. She could have easily turned around in the bank and executed you guys. I didn't understand why she didn't just kill you and Emily at Mel's Sporting Goods."

Harris gestured toward me.

"Keep an eye on the *Tribune*, you never know what you might find out."

As the woman walked away, he said, "It's not easy being an urban legend. Where were we?"

"The SLA was trying to figure out how to arm Patty without getting killed."

"Right. Her previous experience paid off, and she quickly became a star at our indoor target practice. She sharpened her skills by firing a BB gun into a target drawn on a shopping bag and taped to a large pillow."

Harris made it clear that taking control of Patty's life and gaining her trust forced the SLA to make many important decisions.

"Inexperience led to overconfidence. Her family's resistance to negotiation forced Patty to hate us a little less."

"In her book she wrote that the men, including you, assaulted her, even on the night your six comrades died in that firefight."

"Our Army was guilty of many things," Bill said, "but perhaps the most preposterous charge concocted by the Hearst defense team was the lie that we harmed her. This was a cell with five very tough, independent women. All of them were good shots and none of them would have let the guys assault her. Her lover Willie Wolfe would have also gone after anyone who tried to abuse Patty."

"Could something have happened to her that you didn't know about?"

"I doubt it. We were living in extremely close quarters. Within weeks of her capture she was one of us."

"Patty was ready for the revolution."

"Exactly."

"At the trial Emily mentioned that Angela Atwood was worried about closeted Patty being lonely."

"A lot of the SLA members, myself included, weren't into exclusive relationships. That wouldn't have worked in our cell. This was all part of a thing going on in the '70s when people were experimenting with alternatives to monogamy. For example, after her bitter divorce, Angela was a lover of Joseph Remiro and Russell Little.

"A threesome."

"No she preferred them separately. She was devastated when they were both arrested for the murder of Oakland Schools Superintendent Marcus Foster. She missed them desperately."

"If you could have exchanged Little and Remino for Patty would the crisis have ended there?"

"We were so hot it would have been impossible to escape. There was now an international effort to track us down. We had very limited mobility. We couldn't just leave the country and head for Cuba or Brazil. We were stuck until something changed.

"Finally, in late March, her father put $4 million into an escrow account to be given to the SLA upon Patty's release. We saw it as a trap and she made it clear she was not going home."

"Was Patty worried that after being ransomed, all of you would be easily tracked down and killed?"

Harris, now noshing on a spinach croissant, nodded.

"She didn't want us to die. She was worried that the FBI would break down our door and murder eight people she had come to trust. We made many stupid mistakes but we never tortured Patty or hurt her. Our goal, always, had been to make a statement. Slowly she was becoming the most credible voice of the SLA. Unlike our denounced communiques, her public statements led to a public debate about her decision to join our family. All our assumptions about her were wrong."

"What about her engagement? Was she coming to the conclusion that her mother had been right about Steve Weed?"

"I don't know. His name never came up in our discussions and we never asked. He appeared to be dead to her. She never responded to any of his public pleas. Look, we never had anything against the guy. He got hurt because he wouldn't stop screaming. Politically he seemed to have a good history."

"Do you think she was playing all of you?"

"We felt as if we were dictating our own coverage in her family's paper. It never occurred to us that she was trying to manipulate us. We were all convinced she had come over to our cause. Consciousness raising was something we knew how to do. Perhaps the turning point for Patty was realizing that the family could no longer protect her. She had to make her own decisions.

"Think about it. Could she go back home to that San Francisco media circus, where reporters were hanging phones from trees in front of her house? She would have been endlessly harassed. We were protecting her from the FBI, a trial and a long prison sentence. I argued, correctly as it turned out, that her family would hire the wrong lawyers who would attempt to shift all the blame to us. Pleading for special treatment because of her economic status wasn't going to work. She was front and center while we were robbing Hibernia Bank."

"Did she really write those terrible attacks on her family and Weed?"

"Yes, she's from a family that built a fortune with a propaganda machine telling the masses what to think based on their blizzard of lies. They set the table for both Hoovers, Herbert and J. Edgar. They fought the New Deal and were determined to water down the Civil Rights Act. They opposed the Voting Rights Act and Equal Rights Amendment for decades. At one point over 600 newspapers worldwide carried their venomous columnists to an audience of over 20 million. The notorious red baiting of their papers during the McCarthy era helped destroy thousands of careers.

"Patty's first drafts were such a vicious attack on her family and the ruling class that we insisted on toning them down, lest people think we were ghosting them. I remember at one point she wrote that 'the only good thing my dad ever did for me was teach me how to shoot a gun when I was nine years-old.'"

"This sounds like the *Ransom of Red Chief,"* I suggested in reference to the classic O. Henry story where the kidnappers discover they can't rid themselves of a very difficult young hostage.

"Not at all, we all welcomed her decision to fight with us."

"You trusted her?"

"None of us had even heard of hostages identifying with their captors, the Stockholm Syndrome. That's a great space for courtroom witnesses being paid $5,000 a day to dazzle jurors with their infinite wisdom. Do I think she was brainwashed into dumping Weed, having an affair with Willie, saving our lives at Mel's Sporting Goods by covering us with gunfire..."

"She was a great asset."

"Hey I'm just a so-so kidnapper, not some academic delivering sound bites on public radio. I was there from the second we took her and I would be the last person to try to psychoanalyze Patty."

"After the bank robbery you got the feeling she was loyal to her new extended family."

"Patty realized that she'd been living in a fantasy world where it was impossible to empathize with anyone lacking her endless perks. She chose to join our struggle for human rights. Certainly the bank robbery jury didn't buy the losing legal argument that we had forced her to run with us. In early April 1974, we gave Patty the right to be released in a safe place or stay and fight with us. We knew this decision would change her life. None of us imagined how much she would change ours."

The SLA's Minister Of Strategy

October 1986

Oakland, CA

A few days later Bill and I were walking the Lake Merritt shoreline flanked by joggers plugged into their Walkmans.

,"You took Patty's freedom away and then, paradoxically, you gave it back."

"Once she joined our Army, Patty had complete sovereignty. As a comrade she was central to all of our decisions. Emily called her our Minister of Strategy."

"She went public by joining you in the Hibernia Bank robbery."

"We chose the bank to maximize news coverage. We didn't wear facial disguises and picked a branch with closed-circuit TV cameras because we wanted to let the public to know she was now one of our soldiers"

"And you needed the cash..."

"It was expensive to keep renting safe houses and buy cars that were compromised and ditched to avoid being tailed. We were a fixture in the used car market. When the FBI was chasing us they never knew that at one point we were riding around in one of their former sedans. The bank job was also a good training exercise.

"You have to realize that 75 percent of the FBI's local field force was investigating the case at one time or another. Their reputation and budget was on the line. Murders were happening pretty much every day in Northern California but we were a far higher priority. Special agents interviewed everyone who had ever known me all the way back to my kindergarten classmates. There was no way we could go to our friends for help."

"It must have been tricky to pull off a bank robbery with zero experience."

"On the way into the bank Nancy Ling Perry's ammo clip fell from her submachine gun and hit the floor. As she stooped to pick up the ammo, Patty pointed her gun at customers pancaked on the floor."

"You made $10,000 on that robbery for a few minutes work. Was it worth it?"

"Not really, no. Perry panicked when two customers walked into the bank and refused to obey her command to get down. As they ran out the door, she opened fire, hitting one man in the hip and the second in the hand. She overreacted. There was no way those two men should have been shot. Our weapons training was weak. That's the problem with armchair revolutionaries."

"Could Patty have quit after the robbery, turned herself in, gone state's evidence and told the police that she was forced to rob the bank as part of a publicity stunt?"

"Sure and it might have worked. But by that point she had gone from being an innocent victim to a wanted felon showing up on post office billboards—she absolutely hated that camera angle."

"She was terrified?"

"We all were. We were broke, on the run to South Central Los Angeles, hiding out in a minority neighborhood, definitely a first for Patty."

"Instead of a society wedding at the Claremont she was joining you at the Inglewood Mel's Sporting Goods debacle."

"We made a bad choice."

"You bought some jeans, socks and a few odds and ends."

"I also stole a bandolier. After my wife and I checked out, the owner spotted a bulge under my coat. I was not about to let a security guard see my handgun. We scuffled and the guy got me down on the sidewalk. Another 300 pound guard had my wife Emily in a bear hug from behind and three more men leaped on top of me, including one guy who pulled over and leaped out of his car.

"They had one handcuff on me and were going for my other wrist. I knew our revolutionary career was over. Watching all this, Patty knew police were on their way to our latest crime scene. Instinctively she began spraying the store, covering Emily and me perfectly. She fired off 30 rounds and, when the magazine was empty, picked up my semiautomatic and fired off 20 more. As the guards ducked for cover Emily and I sprinted across the street to the van."

"I don't remember that scene in the movie."

"Or her book, but that's what happened. She was sitting in the van, with the keys in the ignition, parked far enough away to escape detection and flee. Opening fire to cover me could have easily led to her arrest or death."

"The same Patty who rescued you and Emily would, years later, accuse you of rape."

"None of the other army members would have reacted as quickly as she did," he said as we walked past a father helping his daughter fly a gold kite above Lake Merritt. "Patty looked up and saw us tussling in the street."

"She saved your lives."

"Correct, which is why they left that key moment out of her book and movie. It would have destroyed the Stockholm Syndrome narrative critical to her legal defense."

"You had to abandon the van?"

"Yeah. We carjacked 17-year-old Tom Matthews's pickup."

"...your second kidnapping?"

"Yes, but we only held him one night. Nice kid, by the way, he really connected with Patty. They really hit it off, especially when she handed him a $100 bill for a night at Disneyland."

"It's not every day a kidnap victim goes out and kidnaps a high school kid."

"Since returning to the South Central safe house was out, we headed to an Anaheim motel and waited to rendezvous with everyone else, late that night, at a drive-in."

"A drive-in?"

"That was our plan B–as we checked into the motel, I suddenly realized we'd left a parking ticket on the abandoned van. The worst mistake of my life."

He stopped, reliving the decision, then continued.

"This ticket led to the crazy shoot out and the inevitable beginning of the endgame."

For the first time I could see he was no longer simply answering my questions. Bill grimaced as he stumbled backwards in time.

"Roger, there is no rational explanation for my stupidity. In that terrible moment I was no better than the people I was trying to take down. I should have been court-martialed by the SLA."

"In other words the van you borrowed from the owners of the safe house on West 83rd street was registered to that address."

"Yes, the police traced the citation to our hideout."

"By the time the cops arrived, the other six Army members had moved to a new location. But it was too late. Thanks to a neighbor the police were on to them and quickly nailed their location."

"You holed up at the motel?"

"We had no place else to go."

For a moment I felt sorry for Bill as he stopped to hand a dollar to a panhandler and then wiped away a tear.

"When I flipped on the television we were stunned by live coverage of the police's armed siege of the safe house where Donald DeFreeze, Angela Atwood, Camilla Hall, Nancy Ling Perry, Patricia Soltysik and Willie Wolfe died."

"What was your first thought when you saw flames engulfing the house?"

"Suicide."

"Because you forgot to pull that ticket before abandoning the van."

"Yes. They all died because of me. Revolutionaries can be as imperfect as the system they are trying to defeat. We should have listened to Patty. She argued against going down to Los Angeles and knew we would stick out in that mostly white neighborhood. Willie Wolfe agreed but DeFreeze claimed this place would be good for a night or two.

"Why didn't you say something, do something?"

"Roger, if we hadn't gone shopping at Mel's, I wouldn't be here. Patty and Emily would have probably been dead."

"A revolution upended by a parking ticket," I quipped.

"It was the kind of problem Lenin never had to worry about when he toppled the czar. Watching the firefight on television Patty was in shock, devastated, saying things that no one has ever reported like: 'Let's kill pigs.' It was angry rhetoric that helped explain her behavior over the next year."

"You fled that night."

"We should have left her in that motel where she could have turned herself in."

"She insisted on fleeing with you?"

"Right. We drove up the coast toward moonlit Pismo Beach."

"And nearly a year later you robbed another bank in Sacramento."

"A woman depositing a church collection was accidentally

hit and died during the holdup. We were amateurs who had run out of cash. Patty, now an old hand at bank robbery, scouted the location and was waiting for us outside, preparing our getaway."

"After covering you with her machine gun in Inglewood and joining two bank robberies why didn't she just give up then? Most of the SLA were dead. Your trio had nowhere to go."

"It would have been easy for her to turn herself in at any point. One time a team of coastal park rangers helped her get up a steep ocean cliff. Again, she could have surrendered safely."

"Why didn't she run?"

"That would be a good question to ask her."

"I'll put it on my list."

"Be sure to point out that by the time we were apprehended in San Francisco on September 18, 1975, Patty had her own apartment. There is no way things would have happened the way they did if we had been the people she now says we were.

"Seen from a revolutionary perspective some of the methods we used made no sense. Things got lopsided with us, the ends started justifying the means. That was wrong and I regret it. Everyone knows you can't attack powerful institutions from positions of weakness. One of us should have had the sense to say, 'Hey we don't have our act together, how can we be talking about kidnapping an heiress? Are you crazy?'"

By now Bill and I were walking across the estuary bridge toward the Cameron-Stanford House. We had circled Lake Merritt and he was sounding repentant: "I don't feel good about the way so many people's lives were affected by what we did. Six people I loved died. We spent all that time in prison, yet my perspective hasn't changed."

Working as a private investigator, Bill, remarried with two small children, had made a new life for himself on behalf of criminal defendants. As part of the legal system, he now redirected a portion of his rage that motivated him to join the Symbionese Liberation Army.

As we headed back toward our cars, customers were lining up outside the Grand Lake Theater to catch the next screening of Patty's movie, a big hit in the Bay Area. It was a believable narrative that would have made her grandfather proud. Some of it was even true.

"We got rubbed out," said Bill. "Having survived the antiwar movement, the Symbionese Liberation Army and prison it's a miracle that I'm standing here talking to you right now. My karma should have been used up a long time ago."

Roger, I think this is one of the best chapters so far. Harris is just about the kindest, most gentle kidnapper ever. Are you going to nominate him for the Nobel Peace Prize?—SW

When Death Didn't Take A Holiday

Memorial Day Weekend 1991

Los Angeles

"People ask me," said Dr. Thomas Noguchi, "if it was difficult to determine the identity of the people lost in that terrible SLA firefight. For me it doesn't matter if someone died in a bowling alley or perished in a burning house. All my cases are difficult."

I had flown down from San Francisco on Memorial Day, the night after taking my family to see Herb Gardner's classic *I'm Not Rappaport* at the Geary Theater. We made sure to get a memorable 'family photo' in front of the marquee.

When I got home from San Francisco late that evening, a voicemail left by Noguchi's wife Hisako, invited me down to meet the famous Los Angeles coroner on one of his few days off. He frequently granted interviews on big cases he'd handled such as Marilyn Monroe, Janis Joplin, John Belushi, Natalie Wood and Janis Joplin, however Noguchi had held me off for over 15 years.

A major league workaholic—he told one journalist he didn't just plan to live to 100, he planned to work until he was 100—Noguchi was probably the most famous Japanese-American public servant in California. During his time as county coroner he was well known for only asking his employees to work half days, i.e. any 12-hour shift they wanted.

"My husband's office will be closed for the holiday and we would love to take you to lunch," Hisako Noguchi explained apologetically in her message. "I am sorry it took us so long to get back to you. There's a little floating sushi boat place we both adore. Please join us."

As my flight descended over Hollywood, banked into a 180° turn at the Civic Center and then headed west toward the Pacific, I remembered the first time I had been on this landing path, descending over Inglewood where my family lived for a year spanning 1957-1958. My father had left his plant manager job in Detroit for a similar position in Glendale, unaware that his new employer was on the brink of collapse. Just six weeks after I enrolled at Century Park elementary school he was laid off and for the first time in his life, on unemployment.

It was a difficult year in many respects. My mother had a miscarriage, the driver for Jewish Community Center Camp Wise nearly backed over my sister Carla, and tracking down relatives, a game my mother called Jewography, had its ups and downs. I loved the place, especially my paper route where I could coast from the top of a hill, hitting lawn after lawn with the Los Angeles Times, never pausing to use the brakes.

I was thrilled to be back there to meet the Noguchis at Floating Sushi. A small stream cut through the circular counter with a tempting array of tuna, crab, salmon, yellow tail and red snapper delivered fresh off the toy boats.

"You should know," Hisako, a pathology professor at the University of Southern California, told me as we waited for her husband to arrive, "Thomas still has nightmares about that terrible shootout and the death of those SLA people in the fire blaze. There was no reason to cremate those victims before their autopsies. Sometimes he wakes up screaming. It has taken him many years of treatment to get back to who he was. It's great that his job has special insurance coverage for this kind of emotional disturbance. If he were committed to a public psychiatric hospital his enemies would get him fired in a minute."

"You're talking about the stigma of mental health treatment."

"Break an arm, everyone understands and sends bouquets. Have a breakdown and your enemies use it as ammo to get you on unemployment."

After he arrived Thomas talked candidly about the well-organized opposition trying to take him down: "The med schools don't like me because my office pinpoints mistakes their surgeons make. Insurance companies always want a suicide diagnosis because it means they don't have to pay a death benefit. Families get upset when I have to report cases where a loved one dies in the arms of someone else's wife or husband. Conspiracy theorists are always giving me trouble about autopsies of politicians and rock stars. Don't even get me started on the mob murders."

Plucking a California roll off a miniature scow bobbing in this culinary marina, Hisako said: "It's important to de-emphasize the negative aspects of death. Of course death is never a happy experience. But at the same time we want people to understand and appreciate the positive side of death."

"You see," said Thomas after taking a sip of Saki, "the deceased generally wishes to have his body used to help the living. We can learn from the dead. They can help us have better lives. A bus crash is a terrible thing but it can be a field day for organ transplants."

Helping himself to a jumbo spider roll arriving on the back of a tiny tugboat, the coroner explained that an essential part of his job was building public trust.

"Any case I handle may become the most interesting one of the century. As public servants we can't afford to make a mistake on big cases such as Marilyn, Bobby Kennedy, Sharon Tate, or Lenny Bruce. Our community must have faith in the integrity of the coroner's office. Skepticism undermines the judicial process.

"A big part of our job is training police to never touch anything until we have completed our work. After examining all the evidence I'll instruct an employee to take the pictures and only after he is finished will I let the police cut the crime scene tape.

"Case in point, I pleaded with the police chief not to burn out those SLA members. Patty Hearst could have been inside that house. The last thing you want in a situation like that was charred remains, particularly with an innocent victim like her."

"In that terrible moment he lost control," said Hisako.

"Instead of being able to take the corpses back to our lab," said the coroner, "we were left with charred mandibles and other body parts requiring special analysis. I had to personally take charge of each autopsy to make sure everything was done perfectly."

"It was my job to make arrangements for the families at the Bonaventure, away from the media staked out at the coroner's office" added Hisako. "We set up a small breakout room to keep everyone up to date. It took us the better part of a week to positively identify who had died and who had escaped that terrible inferno. It was the sort of thing you associate with coal mine disasters, with families waiting at the mine head to learn whether their loved ones made it, or not."

"Each time Thomas confirmed another victim," said Hisako, "I had to go with a priest, a minister, a rabbi or a psychologist to deliver the tragic news. Then I sat silently with each family for an hour to help them begin processing their grief. There is no right or wrong way to do this. Everyone must create his or her own path. After each new confirmation, I went back to the remaining families to let them know that their son or daughter was not the latest identified victim."

"How did the Hearsts and the parents of the Harrises take it when they learned their son and daughters had survived?"

"Their sense of relief was tempered by the fact that their loved one remained on the FBI's most wanted list," said Thomas.

"I remember Mrs. Hearst asking me if she thought there was any chance they would turn themselves in," said Hisako.

"Did you reject that idea?"

"Yes and I told her the FBI is not in the business of trusting armed revolutionaries. Any attempt Patty made to turn herself in was every bit as dangerous as staying with the Harrises. She asked if there might be an agent somewhere with the ability to capture them without incident. Sadly, I had to warn her that based on what Thomas sees all too often, the FBI and the police are apparently plagued by a lack of insight."

Inevitably this kind of talk began attracting the attention of adjacent guests After Hisako threw her husband a knowing look he glanced down at his plate full of sushi and said: "Perhaps we should relax and enjoy our meal."

Realizing we needed a more private setting to continue our conversation, Hisako mentioned that they were taking a couple of days off at a friend's place on Catalina Island. Perhaps I would like to ride the ferry over to Avalon the following day.

"He's loaned us his sailboat and maybe you'd enjoy being out on the water. The forecast is promising."

After checking in at the Zane Grey Inn the following afternoon, I walked down to the harbor and joined the Noguchis for a cruise along the Catalina shore. While Hisako handled the boat, her husband took a nap. Moored up at the Two Harbors marina, we headed down a trail to a picnic area.

Thomas began talking about the post-traumatic stress that led to treatment.

"I handle many difficult cases."

"His 40-page report on Bobby Kennedy is considered a classic," said Hisako as she touched his hand gently. "People need to have absolute trust in the police, in the coroner's office," said Hisako.

"A major reason why America is the best place to commit murder is that most coroner's offices don't even have a staff pathologist," said Thomas. "Unlike many other countries, most American coroners aren't even MDs. A lot of them are elected and subjected to all sorts of political pressure. Everyone is twisting their arm."

"That's why we were so horrified by the decision to set fire to the house and destroy so much critical evidence in the Symbionese Liberation Army case," said Hisako as we walked back to the sailboat. "In that kind of situation you must have everything. A fire destroys evidence."

"But they were firing on the police from the house."

"Yes," said Thomas, "but the police could have correctly used tear gas to avoid burning them out. It was important to do a full autopsy of those victims."

"Were you worried that you couldn't positively identify who died that day?"

"There was little chance of that. We have one of the most modern forensic labs in the world. Our ability to win the public's cooperation depends on our reputation. Yet even in cases like Marilyn Monroe, where we have the intact body, there will always be skeptics."

"Like the people who still think President Kennedy and his kid brother, Bobby, had Marilyn killed to quash allegations that they both had affairs with her."

"Precisely," said Thomas.

"It's taken him all this time to be able to talk about what went wrong on the day of that terrible fire," said Hisako as we left the picnic area and began walking back to the sailboat. "Fortunately his treatment continues. I've worked hard to find a sport that can get him away from all this painful work."

"I tried tennis and all I could think about was how the racket could be used as a murder weapon," said Thomas.

"Fortunately sailing seems to be good therapy," said Hisako. Her husband agreed:

"I like being here when I'm burned out. When I'm on the

water I can put my work behind me."

Hisako smiled as we left the small port in good wind and set a course for Avalon. After her relaxed husband stretched out on the deck and dozed off, she grabbed my hand and said: "Thank you for being so patient and understanding. Just between the two of us, I always make it a point to avoid sailing into the Catalina waters where Natalie Wood drowned."

Not too shabby my friend. And the guy is still very much alive at 98. I wonder who is going to do his autopsy.—SW

Dealing With Her Lawyer Must Have Been More Painful Than Being Kidnapped

May 29, 1991

Bel Air, California

After stepping off the Catalina ferry in Long Beach I phoned my great aunt, Estelle Brandler. Although we had been out of touch since 1958, her cheery voice quickly circled me back to the first time we met. Estelle and her husband Judge Mark Brandler lived in an enviable neighborhood that was home to movie stars, directors and even a screenwriter or two.

Mark was one of the city's best-known jurists. He had presided at a number of famous trials including the Onion Field murder case immortalized in a book and movie. After Patty was convicted for robbing San Francisco's Hibernia Bank, Mark had presided at the Mel's Sporting Goods robbery, assault and kidnapping trial.

At 19 Estelle had married a wealthy businessman who made millions in the Chicago window washing business. After his death she had a whirlwind courtship with Brandler, 20 years her junior. They married beneath a huppah at Malibu's Zuma beach where a klezmer band delighted the guests.

During my 1958 family visit I was dazzled by their multi-level estate with a pool house bigger than our living room. Mark served cheeseburgers on the patio as the pool vacuum snaked through the water sucking up yellow forsythia blossoms that had drifted into the warm pool water.

Estelle, who followed a rigid exercise program, furnished the living room with ivory sectionals and white carpets that matched their poodles. The white Jackson Pollock paintings matched the white walls and the translucent chemise covering her white bikini. Her quiet elegance, perfectly manicured nails, lacquered hair and understated makeup met a sharp wit and considerable intellect. She was in three books clubs and frequently led seminars on the Japanese floral art of Ikebana. She had designed their home and was her own general contractor.

"Roger," she asked as water flowed forth from a plaster cherub's penis into the shallow end of the pool, "are you happy in your little place in Inglewood?"

"I love living across the street from Century Park Elementary. We have a lot of fun riding our bikes to the Hollywood Park track."

"Do you wake up every morning and thank the Lord that you aren't stuck in Detroit? Such an awful place."

"Have you been to Detroit?"

"No, but I've seen scary pictures. I spent years trying to talk your grandmother into moving out here. Since she and your grandfather arrived I think she looks at least ten years younger."

"I loved Detroit."

"It's just beastly there. If you own a pool you can only swim three months a year. Mark and I swim every day, year around. If we want snow we drive up to the mountains and then return home at night to jump in our hot tub. This is the kind of place where God would live if he could afford it."

"We'll never have the money for a pool."

"You tell your mom and dad that you can swim in our pool whenever you like, even if Mark and I are away. Just give us a jingle. I'll make sure the housekeeper lets you in."

Then she put a finger to her lips and whispered:

"You can even skinny dip if you want. I won't tell."

When it was time to leave, Estelle handed me a little bag of chestnuts picked from her own tree.

"You know what they say," she jested with a big smile. "A chestnut a day will keep the doctor away."

Returning 33 years later, I found the Brandlers aging well in place with the help of a live-in nurse. Estelle greeted me at the door with her walker and we headed out toward the patio. Mark was in the pool doing laps. After he toweled off and changed, their aide served lunch.

"So young man," Mark asked me, "what brings you back after so many years? Did you miss us?"

Over the next several days we visited their favorite club, Hollywood's Magic Castle, where some of the world's most prestigious magicians showcased their talent. We drove along Mulholland Drive, visited Will Rogers State Park and the graves of my grandparents, Max and Rose Goodman, at Hillside Memorial Park off the 405.

'Do you remember their big 60th anniversary party at the Sportsman's Lodge?" I asked after pulling up to their gravesite.

"Who could forget that one?" said Estelle. "Mayor Yorty himself was there to help celebrate all they did for the senior citizens community."

"There was that master of ceremonies who congratulated Max and *Sam*?"

"Right and we all shouted, '*It's Rose!*'"

"Correcting himself he saluted 'Sam and Rose.'"

"You know it's a funny thing about my sister, your grandmother, we invited them over all the time but they almost never came."

"It may have had something to do with the time he spent in jail for those embezzlements," said Mark. "Family made him nervous."

After dinner each night, Mark and I retired to his study where he reminisced about his days in court with the Harrises and Patty.

"I don't think Patty ever realized that life in the hands of celebrity criminal lawyer F. Lee Bailey was going to be more terrifying than schlepping around the country with the Harrises."

"Didn't Bailey fly his own Lear jet to big cases nationwide?

"He made morning appearances in San Francisco Federal Court and then flew himself to Vegas for a big murder trial in the afternoon. The possibility of losing the Hearst case never occurred to him."

"Wasn't there a defense team before Bailey?"

"Yes, the Hallinans—a left wing father and son team, who wanted Patty to plead that she'd been drugged prior to the Hibernia bank robbery. The Hearsts unsurprisingly relieved them of their duties."

"Why weren't the Harrises prosecuted for their role in the Hibernia case?"

"The government strategy was to prosecute Patty first. While that case was in motion, she and the Harrises were being arraigned for the Mel's Sporting Goods case in my court.

"While the FBI worked with the U.S. Attorney in San Francisco to convict her for bank robbery, she was ratting out the Harrises to a second FBI team working on the Los Angeles case.

"Bailey apparently believed that testifying against the Harrises on the Mel's robbery and 18-year-old Tom Matthews kidnapping would help her defense in the Hibernia holdup case. It didn't work because Bailey stubbornly refused to let Patty plea bargain in San Francisco."

"You're telling me a celebrity lawyer takes the case of the only kidnap victim in American history to rob a bank with her captors. He makes a deal to have her secretly testify against her fellow defendants in the Mel's case, without trying to get the charges reduced in the bank robbery case. She's essentially risking everything and getting nothing in return."

"It gets worse, Roger. On their way back home from the Poconos the Harrises robbed another bank in Sacramento where a customer was killed by an errant bullet. Patty helped scout the holdup site and was outside while the robbery was in progress. Her attorneys instructed her to take the fifth on a long series of questions about that crime. She was never able to explain why she helped them plan a bank robbery that led to a customer's death. It destroyed her defense in the San Francisco Hibernia robbery case."

"It sounds like Bailey was making the prosecutor's case. She should have just pleaded guilty on the Hibernia Bank robbery and gone for a reduced sentence."

"You should re-read Bailey's closing argument in San Francisco. He sounded like he was having a stroke as he essentially doubled down on the evidence against Patty. Listening to her lawyer must have been more painful than being kidnapped. At least the SLA let her out of captivity, gave her a gun and eventually let her live independently. They trusted her to help them lead the revolution. Thanks to Bailey she wound up being sentenced to seven years."

"Didn't Bailey have some kind of a book deal?"

"Yes, and part of his agreement with Patty was that his book on the case would come out at least 18 months ahead of hers. He also filed an appeal that helped him rake in another $500,000 in fees from her parents who should have fired him."

"After Patty was convicted in San Francisco her mother said, 'Now that they've convicted the woman who was kidnapped maybe they will prosecute the kidnappers.'"

"She overlooked the fact that the Harrises were already being prosecuted for kidnapping Tom Matthews following the Mel's Sporting Goods shootout.

"I decided on two separate trials because the San Francisco judge had ordered a 90-day psychiatric evaluation prior to Patty's sentencing. The Harrises went first. Patty was planning to testify against them while waiting for her own case to begin.

"The security was crazy. We had bulletproof glass and floor to ceiling steel mesh separating the court from the spectators. Even my mob trials never looked like that.

"Her plan was to testify against the Harrises in my courtroom. Determined to silence her, a radical group began setting off bombs in front of Hearst headquarters in New York, and hit one of the guesthouses at San Simeon.

"The Harrises knew that Patty could only testify against them after they took the stand in my court. Both of them refused to do so which meant she couldn't be a witness on rebuttal. The Harrises actually got a shorter sentence in the Los Angeles case then she did for the San Francisco bank robbery. Patty was convicted in my courtroom for being the third kidnapper of Tom Matthews. At the sentencing the prosecutor recommended parole because she was already serving time for the earlier bank robbery conviction. I also expect he let her off because she had been a cooperative witness for prosecution of the Harrises."

"So, do you think she was brainwashed?"

"Patty claimed she stayed with the kidnappers because they would defend her against FBI agents working on shoot to kill orders."

"Then she turned around and went to work against them

for the federal prosecutors."

"She was a great resource against the Harrises in my court. At one point Patty had a collapsed lung and was rushed from her prison cell to a hospital. The moment she was released from the hospital, the FBI team moved to hold her at a nearby county jail where they resumed their interrogation. The prosecutors wanted her in federal prison and they prevailed. Worried she might have a change of heart, the FBI agents tailed the federal marshals returning her to prison. They were determined to pounce the second she arrived at her new digs."

"Was her decision to work with the FBI part of the Committee To Free Patty Hearst strategy?"

"Maybe. Apparently it worked. As you know, the FBI's San Francisco office supported commutation of her sentence and a later parole."

"After struggling to arrest, prosecute and convict her they turned around and fought for her release."

"Patty was a cooperative witness against the Harrises. Now she is working with the FBI to build a case against them in the Sacramento bank robbery."

"She's ratting them out again in a crime she helped plan."

"I'm sure with her eyewitness testimony they'll be prosecuted and convicted again. Who can argue with her vantage point?"

"I thought you said she was outside the bank when the robbery took place."

"Details, details. The point is the FBI will get another conviction against the Harrises decades later. It will make a great chapter for your book."

"What happened to her lawyer F. Lee Bailey's book? Is he still working on it?"

"He abandoned that idea. No one wanted to publish a book about the only big case he ever lost."

for the federal prosecutors.

[illegible]

You Had Nothing To Worry About

February 3, 1994

Sonoma, California

A blue picket fence surrounded Charles Bates' house, a block off Sonoma's main drag. As I stepped out of my Volvo wagon his greeter, a Labrador named Bruno, rushed up with a lot of love.

At the front door Bates shook my hand like an old fraternity brother reconnecting for a reunion. Life here was a step back in time for the former Agent in Charge of the FBI's San Francisco office on the 11th floor of the federal building. After trying to reach him for years I finally connected via a long letter about my hope that this book would one day honor all those who worked so hard to rescue Patty Hearst:

"With your help I believe we can help people understand why it was such a struggle for the FBI to track down Patty. That search was, as you know, one of the biggest hunts in FBI history."

As long as I didn't ask questions about his own work on the case, Bates was happy to share his opinions. A bright light on the dark road I was traveling, he also had plenty of questions for me.

We headed out to his backyard patio where he lifted the

Weber grill hood to grab a couple of burgers. He poured me a glass of his favorite Cabernet and thanked me for my patience.

"The thing about retirement," he said, "is that it takes a while to decide what you want to do with your freedom. It's a bit like puberty."

A year earlier Bates had gone to Stanford Hospital for open-heart surgery and now, fully recovered, he conceded this was the perfect moment for our long postponed interview.

"I don't want you to think I was ignoring you all these years. I just needed to get to a place where I was ready to tell you what you didn't already know. No point in wasting your valuable time."

"I appreciate that."

"How are you doing? Sure enjoyed meeting your wife when we ran into each other at that restaurant in Napa a few years back."

"My wife and I divorced last year but we're still friendly. We share custody of my daughter, still in high school, and my son is in junior college."

"You seeing anyone or is it too soon."

"Adjusting slowly. Mostly it's about making sure the kids know we are not going to get into any kind of a battle."

"That's good."

"Look I know I've been a while getting back to you. Thanks for being so patient."

"There are some advantages to letting a story simmer.""

"Agreed. Do you have a title yet?"

"I'm still working on that one."

"What about *Patty Hearst: A Love Story*?"

"Possibly..."

"Roger, I read all of your journalism on this case and at one point almost sent you an appreciative note. Steve really fucked you didn't he."

"It would have been a book of lies."

"Sure, but think of all the money you could have made.

Patty's book/movie deal brought her over a million."

"Her book was all part of the Hearst family tradition, monetizing half truths that sell trashy papers. She didn't even pay lip service to any of the inequities in our society. All she did was rewrite the story in a self-serving way."

"Hopefully you'll write a book people can trust."

"I never understood why they tried to get the world news media to hold the story for a day. That's Soviet-style censorship."

"The FBI had nothing to do with that. I thought it was a bad decision. It immediately signaled that there was some kind of media conspiracy against the kidnappers, exactly the sort of thing you don't want to do in this situation. Thank God for the *Oakland Tribune*. At least they were willing to break the Hearst case embargo. We sure could have used Harry Harris on our team."

"The FBI didn't do any better with Steve than I did."

"We couldn't even get him to tell us where he and Patty bought their last supper."

"He said it was Park and Shop."

"Our agents found the receipts. It was the Coop."

Bates interrupted out conversation to take a call from his ex-wife, a sales manager off for a GAP corporate retreat at the Hotel del Coronado. Wrapping up quickly he said: "Hey I bet you'll never guess who I have here for lunch.... one of your favorite writers."

After putting down the phone he told me: "She loved your *New Times* piece on Steve, a classic. Now where were we?"

"The kidnapping."

"It sounds like you're not buying the party line."

"You mean that the FBI screwed the whole thing up by pushing the Hearsts not to cave on the ransom demand?"

"The FBI never told them what to do. It was entirely a family decision."

"Any truth to the rumor that Steve was secretly part of the

kidnapping? You grilled him for days, even subjected him to a lie detector test."

"Of course we were required to check that out. It was part of our job."

"Any new leads?"

"I can't talk about that, but let's just say we double and triple checked every possibility. How much do you actually know about him?"

"He lived with me for six months. I had trouble figuring out why he wanted to marry someone with no interest in the movement. She used to proudly cross United Farmworkers picket lines and was friendly with a Hearst editorial writer who claimed Cesar Chavez had Communist ties. How could two people that far apart stand living together?"

"I can't talk about our investigation but I have done a little digging myself. I filed a Freedom of Information Act request with the CIA."

"I'd like to see that."

"Hang on a minute."

While I finished lunch and poured myself more wine, Bates headed back to his study and returned with a thick folder.

"I made a copy for you which you're welcome to take as long as you don't reveal your source."

"Scout's honor."

After lunch Bates left for a walk and I began reading the file on Steve's undercover work for the CIA. He had spent years spying on leadership of the anti-war, civil rights and student power movements. He also worked undercover with prisoners' rights groups, especially at Soledad in the Salinas Valley. Near the town's mission, the penitentiary was the focal point for numerous protests exposing deplorable living conditions and endless health code violations leading to a series of consent decrees with the state's Attorney General.

Chronically overcrowded, the prison had been plagued by

riots, epidemics, food poisoning and a number of suicides. Here Steve made one of his better speeches that became an anthem of sorts for sister groups around the country. He argued that gang violence was the consequence of prison lock-downs making it difficult for inmates to get critically needed medical assistance. The absence of decent mental health care was a major factor in recidivism.

Thanks to national publicity, Steve connected with many sister organizations around the country where he keynoted successful fundraisers. Equally important, he helped write articulate demand letters to the courts on behalf of the struggling prisoners suing in pro per. His reports on all these groups were invaluable to the CIA. They were especially interested in gangs smuggling drugs from Mexico and Latin America.

Of special interest to me was Steve's work with Soledad inmate Donald DeFreeze. This was the first time I had made a connection between the Revolutionary Army leader and Patty's fiancé. While there was no evidence that they ever met, Steve read from a DeFreeze letter at a number of rallies, including one outside Soledad three months prior to his escape.

I remembered watching a portion of that speech in a PBS documentary. Steve had quoted a poem DeFreeze wrote about his mother being abandoned by his father shortly after she gave birth to a future revolutionary. It was called: "Letter From the Son You Never Knew."

"I miss you daddy," the poem began, "you've been gone far too long."

When Bates returned I asked if he believed any of what I was reading.

"It makes sense but how do you explain it?"

"Steve had the perfect cover."

"All the way back to his days as a *Michigan Daily* editor?"

"Didn't you guys cover Cuba after the Castro revolution?"

"Steve wrote a six part series. Fidel even talked to him for fifteen minutes."

"Didn't he do a tour of the Eastern bloc, winding up in Moscow?"

"He won a prize for that story."

"Yes, from the Socialist Worker's Party. They flew him to New York for the ceremony. He was a valuable asset."

"The SLA saw him as a class enemy marrying the daughter of an evil media lord."

"Patty had become Steve's exit plan from life undercover for the CIA. With her money he wouldn't need to continue spying on his old friends. Leading a double life can be incredibly dangerous for someone as exposed as he was."

"A very early retirement?"

"A great move. He could spend the rest of his life lecturing corporations for big fees on the evils of the left and writing right wing books under the uber conservative tent."

"What do you think happened the night she was kidnapped?"

"It's just a theory, but consider this possibility. As you know DeFreeze escaped from Soledad."

"Steve had nothing to do with that."

"Right. Any ideas on where DeFreeze got the money to pay off the guard who helped him escape?"

"From the left?"

"That seems to have been a trend in prison escapes. The payoff could have been made by some Berkeley liberal who believed that DeFreeze had been framed as an accessory to the killing of the Oakland school superintendent."

"Apparently the Symbionese Liberation Army was disappointed that this murder story faded so quickly. They were looking for a strike that would inspire other revolutionaries around the country."

"Patty was perfect. Kidnapping her would assure endless media coverage central to their mission."

Bates paused to open the door for Bruno, who headed in for his chow.

"Also her family could easily afford the huge ransom needed to fund their prison rights cause. The money would help them bribe more prison guards, and also create huge rallies for their other pet leftist causes."

"They might even have enough money left for a retreat in Puerto Vallarta, where they could pay off the police and enjoy a stoner week."

"Everyone needs a vacation. They only made one mistake."

"They picked the wrong family."

An hour later, as Bates walked me out to my Volvo, I paused to give Bruno a quick hug.

"Just want you to know you're welcome back anytime," my new friend told me. "Roger, please call, if I can answer any questions."

That night I sifted through the CIA report realizing how invaluable Steve's work had been for the agency. In so many different ways he was the perfect spy. He understood how to navigate the left and finger leaders of radical groups who could be hounded by the FBI. Thanks to his work the CIA was able to successfully infiltrate the antiwar movement, left-wing publications and groups like Students For A Democratic Society.

The following day I called Bates to offer my thanks.

"You're telling me that the guy who organized the kidnapping of Patty Hearst escaped from jail thanks to the prison rights movement her fiancé helped create."

"I think so."

"He personally smashed Steve's head in before carrying off Patty ."

"True."

"How did DeFreeze know that Steve was working undercover?"

"DeFreeze assumed, correctly, that a true movement leader on the left would never hook up with a family like the Hearsts."

"He made a good guess."

"After the first Revolutionary Army communique, Steve realized that until DeFreeze was dead this madman could call out a hit on him anytime."

"Steve knew how the prison reform movement set DeFreeze free?"

"He would be considered a valuable prosecution trial witness after the Symbionese Liberation Army was captured."

"This potential assassination target was living with me all the time I was writing his story."

"No worries. We had your place under surveillance the whole time."

I thought Bates was an idiot and if he had done his job right from the beginning Patty and I would have been married at the Claremont. Don't get me wrong, I dearly love my wife and my family. But sometimes I think about what that society wedding might have looked like. Can you imagine me in a tux?—SW

Making Of A Revolutionary

November 4, 1998

Lodi, California

The photos dominating Eleanor DeFreeze's living room wall were a tribute to a legend in the making. During his four years at Lodi High, quarterback Donald DeFreeze led his team to an astonishing 39-1 record.

"Everyone who saw that one loss," she told me at her kitchen table, "knew the Bearcats were victims of racist refs, everyone except my son. He congratulated the winning team, never complained and forgot about it."

"When a sports writer asked him about it afterwards Donald said: 'You can't fire the refs in the middle of a game. They make as many mistakes as the rest of us. Perfection is a myth.'"

I had driven to the central valley on a rainy evening, after a long day at the Berkeley travel guide publishing company where I wore three hats as a writer, editor and marketing director. My life as an author and a journalist had helped me understand the floating crap shoot of book publishing. Unlike the New York scene, the Bay Area was home to one hit wonders like the Whole Earth Catalog and the Guide to Nutritional Healing. Thanks to my background as a travel writer, I was a good fit for Ulysses Press, a company specializing in off the beaten track guides. In the midst of a routine review of a new book on the Yucatan, I suddenly realized a section on Cozumel was disturbingly familiar. Doing a double check, I discovered that the writer had plagiarized over 1,000 words from a Fodor's volume.

After spending several hours reviewing the manuscript I realized that she had selectively stolen from nine other guides. My assignment was to fire her, a job made easier by the fact that she lied when I reached her in San Diego.

"Does this mean you're canceling the 'Unknown Maui' project?" she asked crestfallen. "I already bought my plane ticket."

"'Fraid so."

On the drive over to Lodi I stopped for takeout, arriving shortly after finishing a California roll from a sushi drive-through. One of the things I loved about my new job was freedom from daily newspaper deadlines. Trying to turn around a big story in hours could be risky. Now, as an editor and marketing manager at a small travel publishing company, I enjoyed the luxury of in-depth research. From bounce testing hotel beds, to tracking down hidden beaches and waterfalls, I made sure that our readers got the scoop. As all gold-panners know, you have to sift through a lot of ore to find valuable nuggets.

Eleanor DeFreeze, still living in the family home where she grew up, answered warmly when I called to arrange a visit. Scrapbooks on her son's football career were open on the kitchen table when I arrived. A bowl of fruit and blueberry muffins fresh from the oven sat beside them.

Understanding Donald's story required patience and the ability to put to one side the media narrative surrounding his memory. Eleanor and her husband, Donald's stepfather who had co-parented him from a young age, refused all interview requests prior to me showing up.

"When you wrote us my husband said he still wasn't ready

to talk about Donald. For him it's like it all happened last night. He has these terrible nightmares. I've tried getting him help, but you know how men are."

"I do."

"I've gotten a lot of therapy through my teacher's health plan and it's been such a blessing. One of the things I've learned is how much I still don't know about my own family, my son and myself. I have so much to learn."

"What changed your mind about talking to me after all this time?"

"I want to go beyond the terrible things everyone wrote about him. None of those stories properly explained what turned him into such a short lived revolutionary.

"Donald was not the kind of young man who lowered his expectations. He always believed he could achieve any goal imaginable. He learned how to play the trombone in a single music camp weekend. When he decided to win the school science fair, that's what happened. He easily won the lead role in the high school musical, *Bye Bye Birdie*. Girls from all over the county showed up to see his show. He designed football plays his old coaches still run today."

That was the Donald DeFreeze everyone in Lodi admired. A tireless student who tutored kids in junior high, he worked nights at the UPS depot and was recruited by some of the best football programs in the country.

"Coaches kept flying in, hoping for a chance to persuade the Lodi legend that they would put him in the express lane to the NFL," said Eleanor.

"Part of the pitch was the idea that one day he would be able to take care of us for the rest of our lives. We could go on Mediterranean cruises and African safaris, gift college scholarships in Donald's name and maybe get a vacation place in the Sierras."

"Is that what you and his stepfather wanted?"

"Neither of us was sure it was worth four years of indentured servitude."

"Even for the better life?"

"That's what the slave masters told my runaway great grandfather the first time he was caught, arrested and returned to the plantation in chains. They promised food and shelter as long as he caved to bondage."

"But without the safaris and cruises?"

"Now we know all about the brain injuries, which leads to behavioral problems and dementia. His first concussion was on the JV team and by his senior year he'd been knocked out several more times. Instead of sending him to the hospital for evaluation, the coaches let him sit out the quarter and sent him right back in. If it was really painful they gave him an injection to get him through the game."

"Did you ever try to intervene?"

"Donald was having all these headaches and our doctor wanted to refer him to a neurologist in San Francisco."

"I think I've heard of her. She's a CTE pioneer?"

"Correct, it's a neurodegenerative disease. He finally went in for evaluation and she recruited him for a study focused on football players. When the coaches found out about it they warned him that a workup would go into his medical record."

"Was he worried that a negative diagnosis would scare off college recruiters?"

"Yes, and there was no way we were going to drop the curtain on his dream. On some of those recruiting trips he was treated like royalty. The players introduced him to young women thrilled to show him around campus."

"Black women?"

Eleanor laughed. "I told my husband you'd ask me that."

"Sorry, I shouldn't have..."

"They were white, Asian, Latino and African-American. Several of them sent handwritten letters laying out how their campus would be the perfect fit for the next four years."

I glanced up at a photo of Donald and a young woman with hair piled higher than his six-foot frame. A pink corsage matched the sash on her white dress.

"That's Donald with his love, Anna, at their junior prom."

"She must have been worried about him being picked off."

"She was. After his last concussion in the fourth quarter of his final game she drove him directly to the San Francisco neurologist. They arrived shortly after midnight. The doctor concluded Donald was at risk of permanent brain damage if he played college ball."

"Is that why he gave up the game?"

"No, the very next day he committed to Ohio State. That was when Anna decided to leave him. She couldn't face the possibility of him being hurt again. A month later Donald was badly injured by a drunk driver while walking home from work."

"Did they defer his admission?"

"The day after his release from the hospital there was a letter waiting from the Ohio State athletic director."

"They took away his full ride?"

"Donald knew what to do. He immediately went out and found a great physical therapist that laid out a hopeful plan for recovery. The athletic director wouldn't even take his call."

"Bastards."

"He never complained. Instead he signed up for junior college. After graduating with honors he got a great scholarship to Pepperdine in Malibu."

"Sort of an elite place, with no football program."

"It looked like the perfect campus to pursue his new passion, political science. Donald quickly realized he had made a mistake. Even with free tuition, he struggled to cover room and board. His father and I offered to take out a second mortgage, but he came up with an easier way to cover his bills."

"He started dealing?"

"It started with marijuana and soon he was selling cocaine and ecstasy."

"Was he doing drugs?"

"No. I don't think he was, but he was now making enough money to cover all his bills."

"He was never busted."

"Oh no, the college kids were very cool. He got the good stuff and never ripped them off. After graduating he began volunteering with lawyers taking legal action against the state Department of Corrections."

"Was Anna part of this?"

"No by that time she was at the University of Chicago, interning with the Cook County Prosecutor's Office. They were kaput. He fell in love with the charismatic head of a prison rights group in Oakland. They traveled together to a series of protests."

"Didn't her husband show up at a motel one night in Vacaville and pull a gun on him?"

"It was much worse than that. He pistol-whipped Donald as they walked out of their room."

"She resigned?"

"Right, her successor trained Donald to become a case investigator for the Innocence Project. Within a year he helped win the release of an inmate serving life on murder charges. The key break came when the legal team he was working with finally forced Hertz to release a six-year-old rental car record showing the man was in Reno at the time the killing took place in Redding."

"Why was he arrested?"

"One night DeFreeze got a call from a friend asking him to help out two prison rights workers from Turlock stranded in Oakland after their car broke down. They needed a ride home to care for an ailing relative."

"Little and Remiro?"

"Right. After dropping them off he heard on the radio that they were wanted for allegedly murdering the Oakland school superintendent. They were arrested, arraigned and held in maximum security at San Quentin without bail."

"It sounds like a setup."

"Correct, the person who called Donald on behalf of the prison rights group turned out to be an FBI undercover agent. Giving them a ride made him an accessory to the crime."

"He was sentenced to five years at Soledad."

"Yes and that was when Donald started writing legal briefs for other prisoners. He also began smuggling out impassioned op-eds to the *Sacramento Bee*."

"How did he escape?"

"Not sure, but after that we lost touch for more than a year. The first we knew he was still alive was the night he issued the communique about kidnapping the Hearst girl."

"Were you as stunned as everyone else?"

"Of course. I kept thinking I was in some kind of dream and the moment I woke up my son would be at the door to take me out for mahi mahi. Nothing in his life pointed toward this kind of terror. She was completely innocent and blaming her for the sins of her family was crazy."

"Do you think the concussions led to his undoing?"

"A couple of years ago I got a call from the doctor in San Francisco. She sent me a new Journal of Neurology paper. My son had become part of her study. After looking at many similar cases she confirmed the CTE diagnosis."

"Could that have been a factor in all this?"

"From the doctor's perspective he was a victim. I don't think he saw himself that way. I keep thinking about what would have happened if he had gone to Ohio State, made it into the NFL and become a role model for young dreamers everywhere."

"Did they ever find the hit and run driver who ended his career?"

"They did and he went to court with a wonderful lawyer."

"A suspended sentence?"

"Yes and 400 hours of community service doing driver's training with teens."

Donald DeFreeze was the victim of a non-existent mental health system. Not sure if he was treatable but it's clear that he needed lots of treatment in prison. Instead that's where he became a ringleader. I wish you'd write about that.—SW

Will Hearst

May 13, 2000

San Francisco

A cold wind bounced off Market Street's sleek utilitarian towers as I walked past See's Candies. Normally I would have paused for a handful of almond chews, but I was on a mission. I had come from Oakland where my publishing company hummed from an office a frisbee toss away from one of the quietest places in Oakland for a run, Mountain View Cemetery.

Running an independent publishing company, RDR Books, next door to my landlord, Cole's Honey, was the ultimate role reversal for a former freelance writer. I no longer had to worry about an editor at *Longevity* magazine rejecting a story on successful people working productively into their 80s because his subscribers "didn't want to read about old people."

Now it was my job to get back to biochemists writing about their road to Nobel glory, photojournalists profiling the legacy of Nepal's Potala Palace and the author of a *bildungsroman* previously turned down by dozens of New York publishers. If only I had the bandwidth to bring their prose to bookstores nationwide and sell foreign rights at the Frankfurt Book Fair. Alas, it was my job to sit down every morning and write the kind of thoughtful rejection letters authors seldom receive, always ending with the identical salutation, "Wishing you a long and successful publishing life, I remain, faithfully yours...."

My destination was the Hearst Building, a Spanish revival landmark crafted with pink Tennessee marble sheathed in a terra cotta facade. This was the nexus of the world famous media empire created by Patty's grandfather with largesse from her great grandfather's Nevada silver mines. Rebuilt after the 1906 earthquake, this office tower was once home to the Examiner now operating a few blocks away on Mission. For many years two competitors, the *Call* and the *Chronicle*, flourished across the street, hence the 'Third and Market' intersection nickname, newspaper corner.

I arrived early to explore the building's landmark lobby, remodeled in 1938 by the legendary Julia Morgan. The patriotic red, white and blue lighting illuminating the cast bronze animal medallions would have been perfect for a zoo entryway.

When Patty's cousin, Will, stepped off the elevator we hugged like old teammates. I had happily written for him during the years he edited *Outside*. Among my assignments was a piece on the courageous Greenpeace activists who bravely boarded whaling ships, challenged petroleum cartels, and fought clear-cutting.

Will's greatest joy was his sailboat, which he raced in the America's Cup. His wife wrote historical novels about 18th century France and they both did charitable work in the Hunter's Point community, endowing a teen center destined to become a national model.

After valet parking at Pier 39 we headed up to Swiss Louie, Will's favorite lunch spot. The *maitre d'* seated us on a small table overlooking the docks where invading sea lions displaced boat owners to become one of the city's tourism hotspots.

We caught up on the whereabouts of mutual friends working at *Sports Illustrated*, the *New Yorker*, Time-Warner books and *Rolling Stone* before segueing to my work in progress.

"I assumed you had moved on. Then I heard from Patty's

lawyers that you were talking to everyone. Didn't you have some kind of settlement agreement with Steve?"

"He repaid the publisher, wrote me a check for $15,000 and I agreed not to publish what we wrote together."

"He sued you for $450,000 and ended up paying you off to write his own book."

"It wasn't much of a sacrifice, given the fact that I had no way to know if anything he told me about their lives together was actually true. I understand he sent Patty a copy of his own book."

"And she returned it, unopened."

"Did you read it?"

"I tried."

While we lunched on Dover sole, I told Will a little about my 200 plus interviews.

"When is your book being published?"

"What's that old saying? A book is never done...

"...it's abandoned."

"Maybe I can help."

As the sea lions interrupted their sunbathing to dive off the piers for a quick lunch, Will spent the next three hours illuminating the taking of his cousin. He believed Donald DeFreeze conceived her kidnapping as a flashpoint that would recruit fellow revolutionaries. He was convinced it would turn his tiny band into a Symbionese Liberation Army capable of marching on corporate America from sea to shining sea.

"Our country was founded in revolution, yet some radicals–DeFreeze was certainly one of them–see that as a failed uprising. In his manifesto, the one he forced my uncle's paper to publish as part of a potential ransom deal, DeFreeze argued that our economic system is built on the premise that all men and women were not created equal. He said that by the end of the late 19th century, two percent of the country owned 60 percent of the nation's wealth. Over 35,000 workers were killed in industrial accidents every year, a fact that contributed to strikes met with violent attacks on labor. That led to anarchism, bombings, and assassinations, the kindling for the explosive growth of my grandfather's newspaper empire. Hearst papers lit up the newsstands with their beautifully written exposes attacking the working class."

"Some of them were true."

"Occasionally they got the facts right...a stopped clock is right twice a day and so on. Although these events impacted a tiny fraction of his readers, hysterical Hearst coverage terrified the public. My grandfather's yellow journalism was a great business model creating a mass market built around false narratives, conspiracy theories, misquotes and nonstop editorializing on the news pages. His editors and writers never explored what triggered these revolutionary acts. They campaigned against women's suffrage and the equal rights amendment. They thought it was a good idea to ban married women from teaching in public schools. They had no problem with employers firing visibly pregnant women when there was no unemployment insurance. The Hearst team did not cover the fact that state colleges were refusing to admit blacks. They used the news pages to trash muckraker Upton Sinclair's End Poverty In California 1934 bid for Governor. Ku Klux Klan inspired lynchings were often downplayed or ignored entirely.

"When brave black veterans returned from World War II battlefields to their home towns in the South, the Hearst papers did nothing to protect their voting rights or help them crack redlining that blocked integration of white neighborhoods. The fact that GI bill scholarships and home loans were essentially unavailable to black vets was ignored. Even if they could win scholarships many colleges refused to admit them."

"What does any of this have to do with Patty?"

"Anarchist terrorism fueled subscriber growth at my grandfather's newspapers. Or, as they put it around the circulation department, 'There is no such thing as a bad bombing.' Sensational racist profiles boosted the bottom line, leading to targeting of immigrants and a national call for their deportation.."

"The anarchists provided the ammo for circulation growth."

"Yes, and police raids on workers striking for a living wage were the perfect recruiting tool for aspiring revolutionaries. Those who joined the underground may have been short on political theory but they loved the idea of belonging to a movement larger than themselves. Suddenly their personal grievances were transformed into a larger cause. Some of these radicals were so obsessed with newspaper coverage of their battles for a living wage and racial justice that they kept scrapbooks."

After we finished lunch Will dug in to his favorite desert, sticky toffee pudding. Looking out at the ferries returning from Sausalito and Larkspur, I nudged Will to push the fast forward button.

"DeFreeze's genius was turning the tables on the Hearst empire. He accomplished something no revolutionary ever tried, transforming a reactionary media conglomerate into his personal mouthpiece. By taking Patty he knew they would be forced to give him millions in free publicity. Burying this humiliating story was impossible. When my family failed to meet his ransom demands he got a bonus."

"She was forced to run with the kidnappers," I added.

"In the process she destroyed sympathy for all things Hearst. My cousin, the bank robber, suddenly became a sexy advocate for DeFreeze's cause, a poster child for the revolution on post office walls from Miami to Honolulu. She was now a wanted bank robber, sure to be convicted and jailed."

"Did you discuss this with your uncle during the ransom negotiation?"

"No,' Will said. "The FBI director called him, explaining that caving in to DeFreeze's demand would only lead to a new wave of kidnappings. Governor Reagan and the company's hostage advisors were dead set against bargaining with black revolutionaries.

The FBI feared that the Symbionese Liberation Army was trying to open up a race war. Without Patty as their hostage, I believe they would have been quickly crushed. Now the cops had a dual agenda, bringing Patty home alive while exterminating DeFreeze and his white teammates."

"DeFreeze used the kidnapping to make the media his own personal instrument of power," I said.

"He was borrowing a page from John Brown, who inspired abolitionists with his random acts of violence."

"Those actions helped trigger the Civil War."

"Yes, and every time he staged another raid, the press went wild. National notoriety was his goal. Although his numbers were small, the papers made it look like these crusaders could strike anywhere in the middle of the night and liberate slaves. They marketed the idea that he could arrive like a tornado and bring down an entire plantation. Instead of conceding that indentured servitude was immoral, the Southern aristocracy sacrificed their young men in a Civil War they could never win."

"I think that's what psychologists call continuation bias. You keep going even when it's obvious that the path you are taking will fail," I interjected.

"Brown's random actions inspired endless media coverage of his vigilante campaign to stop slavery. DeFreeze wanted to turn the kidnapping narrative into a crusade that would build support for the homeless, the hungry, the unemployed and victims of racial injustice. In the process he went from obscurity to celebrity status overnight."

"He pole vaulted into the exclusive universe of politicians, billionaires, sports figures and entertainers."

"All that coverage gave him the power to negotiate with my family. Patty showcased his cause free of charge. DeFreeze turned a one-day story into a national apocalypse. Her fate became America's leading television drama. Obviously the family could have borrowed the money to meet the ransom demand.

They had plenty of collateral," Will Hearst concluded for the moment.

"I know Randy got a call from Catherine's old college roommate at Harvey Mudd, CFO at the family-owned Hibernia Bank. They offered him an open line of credit to cover the ransom."

"Why didn't he grab it?"

"The plane, the place at Tahoe, the house in Maui, even his home in Pacific Heights were all company property. The Hearst Corporation board of directors was reluctant to cross the Governor and the FBI."

"How did Catherine react when the board said no to a loan?"

"That was one of the key reasons she moved out to a suite at the Claremont."

"She never forgave him?" I asked Will.

"She believed that as board chair my uncle could have had his way with them. They were now up against an opponent already two-steps ahead on the kidnapping chessboard. Like Martin Luther King, DeFreeze understood that he would not live long enough to realize his dream."

"He was living on the house's money."

"DeFreeze risked his life knowing that the narrative he set in motion would be common currency in the mass media. There would inevitably be films, documentaries, Steve's book, Patty's book, perhaps your book, if you ever finish it."

"He wanted to become an icon that would inspire future revolutionaries ready, willing and able to complete his mission."

"His white comrades hauled off a young woman who belonged to my legendary family that built a fortune committing editorial hate crimes against minorities. DeFreeze knew Patty was the perfect victim and, as a bonus, there would be endless speculation about the possibility that she was defiled by these American monsters."

"How could that be a plus?"

"Nothing lights the fires of racism faster than the image of a white woman being brought to her knees by a black man. This is the myth that built the Klan and fueled far too many lynch mobs."

"Do you agree with the contention of Patty's lawyers that, at its heart, the kidnapping was a sex crime?"

"Certainly the jury didn't view it that way. That was a risky argument, given the fact that she decided to run with her kidnappers."

"Was her professed love for Willie Wolfe simply a convenient way to dump Steve?"

"I don't know."

"Do you think she was more afraid of Steve and her family than the Symbionese Liberation Army?"

"Considering the way both of them botched the ransom, she may have feared they would do a lousy job finding a lawyer to defend her in the inevitable bank robbery trial. When she was finally caught the family hired the wrong lawyer who self-destructed."

"You're saying she wasn't brainwashed."

"If she was brainwashed she would have celebrated her crime and pleaded guilty. I read your interview with Bill Harris where he disputes her story about the kidnappers using coercion to win her over. He claims their humane treatment of her, in accordance with the Geneva Convention, was one of the reasons she enlisted in DeFreeze's army."

"You don't consider him a reliable source."

"In times of great stress people are frequently unreliable narrators."

"Do you believe the kidnappers discovered Patty when her engagement photo ran in the *Examiner*?"

"The Symbionese Liberation Army had been planning this action for a year, probably longer. By the time that piece ran they had mapped out their action like a strategic strike. Every detail had been carefully rehearsed. Some of their demands were fashioned in a way no one could ever meet their terms Do you think my uncle Randy would have agreed to join them on a plane headed for asylum in Havana? Would Castro have cleared them to land?"

"DeFreeze realized Patty was the perfect target."

"At the time of the kidnapping they probably understood her as well as Steve, me, or anyone else in the family."

"How was that possible?"

"After the kidnapping the FBI discovered a wire on their home."

"That would explain the break in a few months prior to the kidnapping. It was so weird that the thieves didn't take anything valuable."

"They knew Patty and Steve were battling, that she wanted to call off the wedding. They understood she was at odds with her family. They also knew something else about Patty that you will want to add to your book."

"Was she unwell?"

"During the weeks before the kidnapping she'd been seeing a psychiatrist in Alameda."

"How do you know that?"

"After she was arrested, he volunteered his records to her defense team."

"Is that the doc who wound up losing his license after one of his patients was found dead in her car?"

"That woman was parked in his driveway."

"I remember that case. Several women came forward for the prosecution claiming he had drugged them in his office."

"He was that infamous Dr. Feelgood who shot up his patients with meth."

"Yes. According to him, Steve threatened to jump off the UC Berkeley Campanile if she didn't go through with the wedding. She claimed he had become obsessed with rugs and art work they had purchased from the Wyntoon estate at a huge discount. He worried that losing Patty would mean giving up all the Oriental rugs and paintings they had so carefully purchased from the estate. She was processing the idea that he was marrying her to win a key to the Hearst kingdom. Apparently Steve wanted to live happily ever after in the bosom of a media family."

"I was wondering how they managed to pay for all those family treasures. Patty wasn't coming in to her inheritance until she was 21."

"I had the same question. A thousand dollars here, a thousand dollars there, it adds up."

"Was Steve borrowing to buy all these heirlooms from the estate?"

"I don't know. Clearly he was in a good financial position."

"Did you know that he spied on the Students for a Democratic Society, the Student Non-Violent Coordinating Committee (SNCC) and the Southern Christian Leadership Council for the CIA's CHAOS operation that disrupted political groups with agent provocateurs?"

"I'd heard that rumor. Not sure I buy it."

Will paused a moment before adding: "Did you know they had an art appraiser?"

"An art appraiser? Why on earth?"

"His name was Massey. They wanted special permission to sell off appreciating acquisitions to buy more art at a reduced price. According to the family's terms of sale, which I have been managing, resales weren't allowed."

"Was that part of The Chief's will?"

"Correct. For example when Randy and Catherine divorced family artwork was excluded in their settlement."

"How did Steve take that news?"

"Patty brought it up in therapy after Steve stopped showing up for their joint sessions. She worried that he was obsessed with these family treasures. Then she discovered he was using her appointment time to hook up with one of her old girlfriends."

"Megan... Walworth?"

"I think so. That was the night she began locking him out of the bedroom."

"He never mentioned that."

"The FBI discovered Patty had quietly visited Trips Out Travel on College Avenue a week before the kidnapping."

"To discuss their honeymoon."

"No, that was already set for Wyntoon."

"Where was she headed?"

"She'd bought a ticket to Wales. An old family friend had offered to put Patty up while she worked on the next chapter of her life, down the street from the place where Dylan Thomas wrote some of his best poetry."

By now it was time for Will to return to his office. Walking out to the Embarcadero I thanked him and asked a question I'd been thinking about all afternoon.

"Is any of this true?"

"Would I lie to you?"

Since my breakup with Steve I had struggled to find the truth. Were all these family, friends, experts and officials believable? I liked many of these people who had welcomed me into their ranch homes, served me homemade cookies and barbecued shish kebab dinners on their backyard grills. They had shown me their scrapbooks, picked me up at train stations on moonlit nights and miraculously opened the doors of the silent majority of Hearst friends, extended family, officials and experts, people who never previously considered going public on the case.

I wanted to believe every one of them. Yet, like any historian worth their PhD, I knew it was impossible to reconcile the vast differences between these eyewitnesses. Multiple vantage points yielded endless contradictions. Trying to get a bird's eye view of the case meant sifting through the memories of people reaching back nearly half a century. Some days working on this book felt like trying to take out my own appendix.

I always admired Will. Patty trusted him. Glad you had a chance to work with him at Outside. I keep inviting him down to meet the family. Maybe one of these days....—SW

Patty's Will Arrived Postage Due

August 2003

Honolulu

My fellow University of Michigan class of '68 alum Wendy Yoshimura and I were snorkeling off a beach near Buzz's in Kailua, where my second wife, Marty, and our family were lunching without me.

For years I had tried and failed to get hold of Wendy, hoping she would open up to me about her life on the run with Patty. On the first day of our long-awaited family vacation in Oahu, I suddenly had the realization that she was living and working in Honolulu. The stars had finally aligned.

"I might as well give her a call and just see if she's about," I proffered.

Needless to say my wife, her son Will and my daughter Elizabeth didn't quite see it the same way. My daughter had flown in from London for our mini-reunion, but by now Elizabeth was used to my disappearing for work. It was an occupational hazard, an opportunity popping up at the very last minute, screwing up time off with my family. My disappearing act always had a decent alibi. Or as Marty liked to put it: "I never have to worry about Roger being shot by someone else's wife or husband. He's more likely to be found in bed having a liaison with a typewriter."

Although this vacation had been planned for months, I was unable to resist this once in a lifetime opportunity to learn more about Wendy Yoshimura's pivotal role in the Hearst story.

"What an amazing co-incidence dad, this Wendy happening to be right in the same place we're taking a vacation." remarked Elizabeth.

"I guess it's more important than being with us," added a snarky William.

Marty, the patient librarian who had sympathy for the people behind the books that filled her shelves tried to explain my dilemma: "I'm sure it's extremely important if Roger has to ruin our trip," she added while shooting me a sweet and sour look.

Now in her late 50s, Wendy remembered my *Michigan Daily* expose of Regent Eugene Power who resigned after the state attorney general ruled he was in a conflict interest. Employees of his University Microfilms Inc. checked out thousands of books to copy and sell along with the university's card catalogs. This intellectual property was merchandised to other colleges for big bucks without compensating the university. Students were dismayed by the fact that books needed for coursework were unavailable because Power's staff took weeks to film them.

"A lot of us in Ann Arbor hated you for that expose," Wendy told me after we finished swimming amidst schools of parrot fish, angel fish and cardinal fish near the reef.

"He was one of the key liberal Regents and getting rid of him tipped the board balance to the right."

As she nibbled on a perfect cheeseburger from Buzz's, I knew it was pointless to try to explain why our paper was obligated to publish this story. The fact that Power was a Democrat did not excuse his malfeasance. The same argument could have been made for all the Democratic southerners who promoted their racist agenda in Congress for the better part of a century.

"The thing I hate so much about writers is that they are always in it for themselves. I honestly don't even know why I agreed to talk to you. "

"Thanks for finally caving."

"Maybe it's because I know no one will ever want to publish what you are trying to write. Don't you think it's ridiculous that you are beating this dead nag? Walk over and talk to those lily white spring break college kids from Minneapolis. Most of them have never heard of Patty Hearst."

"I'm a period piece."

"A fossil that should remain buried beneath bedrock."

I knew that Wendy, a social worker, had gone home to Hawaii after "harboring a fugitive" charges were dropped in exchange for valuable testimony against the Harrises. A star witness, she had given the prosecutors details that led the jury to convict those two defendants in less than an hour. Alas, her attempt to portray Patty as a victim of the Stockholm Syndrome, was less persuasive. Two other juries did not buy Wendy's contention that her roommate had been brainwashed into robbing banks and spraying security guards with her semi-automatic rifle to allow Bill Harris to escape.

Lover of an anarchist who planted bombs at government facilities, she had fled Berkeley after police found a stash of incendiary devices in her garage. Wendy's six months with Patty began in Pennsylvania where she cooked for them. Having fled in a rush, she and Patty traveled back from the Poconos and set up housekeeping in a San Francisco apartment. Their life on the road remained the subject of endless speculation among reporters covering the case. This time was part of the "lost year" following the May 1974 kidnapping of Tom Matthews and the firefight with the Los Angeles police.

After Wendy slipped on her sandals, and pulled a cover-up over her swimsuit, we walked over to a shave ice stand. I went for the pina colada, she choose tangerine. There, on a bench beneath a swaying palm, we time traveled back to 1975. Thanks to her photographic memory she quickly demolished most of the myths leading up to Patty's capture and arrest.

"Both of us were pretty sure we would never make it back to San Francisco. We had a vision of being surrounded by police cars and helicopters somewhere near godforsaken Winnemucca. Patty even wrote out a will I mailed to my parents in Honolulu for safekeeping."

"Did you keep a copy?"

"The crazy thing is the will arrived postage due. My parents thought it was some kind of a prank and they burned it."

"So it's long gone. Do you remember anything that was in it? Did she leave everything to Steve?"

"She decided that it made more sense to leave everything to me as her executor, a job I was happy to accept. Of course if they killed me, she needed a number two and that was her sister Anne."

"Were you in danger?"

"After we left the floating Shakespeare company on the Mississippi, I decided to drive the southern route."

"You headed through Kansas and Oklahoma?"

"Right and then we drove across New Mexico and up into Colorado."

"Were you worried about the police?"

"Neither of us was armed. We never drove at night, always checked into motels during daylight, ate in our room, never went to restaurants."

"What about gas stations?"

"That was difficult. We paid at the pump and only used campground bathrooms."

"Did you actually camp?"

"No, small motels seemed safer and we never stayed in the same place more than one night, always paid cash and had the television on nonstop to make sure no one could listen in. Patty was a huge Johnny Carson fan and we always checked the TV listings to make sure we got off the road in time to catch the *Tonight Show*."

"How long did this take?"

"The Harrises wanted us back in Sacramento right away but Patty felt we should avoid them for a few weeks."

"Was money tight?"

"Fortunately our theater directors Michael and Cindy gave us enough cash to cover the trip. That meant we didn't have to talk business."

"Did you do any sightseeing?"

"When we reached Mesa Verde a strange thing happened. Patty wanted to see the cliff dwellings."

"That sounds impossible."

"What could be worse for us than a national park? She persisted and discovered a Native American tribe running their own private tours nearby."

"They operated separately from the park service?"

"Yes, on Ute reservation lands. Exploring those cliff dwellings was a transcendental moment. Our tribal guide gave us a chance to see a number of sacred spots only open to special guests."

"You felt safe there?"

"Not at all, I warned Patty we would be caught."

"Disguises can only take you so far."

"Yes, after a couple of hours I let my guard down. We had been paranoid for so long that this hike on the trail of the ancients nearly put us into a trance. Both of us trusted these tribal people living outside the American police state.

"Our guide, talking nonstop, told Patty about her decision to move back home to the reservation during her senior year at Oberlin. It was a dark time when she had to flee an abusive ex-boyfriend in hot pursuit."

"All my life men have been deciding what's best for me," the guide said. "The problem is they filter out what we have to say."

"Men only remember what they want to remember," said Patty .

"Unless by some miracle they happen to agree with what we said. When I came back to this place, I suddenly discovered a new voice, my own."

"Wonderful."

"I understand why they trusted you and let you join their ranks. They saw you as a gift, a leader who would help them recruit fellow revolutionaries."

"And I trusted them," said Patty.

"You had no choice. They were the only family you had left," echoed the guide.

"Patty hugged our guide wordlessly," said Wendy. "We had finally found someone we could trust. They were both in tears. It was getting late, the sun was beginning to set and, as we left the cliff dwellings and headed downhill, the guide invited Patty and me to stay for dinner. Of course that was impossible. When we reached the tribal office, Patty asked our guide to advise us on the best route to Reno. She took out a map and suggested we try an old Indian trail that had become two lane blacktop leading though Monument Valley and then west to Nevada."

"'Why do you stay here?" Patty asked. "Family?"

"Oh no, they left years ago to live in Tucson. I'm here because I don't want to live in America."

"You're free as long as you remain on tribal land."

"I've left America to move back here among the cliff dwellings that were home to my ancestors."

"Before all this happened, I thought I was free."

"You thought your family would always be there to protect you."

"I never imagined they would abandon me."

"You could stay here Patty . We can keep you safe."

"I'd love that, but I can't turn your sacred place into a target. Someone might say something to someone and suddenly your reservation would be surrounded. We would be in the midst of a hostage situation."

"This isn't Los Angeles!"

"No, and for your sake I want to make sure it stays that way."

By the time I returned to our family's rented cottage late that night I knew the only way to save my vacation was to postpone my next interview with Wendy.

A week later, after dropping my family off at the Honolulu Airport, I met Wendy at her Honolulu Health Department Office to resume our conversation. Over the following week she narrated the story of the trip to Sacramento where she and Patty reconnected with the Harrises. By now the money from the theater work had run out and they began planning another bank robbery.

"I was opposed, but we had no money," Wendy told me. "Patty insisted this was going to be their last holdup. The plan was to score enough cash to find a new safe house while the SLA began recruiting. That Sacramento holdup led to the accidental death of a customer depositing receipts from a church bake sale. Bank robberies were no longer possible. Our future depended entirely on the kindness of fellow revolutionaries."

Conversations during my extended stay happened during moments Wendy stole from her busy career running the state's contact tracing division. Her hostility began melting away as she answered many questions about her life on the run with Patty.

Since leaving the revolution she had become a nationally recognized leader in halting the spread of sexually transmitted diseases.

"We have the best staff in the country," she told me over lunch at a cafe near the Mission House. "If someone gets an STD, it's our job to find the names of everyone they may have infected and arrange quick treatment."

"That must be a little tricky."

"You mean marching up to someone's front door and telling his wife, or husband that their spouse has a confirmed case of chlamydia?"

"No one wants to know they are married to someone who is cheating on them."

"Actually the marital partners handle it pretty well. It's the people they, in turn, have been cheating with that lose it. Sometimes a single case can lead to dozens of infections. Fortunately we work with a great emotional support staff."

"It's wonderful that you have a contact tracing network set up. If America was ever hit with a pandemic, you'd be all set."

"Yes, but that would devastate our tourism."

"Is it a struggle to get people to come clean?"

"Doctors are required to report anyone with an STD. That's where our work begins. Then we're dependent on instant honesty. Some are very reluctant to share their contacts. Of course when we do reach them we have to find all the people they went on to connect with."

"Do people forget the names of their sex partners?"

"That's one of our major problems. Fortunately some of our clients are detail oriented. We had one guy who came down with gonorrhea. He was just amazing. His business was setting up sex vacations for tourists from all over the world. He met customers at the airport, put them up in his apartment, provided full board and unlimited coupling.

"When we caught up with him he had reservations out for

the next six months. Fortunately he kept a spreadsheet with contact details for his last 150 customers. Some days he had as many as five contacts. We asked him why he kept such detailed records and he said, 'I knew I was going to come down with something one of these days and I wanted to be prepared. I 'm kind of a fanatic when it comes to great customer service."

This is actually pretty funny. Wendy took good care of Patty. I just wish she had talked her in to surrendering before the Sacramento bank robbery. Hard to understand. Any thoughts? -SW

A Night At San Simeon

May 24, 2004

San Simeon

The hand-written invitation arrived in a number ten business envelope with no return address. I immediately RSVP'd for this "special night honoring Harry Harris with great food, live entertainment and a pool party you'll never forget."

The sendoff was happening a few days before I was set to move back to Michigan, after more than eight years of commuting from Berkeley to the Midwest. I was returning to the Lake Michigan community of Muskegon, where I had gone to high school, for a wonderful reason: my second wife Marty. Although we married in 2000, the two of us continued commuting for another four years, while we pursued our respective careers as book publisher and librarian. With my son and daughter in California and London and her son in Michigan, this long distance life made sense up to a point.

I was going to miss this place with its micro-climates guaranteeing a choice of weather. On a single weekend you could ski to Yosemite's Glacier Point, go white water rafting on the American River and have a dip in the Delta. I was going to miss my friends, colleagues who had looked out for me, my publishing office on Oakland's Piedmont Avenue and Shirley Lee, my buddy at Summit Bank who always gave me a reminder call when it was time to avoid a dreaded overdraft.

While I planned to return often to visit my son, other family, friends and bookstore owners central to my business, I knew this move would slow my search for Patty Hearst. There would be little time left for the kind of serendipity that had been critical to my investigative reporting stretching out over the decades. I would no longer be able to jump in the car for a quick trip to San Francisco for an interview with a St. Jean's nun, or catch a short flight to Los Angeles to chat with the reporter who knocked on the door of the Symbionese Liberation Army hideout just before the deadly police firefight.

Now, at the end of thirty-six unforgettable California years, I was headed down Highway 101 through the Salinas Valley immortalized by John Steinbeck. In light traffic I passed Soledad Prison, where Donald DeFreeze made his infamous escape in a laundry cart. Unlike so many other trips I had taken down the mission trail, it was hard to know where this journey was going to end.

The invitation sitting next to me on the Volvo passenger seat opened with a tongue-in-cheek story:

CRIME WRITER MISSING, UNACCOUNTED FOR, BAY AREA ON EDGE, POLICE ON HIGH ALERT

East Bay readers feared the worst as news spread that veteran crime reporter Harry Harris was the subject of an all hands on deck nine county search. His family last saw this intrepid reporter, a front-page fixture at the *Tribune* for decades, when he headed out for a Jersey shake at Dreyer's on Piedmont Avenue.

At a news conference Oakland Police Chief Mel Francis told reporters that his detectives have been sifting through a series of leads on Harris who was scheduled to retire the following week after 40 years on the crime beat.

"While there is no evidence of foul play we are urging the public to share tips about his whereabouts via our anonymous hotline.

RSVP: 345 Sunview Drive, Morro Bay, 93442

At the very bottom of the invite was the address of a Morro Bay lodge where all party guests were expected to gather. Our destination was next door to a great state park where I had camped with my kids years earlier. This coastal sanctuary, with its eucalyptus lined roadways and oceanfront restaurants famous for their wild caught salmon and clams, remained hypnotic. After checking in at the hotel I boarded a yellow school bus ferrying fellow guests down coastal Highway One.

Half an hour later our driver swung left onto a road that led past free roaming zebras, the last remnant of The Chief's once flourishing zoo. While the menagerie may have been sold off in the depression to help the Chief settle his debts, this monumental Julia Morgan designed castle was a tribute to his place in California history. Now, finally, I was at the epicenter of his empire, not as a tourist but as an insider. All those years of struggle, digging through archives, trying to reconcile conflicting accounts, and begging eyewitnesses to sit down for a chat, slipped away as we arrived at the front door of the former Hearst estate, now the crown jewel of the California State Park system. For the first time all of my trial and error felt like it had been worth it.

A mariachi band serenaded us as we alighted from the first of several buses. Our group was led down a tiki torch lit staircase to the Neptune pool deck where waiters greeted us with caviar on silver trays. Prime rib, chicken cacciatore and shrimp towers headlined the buffet table. While my fellow guests bellied up to the open bar, I headed over to the displays featuring the best of Harry Harris. A big poster made the most of his many awards.

Bankrolled by an anonymous admirer, this gathering of the tribe at Hearst's inner sanctum was a testimonial to a classy reporter who deftly approached a breaking crime scene with the tender loving care of a jeweler handling an uncut diamond. The king of the cop shop, it was Harry's deathless prose about the dearly departed that reminded me of what 1984 author George Orwell said after reading James Joyce's *Ulysses*: "I feel like a eunuch who has taken a course in voice production."

We all knew it was pointless to try to compete with leads like: "After a hard day working on tax returns, accountant Mark Meadows stretched out on the diving board of his Orinda pool, fell asleep and rolled over. He was 54."

Predictably, Harry showed up half an hour late to his own retirement celebration. Fortunately he had a great excuse. On his final day at the *Oakland Tribune* he was delayed by a double homicide on the Embarcadero. Grabbing our drinks, all of us gathered below the estate's cupid statue, as Charles Bates, the FBI man who had been so helpful to me, kicked off a series of tributes to the journalist who arrived with no idea he was guest of honor.

The idea of renting San Simeon for the Harris bash evolved over drinks with the anonymous donor at Oakland's Jack London saloon. It was here that a group of retirees quietly put together the guest list. As they talked to some of the cops who had worked with him over the years, everyone agreed this event needed to go beyond traditional venues such as The Old Spaghetti Factory or a Hornblower yacht.

As one of the many reporters who had benefited from Harry's generosity, I added a few words of my own:

"I first met Harry Harris when I was covering the Patty Hearst story for *New Times*. His sources were legendary, people who always went out of their way to make sure he got it right. Often he volunteered information, provided contacts and, above all, made sure that we treated our subjects with the dignity they deserved. We've all been honored to work with him."

After dinner we headed to the cabanas with swimwear we'd all been asked to bring along. One by one the guests belly flopped into the aquamarine Neptune Pool. I had forgotten my suit but one of the attendants quickly solved the problem with a lime green Speedo that gave the crowd a good laugh.

In the chilly water with the other guests, I glanced up at the castle on the hill and imagined what it must have been like for The Chief's guests who had the run of the place for weekend galas. Unlike the celebrities who dominated San Simeon during his golden era, none of the guests in the Neptune Pool that night were household names. We sought neither fame nor fortune. We loved going beneath the surface to set the record straight. Immortality was seeing our *grande reportage* footnoted by historians.

Harry began with a doff of the hat to his old friends honoring him at the cathedral of American capitalism's pool deck. Then he moved into his origin story.

"As a kid I was a paperboy. Then I discovered you could make more money writing for a paper than you could tossing it on people's porches. Editors were good to me and after a dozen years on the crime beat one of them took me to lunch to find out if I was interested in joining their ranks. When I turned him down, he was puzzled:

"Why do you want to be stuck in the trenches for the rest of your life when you could become a leader?

"Because I don't want to be like you."

"In that moment I think, for the first time, he understood why I never wanted to join corporate, where the bottom line was the holy grail. In my world there were no filters between my stories and my readers. I worried that becoming an editor would inevitably make me a class enemy of my fellow reporters.

"For me covering crime was the best job in the world. Most of the people I wrote about were victims who only made it into our paper once in a lifetime. It was my job to treat them with the kind of dignity they deserved, something that would give their families good memories to carry forward. When I turned in my copy I knew that our paper never flinched, we always told the truth. Sometimes we were under pressure to hold back big stories. Fortunately my publishers never buckled. While the chamber of commerce despised all our crime coverage, no story was ever killed."

After the ceremony, fellow guest Charles Bates came over with an old FBI colleague, special agent Cindy Winton, who had retired from the bureau days earlier.

"I think the two of you ought to get to know each other."

The following afternoon she and I began a series of interviews that forced me to delay my planned move to Michigan. It wasn't easy to find time in her busy schedule because she was moving to a new home her husband had just finished building in Santa Rosa. Many of our talks took place while I helped them move boxes into their mission style place that had plenty of space for visiting grandchildren.

Our focus was on how her painstaking undercover work led to the day she arrested Patty Hearst outside her apartment in San Francisco's Cow Hollow. When I called Marty to explain why I had to delay my move back to Michigan she laughed:

"If you added up all those airline change fees you've been racking up, I bet you could've afforded a time share in Maui."

Cindy Winton

May 27, 2004

San Rafael, California

Helping Cindy Winton and her husband Mike unpack boxes at their new home, it was clear they had spent years carefully planning their retirement. Everything was neatly organized into files all the way down to funeral arrangements. He had led an outstanding homicide team for the San Francisco police. She had won many honors for her work at the FBI. Now they would have time to spoil their grandchildren, entertain friends and join new book clubs.

Shelving their hundreds of books it was obvious that fiction was their passion.

"Do you know the difference between a mystery and a thriller?" asked Mike.

"Not really."

"In a mystery you're trying to figure out who did it," said Cindy. "In a thriller you know who did it and you're tracking them down."

"That makes my book a mystery and a thriller."

Together they had written a series of mysteries under a *nom de plume*, books that won them several nominations for the prestigious Edgar awards.

"These books were our escape, but now that we're permanently off duty, we've decided to start a band, maybe play weddings, holiday parties, corporate events," said Mike. "We're calling it *Life Without Parole*."

When we finished unloading each day Cindy, invited me to run with her in the shadow of Mt. Tamalpais as the fog rolled in from the Pacific. Back at the house she and I dined on Chinese food out on the patio while Mike worked on a sailboat in the garage. Our conversation began with a subject that seldom comes up in books like mine, the human side of the FBI.

I had worked every possible channel to reach the FBI and read many of their heavily redacted documents on Patty's case thanks to Freedom of Information Act requests. As it turned out Cindy had done her own homework on my own family's long and very complicated history with the bureau.

"One of the reasons I decided to talk to you was your uncle Melvin. Our records show he was one of our best west coast undercover agents during the Communist scare in the 50s."

"Funny, my uncle never talks about that."

"He did extraordinary work for us thanks to his long leftist past. Around the office we called him Melvin the Red Nose Reign Dear," Cindy said.

"When exactly did the bureau begin following my parents?"

"That would have been in the late '30s when they were active in the African American Students Union at the University of Illinois."

"And my uncle Kenny?"

"That would have been in the late '40s when he was busy with a group trying to desegregate the Detroit Tigers, which didn't happen until the Tigers hired Ozzie Virgil in 1958."

"The FBI got my uncle fired from his tenured job teaching 8th grade at a Torrance, California school in 1953. Like thousands of other suspected Communists, he was blacklisted from public school teaching across the country for the rest of the decade."

"Ah yes, Operation Textbook. The agency helped purge thousands of leftist teachers. That was a high priority for the director. Many of those teachers never taught again."

"Fortunately Kenny got a PhD at UCLA and wound up being a world famous reading educator, President of the International Reading Association."

"We heard about that."

"Did you know that eventually he was invited back to the Torrance schools to run a week long staff training workshop."

"Good for him. You must be very proud. Our Mr. Hoover ruined a lot of lives. Glad to know your uncle wasn't a victim for life."

"You knew Hoover?"

"My father worked for the bureau in Baltimore. Thanks to him I became one of the first women special agents in 1972."

"J. Edgar Hoover was at your swearing in?"

"No, his mother was throwing a big dinner party for her bridge partners that night. He lived with her until he was 40. She came first."

"You never actually met Mr. Hoover?"

"I can't be sure. My dad was close to his personal secretary. They dated for a time. She arranged a private meeting but when we walked in the director wasn't there. Instead there was a woman sitting at his desk."

"Was he cross dressing?"

"I've always wondered about that."

"What was it like working for the bureau in those days?"

"We did a lot of stupid stuff back in the Joe McCarthy era. The Senate witch hunts were crazy."

"I know that when the FBI's Detroit office called my mother in for an interview in 1953, she couldn't get child care. She had to bring my infant sister Carla along. It was terrifying."

"Yes, I've read that account. They were pre-interviewing her for the un-American Activities Committee hearing about some of her leftist activities," Cindy said.

"How could a kindergarten teacher be a threat?"

"At that time the FBI went for as much publicity as they could get to expand their aegis. Hoover had a saying: 'Leak a good story and you'll plug a hole in the budget.' He was very Machiavellian."

"The Hearst case must have posed a difficult challenge."

"I, and other agents, knew that the agency was bitterly divided between the kind of take no prisoners approach you saw during the Los Angeles firefight with DeFreeze's revolutionary army and what my team wanted. These were common criminals cloaking bank robbery and murder in revolutionary rhetoric. Turning kidnappers into martyrs simply inspires more politically motivated crime. Clearly what drove the Symbionese Liberation Army was their lust for the front page by any means possible."

"How long has this battle been going on?"

"It began the day she was kidnapped. In the beginning the bureau, the attorney general and the governor were adamant that there would be no hostage negotiations."

"The family tried?"

"The bureau leadership was convinced that any ransom deal would simply lead to more kidnappings. The family filtered all their offers through our team completely dominated by men hand picked by Hoover," Cindy said,

"Women agents weren't consulted?"

"Although the bureau employs more women today, girls essentially remain an afterthought."

"There's never been a woman running the FBI."

"I doubt there ever will be."

"Did you volunteer to work the case?"

"Yes, but they brushed me off."

During our many interviews, Cindy Winton laid out a theory of the case that was both novel and troubling. Her 1973 masters thesis at the University of Chicago's department of psychology created a world view that put her at odds with her employer on this critical case.

"I don't mean to belittle the FBI's concept of agents working in pairs but from the day she was kidnapped I knew I was uniquely qualified to track down a suspect like Patty. A show of force was unthinkable. We had to find a way to take her without incident. Again and again I successfully troubleshot difficult cases. This time I spent months trying to persuade the bureau to trust me. No one was listening."

"Why?"

"Definitive research shows there are many ways our brains can 'trick' us into a misconception of the truth. These biases serve as filters, hindering our ability to make good decisions. In high-risk situations a decision improperly filtered by cognitive bias can end up being fatal."

"The cops lucked out when they opened fire in Los Angeles."

"For sure. The cops had no way of knowing whether or not all the SLA members were inside. If Patty and the Harrises had not gone shopping they could have been killed with enormous consequences for the LAPD and the FBI. This time there was no question she would be our target. This was our one chance to take her alive. If she came at us armed we would have fired back.

"After she and the Harrises robbed that bank in Sacramento I was certain they would head home to San Francisco. When a tip came in that a woman resembling Wendy Yoshimura was seen leaving a grocery store in San Francisco, I asked the office to let me run our field operation."

"No woman had ever done that?"

"Junior special agents like me seldom got out of the office without a seasoned veteran. The FBI sells itself as an elite unit fighting interstate crime. As you've seen in other large crime-fighting organizations, leaders can be subject to the overconfidence effect. As soon as the bureau confirmed Patty was back in San Francisco a task force went to work planning a strategic strike with plenty of firepower. This kind of one size fits all approach can backfire."

"How did you talk them out of it?"

"I told them I was going in alone with zero backup."

"That sounds dangerous."

"Not nearly as dangerous as sending in a crisis team."

"You had no way of knowing if Patty would even open the door. What if she started shooting?"

"We'd confirmed, by then, that she and Yoshimura were living separately from the Harrises. We didn't have to worry about a big firefight."

"Didn't the Berkeley police find a cache of weapons from Yoshimura's garage in 1973?"

"Yes, but she'd been 'storing' them for a boyfriend who we'd locked up a while before. When I made my move, Yoshimura had gone jogging on the Marina. We'd been tailing her for a while. We knew Patty was alone.

"We had been watching her movement for days I knew she always took the garbage out every morning to get a little fresh air. When she stepped out with a bag full of trash and lifted the lid I just walked up behind her."

"No weapon drawn?"

"It was just me unarmed. As she turned around I handed her my business card."

"What did she do?"

"Patty held out her hands to let me cuff her. As we headed down the alley to an unmarked car the first thing she said was: 'Can you get someone to pick up the new meds for my cat? It's at the People's Pharmacy on Stanyan.'

"Just minutes after Patty was taken, Yoshimura returned to the apartment to find agents inside waiting for her. By this point the Harrises were also in custody."

"None of this ever made the news. Did you mind not getting credit for bringing her in so easily?"

"The key to the whole thing was going in without a weapon. Telling the truth would have been a publicity nightmare for the bureau. They didn't want to give credit to a woman succeeding singlehandedly. They preferred the fictional portrayal of an overwhelming strike force subjugating the bad guys. I promised my boss back in Washington to never tell anyone what I did that day to save her life."

"What changed your thinking?"

Cindy looked out at the magnolia in her new backyard and then paused for a sip of mint ice tea. "I read what your uncle Melvin did for us. Spying on all those Communists was a far greater risk than arresting Patty. One slip and he could have been assassinated. Your family can be very proud of the way he protected our country. The bureau would be nowhere without heroes like him. Thank you for his service and thank you for telling the truth about Patty. People have a right to know what their public servants are doing with their hard earned money."

"I'm not going to get you in trouble if I put this in the book? They'll know it could only be you or Patty who told me."

"Retirement is great. Where would any of us be if Otto von Bismark hadn't invented it? You should try it sometime."

Roger I am thinking that this chapter leaves a few unanswered questions. If your uncle was in fact an undercover agent maybe you should give him a little more attention. That's so fascinating. You have an incredible family.—SW

Anne Hearst

February 28, 2010

Ojai, California

Patty's younger sister Anne lived in the kind of blissful obscurity that had eluded so many other members of her famous family. Her name wasn't even on my call list. Barely a footnote in Patty's own book, she was 15 when her sister was taken. Documentaries dropped in a split-second shot pulled from her St. Jean's yearbooks. After college she had given up on a career in chemical and environmental engineering to teach chemistry at a private high school in Ojai.

Unlike so many of the other family members and Patty intimates I had previously interviewed, Anne had eagerly sought me out. Her cousin Will had hinted that talking to her could kill any chance of ever getting to Patty. I had finally caved to Anne's request for a meeting after she convinced me that our talk would be in complete confidence.

We met at Bart's Books, an open-air literary shrine built around a courtyard shaded by jacaranda and eucalyptus. It operated around the clock with honor system bookstalls lined up overnight next to the parking lot. Customers trained their headlights on the shelves and browsed at their leisure.

"I met my husband here, we got married in the fiction section," she told me as we sat down with our coffee and blueberry muffins. "For our kids, this place is a second home. They present amazing visiting novelists from Los Angeles and San Francisco. Who knows, maybe one day you'll be here to read from your book."

"I'd love that."

"I'll bring the faculty from my school and all my students. You'll be signing a lot of autographs."

Taller than her sister, Anne was wearing jeans and a maroon sweater, her hair neatly tied back in a bun. She spoke with the calm reassurance of an old friend determined to convince me that I could believe her every word. Our timing was good since I was at one of those troubling moments when the old shit detector was triggering like a hyena.

After all these years I wondered if this was the book I was not born to write. Occasionally I would show a partial manuscript to a potential publisher who typically never got back to me. My literary agent who had peddled the book with Steve for all that money, had sold his agency and retired to a Seven Mile Beach condo next to a reggae bar in Grand Cayman. I heard that he was a neighbor of Iggy Pop who was born in the Michigan town I called home.

Every day I seemed to be drawn away on another project with an actual deadline that detoured my search for Patty Hearst.

"You want to get it right," Anne said when I explained all the delays. "After the blizzard of lies our family has struggled to deal with, I'm happy to finally meet you."

"I'm not sure that there is anyone who can explain this case believably."

"That's why I called you. I am so happy you drove down to see me. I read your Hillsdale College book about the mysterious death of the President's daughter-in-law who happened to be his top aide. I try hiding the fact that it's my alma mater."

"Do you think they were having an affair?"

"Based on what you wrote, I'd say the odds were at least 110 percent."

"What about her husband? Do you think he killed her or was it a suicide?"

"Given the shoddy quality of the police work in that company town we'll never know," Anne said. "They wrote the worst police report in Michigan history. I still can't believe they took her husband, the prime suspect, out for a hamburger before they interrogated him. Hillsdale was one scary place. I still have nightmares."

"Sounds like their right wing Kool-Aid left a bitter taste."

"My family still donates a ton. One of my uncles is on the board."

"You called because you wanted to talk Hillsdale?"

"Actually, I'm a little hurt you haven't reached out to me on your book about my sister."

"I don't believe you've ever given an interview."

"Other writers reached out to me, even dangled cash, but you're the only one I trust. Steve's told me a lot about you."

"You're in touch?'

"Steve and I Skype every Sunday. It began when he moved in with my family right after the kidnapping."

At that moment I knew the likelihood of our conversation remaining confidential had evaporated. I even considered the possibility that Anne was recording my thoughts to share with her BFF Steve.

"He told me you took good care of him while he was recovering."

"I checked in every morning just to make sure someone hadn't killed him."

"That would have taken a lot of explaining."

"He was kind of *persona non grata*. My mother kept trying to shift the blame toward him. The place was littered with experts and consultants offering competing advice from as far away as Kathmandu. I remember at dinner one night these two fortune tellers got into a fistfight. I was the one who had to break them up and clean the blood up off the floor."

"That must have been a scary time."

"It got worse. One of the FBI psychologists was caught raiding the liquor cabinet and a hostage expert from the state police was so wasted he peed in the pool. The reporters were constantly coming in to use the bathroom by the front door. I caught two reporters from competing Los Angeles newspapers humping in a basement storage room. One of the network sound guys passed out after shooting up. We had to call an ambulance."

"Were Steve and Patty fighting in the weeks before she was taken?"

"A lot of it was about his affairs."

"Were you surprised?"

"As the world knows, my grandfather lived with his mistress in San Simeon for over 30 years. She loved the old guy."

"They were very open about it."

"Both of my parents had their share of lousy lovers. One time they showed up at our vacation house in Tahoe with their respective paramours."

"Sort of like Noel Coward."

"Yes, a third rate imitation of *Private Lives*. It was quite a scene when she walked her Asian lover into the master bedroom and discovered it was already taken by my dad and one of his favorite mistresses, an African American."

"Patty had been faithful to Steve."

"Absolutely and, after finding out he was sleeping with her old friend Megan Walworth, she was ready to call off the wedding."

"You argued against it."

"Although I barely knew Steve at that point, I was sure he loved her."

"Because she was a Hearst?"

"Sure, that was part of it. He also loved the way she took him on, put him down in front of friends, didn't just cave."

"Some people are happiest when they aren't being taken for granted."

"That was Steve. Strong, decisive women were his weakness. One week he slept on the futon after a marathon battle over the wedding guest list. He wanted to elope and she insisted on the Claremont. Steve kept pointing out that the wedding money would be much better spent fighting Jim Crow laws in the south."

"At that point he hadn't dropped the leftist veneer."

"No, his eventual pivot to the right came as a complete surprise. My mother was stunned. She couldn't believe he was her secret political soulmate, an undercover agent for the CIA ratting out student radicals."

"Can I ask you something?"

"Sure."

"When Steve realized he could confide in you, why did you trust him?"

"I had no choice. By that point he desperately needed someone in my family he could talk to."

"Patty was gone and he wasn't getting any love from your parents."

"I snuck him out of the house as much as we could. We went for drives down the coast, took ferry trips to Sausalito and Angel Island. One time we went over to Alcatraz, a place I'd seen every day out our living room window but never visited."

"It was Steve's idea?"

"He needed to escape the bedlam. About the only time he could get any traction was when he drank with my father late at night. Besotted, my dad was agreeable to all of Steve's half-baked ideas on how to rescue Patty. By morning he had forgotten everything they had agreed to. That trip to Alcatraz was on the first boat out at 8 a.m. We were pretty much by ourselves for the entire trip. After we arrived the guide, a former prison guard, gave us a VIP tour."

"He recognized both of you."

"No, just Steve. In most stories my photo was a thumbnail."

"Right, I remember your picture in one of my *New Times* articles. Did it seem weird to be hanging out with Steve in the middle of the hunt for the Symbionese Liberation Army and Patty?"

"At that point I think both of us just wanted to play tourist. Making history is not nearly as much fun as studying it. After all those years watching boats head in and out of Alcatraz it was kind of cool to actually be there.

"Steve was curious about Al Capone's cell. We discovered the island's most famous prisoner played banjo and mandolin in a pickup band called the Rock Islanders. Capone also wrote a love song called Madonna Mia that had a half decent ending."

There's only one moon above,
One golden sun,
There's only one that I love,
You are the one.

"In her book Patty wrote that Steve made a move on you."

Anne paused for a moment to get a refill on her coffee and then sat back down as a hummingbird buzzed our table.

"She was just quoting a rumor in Herb Caen's column. He would print anything it took to sell papers."

"You weren't all that close with Steve?"

"I was just giving him back rubs, my contribution to his physical therapy."

"Why was she so angry at Steve?"

"She hated his interview with Marilyn Baker on KQED. He floated the idea that she was just playing DeFreeze and the gang. That really hurt her effort to convince the group that she had honestly become a fellow revolutionary."

"They were skeptical?"

"They had to be terrified about the possibility that Patty

would be the ideal witness against them in the bank robbery trial. Kidnapping makes strange bedfellows."

"Earning their trust was a big challenge."

"Do you remember how Steve got that brave French revolutionary to write an open letter asking her to declare that she had not been coerced by her captors?"

"It was naive to publish that on the front page of your father's newspaper."

"She was furious that Steve meddled in a way that could kill her attempt to be adopted by a family of revolutionaries. Without the SLA's protection, Patty would be vulnerable to just about anyone with a badge."

"Running with them was her only choice at that point."

"There was something else that infuriated her. On one of our little excursions we went over to their Berkeley home and picked up all of the rugs and art they had purchased from the estate. Then we moved it into my parents' basement. On the day mom and dad told him to move out, a friend came over and they quietly moved everything over to a rent-a-space in Berkeley across from Safeway. During one of my Pleasanton prison visits she asked me to have him return everything, even though he had paid for all of it."

"He agreed?"

"Immediately."

"Did he make good on the promise?"

"After her sentence was commuted Patty's lawyer wrote him a series of threatening letters. I've stayed out of it. I never found out what happened."

"And you still trust Steve."

"After your experience with him I don't expect you to believe anything Steve says. All I know is that whenever I've needed a hand he has been there to back me up. When I had to escape from my first husband it was Steve who drove me to a safe place. He's driven down from Los Altos to help my twin daughters write college admissions essays and always sends flowers on my birthday."

"Would it be good for Patty to reach out to him now?"

"That can never happen."

"Is there anything else about Patty you'd like to share?"

"This is a little difficult, but when the trial was going on I visited her in prison daily. She was still in shock and I did my best to convince her that no judge or jury would convict her."

"And after she went to jail...."

"I told her the family would work on a Presidential commutation."

"What was she like after she was released?"

"We had an apartment together for a few months. On a trip to Hawaii she started painting, dancing, doing yoga and taking pottery lessons."

"How often do you see her?"

"Rarely, she hates that I remain close to Steve. She has told everyone in the family not to talk to you."

"Which means I'll never have a chance to see her."

"Well. There is one thing that might prick her interest..."

"What... go on?"

"Have your publisher send her your book."

"That could be a serious mistake, Anne. Her lawyers would come after me."

"That risk is seriously worth it."

"A pre-publication injunction is not really what I'm after, having spent decades on the case."

"You're writing a novel. There's no legal basis..."

"I know that but I don't see why she would want to abandon the 'official story' of why her parents failed to ransom her, why the SLA trusted her with a gun, why she 'fell' for Willie Wolfe."

"After all this time it might be therapeutic for her to abandon her fictional narrative."

"You aren't buying her version of what happened."

"I don't know anyone who knew Patty pre-kidnapping who believes the scripted story her lawyers presented at the trial, the one a jury shot down."

"She was in on her own kidnapping?"

"Of course not, but there is no way she was a victim of Stockholm Syndrome."

"It takes a novel to set the story right," I joked.

Anne laughed, then gave me a big hug.

"A lot of times fiction is just the truth disguised via pseudonyms and a change of venue."

We were both silent for a while. Anne seemed unburdened somehow. I was considering her crazy proposal. Finally I said:

"Is there anything else I need to know?

"I had a dream about you."

"I'm flattered."

"Your Hillsdale book reminded me that every woman I know has a very complicated relationship with their in-laws. In my case I actually adored the parents of the man who made my life hell.

"One of the reasons I put up with his abuse was that I didn't want to disappoint his family. I knew how much they loved me. After I finally had to flee, I wrote a long letter telling them everything they didn't want to know. By that point it was too late. He was so far down the cocaine road there was no way we could save him."

"He loved drugs."

"It was his passion and after he died I realized there was no way I could compete. He said getting stoned alone was better than sex with me. I was married to a hedonist unable to realize how badly he needed treatment."

"You're happy now?"

"I love my students. Both my kids have great jobs and, thank God, I haven't been on a date in five years."

After we left the bookstore, Anne drove me to a hillside

park where parents were playing with their kids, dogs chased balls and families picnicked on barbecue. In the distance a balloon was ascending with a jazz combo.

After a long silence Patty's sister asked: "Don't you have any more questions?"

When I didn't laugh she grabbed my wrist, took my pulse and said seriously, "I think you may have passed out. Sorry I don't carry a defibrillator. Do I need to call 911?"

We both laughed.

"Roger, I have one for you."

"Shoot."

"Why do you do this? There have been like a gazillion words written about this case. So many of the principals are gone. Isn't there something else you'd rather be doing? You could be hanging out with your family, seeing friends, hitting the beach, chasing loose women or men, reading a good novel?"

I paused to consider the person I had become.

"For me research is a joy. I've met so many fascinating people. It's like working on a volume of short stories. This is no longer just about Patty. I'm falling in love with my supporting cast."

"Don't you think that's a little risky?"

"It's an occupational hazard."

'You and Steve were pretty close."

"Very. We were getting ready to invest together in Berkeley real estate."

"You know he feels pretty guilty about what he did to you."

"Which explains why he's never reached out to me."

"I think he could help with your book."

"Excuse me?"

"I'm serious. I told him you were coming by and he asked me to give you this note."

After my Delta flight back home to Michigan took off at sunrise from San Francisco, I ordered a drink and read Steve's note.

Roger

I can't tell you how many times I've sat down and tried to write this letter. My new therapist, a curvy knockout, has been helping put down on paper what I've wanted to tell you. I'm not sure if it was some kind of brain injury from the beating I took that terrible night Patty was taken from me or just my own appalling lack of empathy. What's clear is that I let you down and if there's any way I can help you on your new book, please let me know.

When the plane landed I decided to take Steve up on his offer and sent him my work in progress. Two weeks later he wrote me this letter:

I've read your book three times now and can't wait to see the next chapters. I always suspected there was much more to the story than any of us knew at the time and your reporting is amazing. You have done the impossible, and then some. I've taken the liberty of making notes at the end of each chapter. Hope they are helpful.

If you've got time for a call, I'd like to make a few suggestions, nothing major. I can add a detail here and there, a few more quotes from my time with the Hearsts and, above all, set straight some of the details about Patty that are not in her book or mine.

Please know that I am here for you and if you would like, at some point, to visit with me in Nevada City I will share some important details that your readers will appreciate.

Sorry I was such a jerk to you and I wish you all the best with this amazing book.

Ciao, Steve

Great chapter. Don't change a word of it.

I Always Knew He Would Be The First One Killed

January 2018

Mountain View, California

Just back after a 24-hour journey home from Mumbai, a jet-lagged Dr. Tom Matthews met me outside the Slice of Life company cafeteria. The corporate logo, a neon heart overlaid with a giant DNA strand, floated above the dining area.

"Sorry I'm late, my flight was delayed."

Even now, after all these years, Tom, with his tousled hair, and boyish grin was instantly recognizable. He was the happy-to-be-of-service carjack victim who probably saved the lives of Patty and the Harrises in the moments following the Mel's Sporting Goods shootout. The 17-year-old track star sat in the back seat of his dad's truck with Patty, while Bill drove and Emily rode shotgun.

Matthews was one of the most elusive figures in my search for Patty Hearst. I'd spent more than half my life trying to land this interview.

During my wait outside the cafeteria, Matthews's coworkers, security IDs lanyarded around necks, ran in to grab recyclable plastic lunch boxes crammed with chicken cacciatore, garden burgers, eggplant parmigiana or a salad bar medley of their choice topped off with diet sodas, a kale shake or a latte. On checkout each meal receipt came with a meticulous summary of total calories, fat, sugar, cholesterol and sodium. All these details were automatically entered on permanent personnel records. Those who exceeded the company nutritionist's recommended daily limits were, after three polite warnings, referred to Slice of Life's in house medical clinic for personal counseling.

"It's all part of the bidding war for talent," Matthews said after I was finally permitted entry and handed my multi-chipped visitor's pass from a young guard with a side-arm. "This is my sixth startup and I can tell you food service is a big deal when you are working people 90, 100 hours a week. Some of my colleagues regularly bunk down in their offices. They keep this cafeteria open around the clock. When you're asking people to pull all-nighters you can't expect them to survive on ramen and Doritos. Well-balanced nutrition is critical to our survival. Around here taking sick time requires more documentation than most of us want to share. There's also a big stigma around mental health care, even though it's fully covered."

"A cry for help is a sign of weakness."

"In this company stress is considered a wonder drug."

"What is this place?"

"It's your basic Silicon Valley money pit. Ninety-five percent of the startups here will disappear within five years. For every Bill Gates or Steve Jobs, the streets of San Francisco are littered with the detritus of entrepreneurs slain by the vulture capitalists. We all have our resumes out. You need enough second-round financing to backstroke out of a sea of red ink to an Initial Public Offering. Amazon lost money for many years but the stockholders hung in there, hemorrhaging billions, until they finally made it. Most early stage investors don't have that kind of patience. They want a quick return."

"Do any of these people know who you are?" I ventured.

"Once in a while I am asked about Patty and the Symbionese Liberation Army. There was a new book that came out a couple of years ago that became a CNN documentary."

"It would have had legs if the author hadn't accidentally exposed himself during a Zoom meeting with some of his editors. Gotta keep your pants on and that fly zipped when you're working from home."

"Right. Anyway, there was a short mention of how my dad's truck became the carjacked getaway vehicle after the shootout at Mel's Sporting Goods. Some of the younger people have questions about Patty's journey. They loved the story about me ordering pizza the night I was stuck with her and the Harrises in that Anaheim motel."

"You don't sound bitter."

"I'm not. I was just a high school senior, suddenly on a Symbionese Liberation Army joyride in my dad's pickup. My only my regret was missing a playoff game that our team lost."

"And what's your take on the whole brainwashing angle?"

"I would call Patty a gentle revolutionary. It's not easy being objective about someone who is holding you captive but she and the Harrises never threatened me. They just asked for the keys to the truck and told me to get in the back seat. I remember Patty thanking me for not trying to resist."

"Although they were pretty well armed, none of them wanted to get caught in a second crossfire."

"Yes, and they were grateful that I helped them navigate an unfamiliar neighborhood. Remember this was long before WAZE. It wasn't like they could stop at a gas station and ask for directions."

"Did they try to indoctrinate you?"

"Patty showed me a draft of a communique explaining how

the Hearst empire was built on yellow journalism that destroyed careers, cratered marriages, and ruined lives. She argued that the papers relentlessly pushed their right wing anti-Communist agenda onto breakfast tables coast to coast. Maybe you found out about some of that in your research."

"When I was growing up in Michigan, the House un-American Activities Committee held hearings in Detroit. The Hearst papers fired reporters they thought had left wing ties. One of them was the father of my closest friend. The paper covered those hearings with daily big headlines on the front page, never telling readers there were exactly 123 registered Communists in the state."

"That story in the McCarthy era was the perfect Hearst moneymaker across the country. Terrifying readers was great for business. Nielsen ratings for their TV stations exploded the night after I was taken and most of the Symbionese Liberation Army was exterminated.

"Patty was convinced her family would never ransom her. Now her new family knew that any attempt to surrender could lead to another firefight. Looking back, the action felt like another failed startup."

"Startup?"

"Take this place. Bill Gates, who has more money than God, tossed in a billion followed by Rupert Murdoch and Elon Musk. We've got quite a hill to climb. It will take a very long time to pay them all back."

"You could be one of the fortunate few."

"I don't think any of us will continue working here if the stock options turn out to be worthless. It's tough when you have to pay taxes on the options before you can cash them in. The 23-year-old Stanford biotech dropout who wrote our business plan has already been fired. Security marched her out after the lawyers forced her to sign a series of nondisclosure releases that spared her years of court battles. She didn't even get time to clean out her desk. They sent her personal items to her house COD."

"That's why you all work ridiculous hours?"

"Theoretically we can take as much vacation as we want but most of us barely have time for Hanukkah, Christmas or Kwanza. Our big problem is the endless licensing hurdles. The only thing the FDA hasn't demanded of us is our first born."

"You must be exhausted."

"The SLA had a much more efficient strategy. Kidnap an heiress, demand $4 million for 'the people' and presto they're in business. No lawyers, no consultants, no board of directors, no SEC filings, no initial public offerings, just cash and carry. They got a bonus when they picked Patty. She advanced their cause perfectly."

"Did you believe she was committed to the revolution?"

"By the time they carjacked me, she couldn't run away. She was wanted for bank robbery. Turning herself in would have landed her in jail. Many inmates had a better alibi that she did."

"You didn't feel intimidated?"

"They paid for the gas, and then checked into a cheap Anaheim motel."

"...and ordered pepperoni pizza."

"The Harrises were famished. I met the driver outside the room and tipped him well with Emily's money. When I got back inside they were watching the rest of their comrades die in that firefight. They were all in shock. I remember Patty looking at the screen, crying and saying, 'We're next.'"

"The Harrises?"

"I'm pretty sure they were both stoned. They passed out while Patty kept watching the live coverage in tears. She never flinched, even when the FBI announced they were doubling down on their search for her, Bill and Emily.

"At some point, I don't remember when, I walked across the street to Disneyland in a daze."

"Weren't they worried you were gong to turn them in?"

"You'd have to ask them. Everything about them at that moment was surreal. Apparently they needed time alone to process the tragedy."

"Did you have to wait to get in to Disneyland?"

"Lines at the park were pretty short that night."

"Perhaps everyone was home watching the rest of the Symbionese Liberation Army being executed on television."

"I remember coming down off the Matterhorn thinking this was the greatest night of my life. How many people get a chance to run with folks who have that kind of courage to stand up to the man? When I got back to the room the Harrises were awake, reloading their guns. I tried to hand over change from Patty's $100 bill but she waved me off. We all drove to another motel in the pickup and the following morning they paid for a cab back to my house."

"What happened to the truck?"

"Not sure, my dad was pretty upset. It may have been a beater but he loved that Ford. Worked on it every weekend. He had just put in a new carburetor. It was never found."

"And the police?"

"They interviewed me for a day and a half. I was pretty useless."

"What do you actually do here at Slice of Life?"

"Gene editing."

"Huh?"

"Designer babies. Imagine if you could tweak the DNA of HIV positive parents in a way that would insure their children will not inherit the virus. We believe one day kids could be born immune to measles, chicken pox and tuberculosis. Maybe we could rule out Down syndrome, Autism, Multiple Sclerosis, Asperger's, even the common cold."

"What about the Stockholm Syndrome?"

"Now wouldn't that be something."

"You're trying to put an end to sick days."

"Exactly, productivity would skyrocket."

"It sounds like market based eugenics."

Tom raised a finger to his lips: "We don't talk about the TIME story that tried linking us to the ideology of White Supremacy groups. We're definitely not trying to build a master race here. Our new CEO is a bio-ethicist. He writes op-eds for the *Wall Street Journal*."

"What's your role?"

"I'm running the psychiatry program. Our goal is to give parents an opportunity to rule out the possibility of being forced to raise a child with schizophrenia."

"As long as they can afford it."

"We're not it just for the love of it. Someone has to repay the investors. One day we might tweak the heritable code of a human embryo to create humans less likely to become kidnappers or bank robbers. It all comes down to gene modification."

"That sounds expensive?"

"After we get FDA approval it's all up to marketing. TV ad campaigns designed to persuade prospective customers to beat down their doctors' doors for this stuff cost a lot. If human trials are slow the venture capitalists could get twitchy. Our lobbyists are suggesting we give it a go in Brazil and use those successful blind trials as the scientific evidence we need to jump start this biotechnology here."

"What if the trials fail?"

"Then we just move on to the next startup. Headhunters park alongside our company driveway. They want to catch you when it's time to head home to bathe and see your families for a few hours. They lure you with more money, a family friendly 9-to-5 work schedule and sabbaticals every three years. They are relentless. One of them had the audacity to hand over a written offer to one of my colleagues while he was standing on the sidelines at his kid's soccer game."

"You really think it's safe to mess with human evolution?"

"Nothing is safe. You're taking a chance just driving to this interview on the Nimitz freeway. Most people don't even have grab bars or bathmats in their showers."

As we finished lunch Tom was apologetic:

"I'd love to take you back to our lab, show you around. Unfortunately, as you've seen, the security is a rather over-the-top . You got everything you need?"

"I have one more question."

"Shoot."

"Did Patty say anything about all those killed that night? They'd been such a tight unit."

Tom thought a moment then answered: "She was convinced it was her fault, that she should have been there to defend them, put her life on the line. The Harrises tried to calm her down but Patty insisted that her failure to talk the group out of fleeing to Los Angeles led to their deaths."

"Why didn't they listen to her?"

"For the same reason her parents and Steve didn't think her communiques were believable. No one realized she was some kind of genius."

"Genius?" I asked, astounded.

"Yeah, I think so. Patty did what she had to do to survive and then, after she was arrested, turned on the kidnappers who had fallen in love with her. Jail was not an option."

"You're not buying the Stockholm Syndrome?"

"Actually, Roger, that term was not invented by a Michigan State University psychiatrist until after the kidnapping and it wasn't popularized until her trial was over, much later. Her big-shot lawyer F. Lee Bailey argued she was brainwashed which may have been true in the first weeks, identifying with her captors in the short term, but not in the long term. You can't call it psychological coercion when she ran with the SLA for more than a year after they'd offered to set her free. Patty's hatred of her parents for blowing the ransom attempt and her decision to dump Steve does not add up to this pop-psych analysis. Her lawyer tried to use this as her defense, but in the end the jurors didn't accept his version or hers of the bank robbery and my kidnapping in Inglewood. So why should anyone else? I was with her the night six members of the SLA died and I can assure you she wasn't remotely showing signs of delusion, brainwashing or any 'Stockholm Syndrome'.

"She turned on two families: her own and the SLA?"

"You could say that but you'd be wrong. Your family can imprison you or they can set you free."

"Neither family was able to do the latter."

"Agreed. What I remember most about Patty," Tom said "was the moment a local TV anchor reported that Willie Wolfe was dead. She grabbed my hand and I put my arm around her."

"They were seriously in love."

"Patty looked at his photograph on the TV and hugged me in tears."

"What did she say?"

"'He was the kindest, gentlest man I ever met. I always knew he would be the first one killed.'"

Always wanted to meet Tom Matthews. Tried to track him down when I was working on my book. Glad you finally connected with him. His version of events is so much different than the way Patty tells it in her book. Of course she had a white male ghost writer from the Hearst bullpen. That's pretty ironic when you consider the fact that she attacked Jeffrey Toobin for being the white male writer of a book about the case that she absolutely hated. I don't seem to remember her ghostwriter being a young black female. Too bad she didn't choose you to ghost her book. Keep trying to reach her. I think the two of you would have a wonderful time revisiting the story. Heard a rumor that she has a place not too far from you. Not sure.—SW

Curl Up And Dye

August 2019

Washington Island, Wisconsin

Shortly after my wife and I arrived by ferry for the Washington Island Film Festival, she mentioned it was time to get a haircut.

The gala brought cinema buffs from all over the country to the northern reaches of Door County, the legendary Midwest tourist destination famous for its dark sky parks and cherry orchards. This county of 28,000 is also home to four professional theater companies, a subject I had recently written about in the Los Angeles Times travel section. Although it was a far cry from Sundance or Cannes, this event was, in its own way, a grand celebration of independent filmmaking in flyover country. I was thrilled to be presenting my new mental health drama, *Coming Up For Air*.

After striking out at several barber shops I began calling hair salons. When that failed, I pulled into the full lot beside 'Curl Up and Dye' and double parked behind a Ford 350 loaded with craft beer kegs.

"We're fully booked," said the cheery receptionist dressed in madras shorts and an 'ANY FUNCTIONING ADULT FOR PRESIDENT 2020' t-shirt. After a moment, looking at my forlorn face and even more forlorn hair she came back to me with: "Hang on...Let me check with Emily. I think she may have just had a cancellation."

A couple of minutes later I was sitting in Emily's chair. As this trim blue-eyed woman spread an apron over my lap we both did a double take.

"Aren't you Roger Rapoport? I saw the interview last night with you on Channel 4. I have tickets to your screening. I was going to bring my brother along, but it's sold out."

"I can get you an extra ticket."

"That would be wonderful."

As I did a double take she gave me a smile that quickly took me back to 1974: "Emily....? Emily Harris? What the f..."

"Indeed. I guess we have a little catching up to do. Lean forward for me, will you," Emily Harris said spreading a cape over my shoulders.

We had breakfast the following morning at Emily's small cottage near the ferry dock. While my wife joined a walking tour of local gardens, Emily brought me up to date on her journey back to the place where she grew up.

"I moved back here after Bill and I completed our sentences for the Sacramento bank robbery."

"Your second sentence?"

"Correct, after serving four years of an eight-year sentence for the kidnapping and the first bank robbery in San Francisco."

"What did you think of the judge?"

"Brandler? A pompous son of a bitch. His instructions to the jury were a disaster. Now if we had been white collar criminals..."

"Were you bitter about Patty's sentence being commuted?"

"Hardly. If it hadn't been for her stupid lawyers she might have actually been acquitted in the San Francisco trial."

"Does anyone here realize they have a celebrity in their midst?"

"Given the way I look now, people old enough to remember the case would never make the connection, unless they have been bird dogging the story for decades."

"You look good."

"Thanks, you too. I really liked your interviews with Bill in the *Tribune*; not bad for a pathological liar. Some of the crap he sold you was so convincing I almost believed it myself. Why did he talk to you?"

"He knew I was going to treat him fairly. He had a second wife and kids. Telling the story of his rehabilitation was therapeutic."

"It was good to see him admitting so many mistakes. It's a miracle Bill and I are still walking this earth."

"He only had good things to say about you."

"They say the secret of a successful marriage is knowing when to call it quits."

"My first marriage was great until it wasn't. My second has been wonderful."

"Is that book of yours ever coming out? I mean isn't there some kind of statute of limitations."

"It's only been 45 years."

"You've found potholes in the story nearly everyone agrees is true?"

"Yes. Maybe you could help me fill in some of them. I'm under a self-imposed deadline for the 50th anniversary of her kidnapping."

"You don't believe Patty's book?"

"Does anyone?"

"I hear they ran part of it in *Manhattan* where every syllable is fact checked three times by people who have worked there 40 years. What more could you want?"

"The truth?"

Half an hour later we were bouncing along a coastal gravel road in Emily's Nissan. Sailboats were racing out on Lake Michigan as we came around a bend to a two-story log building with a commanding harbor view. As we pulled into the driveway a small man, sunlight illuminating his bald pate, gave a wave.

The sign over the doorway read: "Massey's Arts and Antiques."

"Roger," said Emily, "I'd like you to meet my brother."

"Can't wait to see your film," said Massey while pouring each of us a glass of fresh squeezed lemonade made by kids down the block. "My grandchildren already have their tickets thanks to a foundation that picked up a block for their school. Mental health is such a timely subject."

Over the next several hours Emily and Massey answered many questions about the kidnapping. Minute by minute they explained precisely how everything had come together and then suddenly fallen apart.

"What you don't know is that it was never intended to be a kidnapping," said Wendy. "Bill and DeFreeze wanted to take Patty but the SLA women refused to participate. At one point we all threatened to quit over their disastrous male chauvinist approach to the revolution."

"I thought the women were in charge."

"Yes in some ways we were. We had the guys outnumbered. But they had this brilliant way of pretending to listen to us and then just running off and doing whatever they wanted."

"It was a stupid way to try to raise millions to jump start the revolution," said Massey.

"We researched a lot of kidnappings and showed the men all the reasons why it would fail," said Emily.

"And get them all killed," added Massey.

"I thought the idea was that taking Patty guaranteed wall-to-wall media coverage, perfect for promoting their cause. "

"Sure," said Emily. "Kidnapping a media heiress was a bold move they believed would prompt similar actions from revolutionary groups around the country."

"The men insisted Patty would be quickly released after the family instantly ransomed her."

"There were two problems with this approach," said

Massey. "First, kidnapping is only the beginning. It's critical to keep the victim safe while ransom negotiations are going on, not an easy job when a big task force flanked by German Shepherds is tracking you down."

"And second," segued Emily, "all the women in the Symbionese Liberation Army were feminists, several of us were bisexual and one was lesbian. Abducting a woman was morally indefensible. Women everywhere would be alienated by this sexist act, especially when the victim was an innocent young woman who wasn't even old enough to buy a beer. Plus we were worried that she could be violated by our men who might view her as community property."

"Was that discussed?"

"At some length and the men guaranteed her safety, promising they would strictly follow the Geneva Convention."

"When Emily described their dilemma I came up with the sensible idea of stealing the extraordinary painting Patty had given me for appraisal," said Massey. "It was worth at least $4 million."

"It was the perfect solution," said Emily. "My brother shows up to meet with Patty and Steve to return the valuable Hearst treasure with his appraisal. As soon as he leaves we steal the painting, sell it and then use the money to help those who need a hand, the homeless, the hungry, the jobless, people desperate for medical care. No one gets hurt and you don't need to feed a painting. There's also less risk of getting shot by FBI hotheads."

"Not to mention the possibility that with the fallout from a kidnapping six of your comrades could wind up in an LAPD weenie roast," said Massey.

Emily nodded in agreement: "It would have been seamless except for one thing."

"I had been in Hawaii for a conference," said Massey, "and after landing in San Francisco I forgot to reset my watch back to Pacific Time."

"He had a 6:30 p.m. appointment at Patty and Steve's place," said Emily. "We wanted to give them a little time to ask questions about the painting before arriving to steal it. When we stormed in at 7 p.m., Massey was missing. My husband Bill and DeFreeze flipped. They tore up the house trying to find the damn painting. Then Steve started screaming. When DeFreeze tried to quiet him down with a rifle butt, he kept screaming and our boys were convinced the neighbors were going to call the cops. After they knocked Steve out, Bill, I still don't know why, instinctively picked up Patty in a fireman's carry and headed out to the car. As they were leaving, Steve came to and ran screaming out the back door."

"Your men didn't want to leave empty handed."

"I've been over this so many times," said Emily. "Bill and DeFreeze spent months architecting this kidnapping before all the women talked them out of it. I and the other women never wanted to deal with the Hearsts. What were we going to do if she had a medical issue? When stealing the painting didn't work the men couldn't accept the idea of retreating to fight another day. Kidnapping was self-defeating. We ended up with no money and were forced to start robbing banks."

"All because I didn't reset my watch," said Massey, as an antique postcard collector from Whitefish Bay knocked on his door.

Great interview. Nailed it. The book just keeps getting better and better. Even if Emily is lying it makes a great story. I think the critics are going to love this chapter.—SW

My Wedding Day

March 28, 2021

Nevada City, CA

I was midway through writing my chapter on Will Hearst when a FedEx package arrived containing an mp3 file on a USB stick from Weed and an invitation to meet at his house to break bread the following day. Obviously he had gone analog to get this digital file to me in a thoughtful effort to tempt me to make the journey to his Nevada City estate.

The following morning I headed north from Berkeley, opening Steve's mp3 on CarPlay as I crossed the bridge above the Carquinez Straits. The bottom of the Sacramento Delta, a maze of waterways that was California's island in time, was the very same roadway that Patty and the Harris's had taken back to San Francisco after the tragic bank robbery in Sacramento.

Listening to his voice I wondered if Steve might be trying to ghost his old ghost writer. There was certainly no reason to trust him. Despite my misgivings I continued east.

Then, 45 minutes later, driving past Davis, I flashed back to the day in November 1974 when agent Sterling Lord called to let me know that Ballantine loved my work in progress. The accounting department was cutting the check for the second portion of our advance.

I immediately called Steve, who had moved out of our house

weeks earlier, to share the good news. My call went straight to voicemail.

"Hey Weed," I told him. "Let's set up another meeting with Arlene Slaughter. There's a four bedroom over on Prince Street that would be perfect for us."

Instead of returning my call to celebrate, he responded days later with a lawsuit.

A speeding Harley driver cut me off on the causeway crossing above the Yolo flood plain and threw me back into the present as I slammed on the brakes. A minute later, I resumed Steve's audio commentary on my book, a supplement to his stream of consciousness comments he'd been emailing chapter by chapter.

It had been a long time since I'd heard his familiar, weak-on-consonants monotone. Just listening to his voice made me consider the possibility that I could be setting myself up for a meltdown, the definition of what today's TikTok brigade would call a 'triggering' event. I felt my heart rate quickening and I pulled off into a taco stand parking lot to catch my breath. I started doing some of the eye movement and desensitization stress reprocessing exercises my Muskegon therapist had prescribed me to follow. After a few minutes of careful breathing and calm thoughts my heart returned to a less alarming BPM and a few minutes later I felt able to resume my journey, heading up into the Sierra foothills toward the Gold Country.

Hearing Steve's audio critique it was obvious that after all this time his anger toward me had given way to a reckoning. For reasons I did not understand he needed me far more than I needed him:

> *It's nice to see Bill Harris describe himself as your friendly neighborhood kidnapper. Inasmuch as I was on the receiving end of an SLA rifle butt the night they snatched Patty out of my life, I'd like to suggest that you seriously revise that chapter. His self serving nonsense is ridiculous. He was a criminal*

psychopath and nothing he says deserves to be published in the Oakland Tribune or anywhere else. Don't fall for his ridiculous lies.

The stuff on Randy was pretty good. If he had put down the $4 million the SLA wanted she probably would have been freed within a couple of days. After she recovered at home and I was released from the hospital we would have gone off to a Zen resort above Big Sur, far from the paparazzi. My book would have been worthless but hers would have been worth millions. I could have helped her out with the screenplay and made sure none of those Hollywood sharks ripped her off with their kleptomaniac accounting.

Nice that DeFreeze's mom made it into your book. What a sad story. It almost made me feel sorry for the guy. I can't believe you actually got to Noguchi, good stuff. I can't imagine sifting through those charred mandibles. It didn't work out for that schmuck Willie Wolfe. Too bad. The FBI interviews are very revealing. If they hadn't screwed things up and the Attorney General had not put a choke hold on Randy regarding the SLA ransom demand, Patty and I might still be together. Just saying....

Woah, Agent in Charge of Monkeys at the FBI sounds like he is on the verge of checking into a memory unit. Next thing you know he's going to be accusing me of being the undercover agent who rode shotgun with Black Panthers head honcho Huey P. Newton. Alzheimer's is such a heartache. Really feel for his family. For all his tenacity I kind of respected him. Painting me as a CIA stooge is cuckoo land stuff. Please dump all that nonsense. I was never an informer.

Nice job with Tom Matthews. Good that you were persistent.

His story is fascinating. I'd love to meet him one of these days. Send me his cell number. Maybe I'll invite him up to the Gold Country for a salmon barbecue.

As I passed the "Keep Out" sign in Steve's driveway and paused at the guard gate to punch in an entry code, it was clear that the Trump years had been a bonanza for Steve's on-line empire. Gold-plated right wing foundations poured big money into Steve's many causes, including Trump's potent 'Stop The Steal' campaign. His website aimed at college youth, *The Dawn's Early Light,* had made him a celebrity with Young Republican clubs. A well-armed five-man security detail accompanied him on his campus lecture tours until Covid-19 forced him to retreat to Zoom. Luckily, birds discovered nesting in an engine forced the cancellation of his American Airlines red-eye to Washington early on the morning of January 6, 2021. As a result Steve was a no show at the Trump 'Stop the Steal' rally on the Ellipse and his prepared remarks were never delivered.

Back in Michigan there was a campaign afoot to give him an endowed chair in political science at uber-conservative Hillsdale College. It was a sweet deal with campus wide lectures, a team of researchers and an annual seminar for alumni willing to pay $5,000 for an exclusive weekend with Steve. His leeward Caribbean "Freedom" cruise was fully booked and provisioned to sail as soon as the Center For Disease Control dropped its quarantine hold on passenger ships. Among the entertainers signed for the voyage were Ted Nugent and Kid Rock. Representative Marjorie Taylor Greene and Fox News's Tucker Carlson had also voiced interest in joining forces for a seminar.

We plunked ourselves down in Steve's den looking out at the cardinals and nuthatches zipping around his 20-acre foothill estate. One of his trusty German shepherds was busy licking its crotch while the other dozed. Weed had become president of the school board, a county commissioner and now a sought-after speaker at militia fundraisers. He was holding the fort digitally during the pandemic, with on-line podcasts and other content. Because we had both been vaccinated for Covid-19, neither of us had to wear masks, but we still kept our six-foot distance.

"Thanks for making the trip," Steve began. "I heard you were wrapping up your book and thought I could help. I sure owe you one. I talked to my therapist about it last week and she suggested that at our age it's important to take ownership of our mistakes. My wife totally agrees."

"Did you ever think that our little story would have such great legs?" I asked.

"*Schadenfreude* sells. What did you think of Patty's book?"

"Predictable."

"The movie sucked. It is perennially ranked among the ten worst crime dramas of all time."

"Did you see the review that said 'at 124 minutes it was at least two hours too long'?"

"May I ask how your book is coming?"

"I'm almost done. Can I ask you something?"

"Sure."

"Anything?"

"Shoot."

After a short pause I asked: "Did you know Donald DeFreeze?"

"Yes."

"Did he work undercover for the FBI as part of Hoover's plan to destroy leftist-backed groups?"

"Yes, when both of us were part of the prisoners' rights movement. But he and the bureau had a falling out when he turned down an assignment to set fire to the UC Berkeley ROTC office."

"Did the bureau retaliate?"

"You know about the phone call DeFreeze got asking him to pick up Little and Remiro and give them a ride back to Turlock?"

"Yes, he didn't realize they were fugitives suspected of killing the Oakland school superintendent."

"The FBI told me that call came from an undercover agent. He and DeFreeze connected on the yard at Soledad. This guy was later arrested for holding up a liquor store in San Leandro."

"What about Patty? Has she spoken to you since the kidnapping?"

"No. Not one word. I send her a birthday card every year. She never responds."

"Because you bolted over the fence after you came to following the assault?"

"No."

"The affairs?"

"No."

"Signing a six figure book contract with me when no one knew if she was going to live or die in the hands of the Symbionese Liberation Army?"

"No."

"Because you moved in with her family after you got out of the hospital."

"I doubt it. Randy and I sat up late night after night trying to figure out the best strategy to free Patty."

"That really upset her mother."

"She didn't take well to my bonding with Randy. When Catherine came home from the Claremont after a few weeks away from the media mess in Pacific Heights, Randy and I were wrecked."

"You'd been up drinking with her dad night after night."

"The *New Times* profile you wrote mentioning my marijuana dealing back in college piqued his curiosity. He'd never tried pot. We were both pretty stoned by the time Catherine surprised us. It was pretty bad, Roger. She just unloaded."

"Blaming you?"

"She accused me of being a spy invading their home to

research a sordid insider account of the family crisis. At one point she actually said it was too bad I hadn't started sleeping with Patty when she was 15, because then I could have been prosecuted for statutory rape. She was skeptical of Patty's story that our affair was consensual."

"How did he handle her?"

"When Randy explained that he and I were just strategizing, she started yelling so loud one of the security guards stepped in to make sure everyone was safe.

"Catherine lowered her voice and glared. 'If Patty saw what the two of you looked like right now she'd probably never come home.'

"She picked up a lamp, started brandishing it and then sat down in tears. I suggested that given the late hour we should all head for bed. As I got up to leave she grabbed me by the shoulders, and pushed me right back into my chair.

Steve, there are some things you need to know about Patty and us if by some miracle she survives and makes the mistake of coming home to marry you.

Everyone thinks I'm some kind of ogre because Reagan appointed me to the University Board of Regents for 16 years. I never could stand the man, a pompous, condescending womanizer who always smelled like an old sock. Unfortunately he had veto power over state funding, the principal source of income for all our campuses. The board had to listen to me because they knew I was the one Regent Ronald Reagan trusted, the person who could sweet talk him into deals that kept the money pouring in from Sacramento."

"There's more," Steve went on. "At that Randy suddenly perked up with a wicked grin:

My wife has always had a special gift for finding ways to

help men open their wallets.... and their pants.

"Ignoring her husband, Catherine continued.

Of course, as a political conservative from a famous family, I started getting death threats from across the state. Following one tumultuous Regents meeting someone took a shot at my car. To be on the safe side the State Police decided to assign me a bodyguard who drove me to subsequent board meetings."

As the sleeping German shepherd began to rouse, his partner continued licking himself. I looked at Steve and guessed: "Now you're going to tell me one of these death threats came from the Symbionese Liberation Army."

"Yes, and there was another, bigger problem. The Hearst family had a credible report the day before the kidnapping that someone was doing surveillance on our Berkeley place. The fear was these were the same people who had robbed us several months earlier. A State Police officer came to warn Catherine but she was out shopping with Patty's sister Anne. Randy was at a board meeting in New York.

"The officer left his card with the maid and, after returning his call, Catherine tried reaching Randy's New York office. Alas, he was already on a plane home to California. He arrived in San Francisco at 3 a.m. and promised to put Hearst corporate security in touch with the State Police ASAP."

"What happened?"

"The following morning, just as the head of corporate security walked in to Randy's office, Patty's dad was called to an emergency meeting about a surprise IRS audit. By now Catherine was beginning to panic. She phoned the State Police to let them know she was on her way to Berkeley to drive Patty and me back to the safest place she knew, her own home in Pacific Heights. The officer insisted it would be better for him to drive over to our apartment."

"Good call."

"He thought Patty and I would be more open to listening to what the police would say rather than a worried mom. The officer who had been assigned to fetch us jumped in his car and got caught in a massive tie-up on the Bay Bridge behind a jackknifed tanker truck. By the time he reached our apartment Patty was out visiting with a nun from St. Jean's to pray for our wedding."

"What about you?" I queried Steve.

"I was out."

"With...."

Steve paused for a moment, deciding whether or what to answer, then continued: "I had decided it was probably a good time to call it quits with this wonderful woman, Delilah, who worked at Nabolom Bakery just off College, right round the corner from our apartment."

"That must have been excruciating."

"She was so extraordinary. Every morning I stopped by for a cinnamon twist. They ran out early but fortunately she always saved one for me. During her break we went for a walk up Russell Street. It took longer to explain about the wedding than I expected."

"Did Patty know about Delilah the Nabolom Lady?"

"...and another woman who cornered Patty as she was walking in from the garage with groceries from the Coop and handed over photos of me buck naked in her bedroom. She thought a trial separation would be a chance for us to decide if our love was strong enough to sustain a lifetime together."

"Was Patty pregnant?"

"Not that I know of."

"Were you sleeping together?"

"Yes, after the STD test she insisted on came back negative."

"What happened to the trial separation idea?"

"She asked her mother to delay the wedding but it was too late. It never happened. By that point there was no way to stop the ceremony. The governess who had raised Patty had already put our invitations in the mail. All the deposits had been made with the Claremont, the caterer, the photographers and the florist. The gift registry at Gump's was swamped. People Patty and I barely knew had made travel arrangements from as far away as Singapore."

"How did the Nabolom lady take it?"

"By the time we reached the Claremont tennis courts she was threatening to hurt herself. I had to walk her through the Uplands to calm her down."

"So, neither you or Patty were home when the state police arrived."

"No. They left us a note to call. When Patty returned she started dinner and then called. They put her on hold. When stuff started burning she hung up."

"Did she say anything when you got home?"

"Yes. I called and they put me on hold. Hungry, I hung up and sat down to dinner. We thought it was probably about the recent burglary at our place a few weeks earlier."

"An hour later Patty was in the trunk of that Chevy Nova and you were in Alta Bates Hospital intensive care."

"We were in the wrong place at the right time."

"Did the Hearsts visit the hospital?"

"Randy did. I suspect Catherine was hoping I'd remain in a coma, at least until Patty was home safe. As soon as the FBI got word of the kidnapping the state and local police lost control of the case. The FBI flooded the region with officers who knew nothing about the Bay Area scene. The bureau's prestige was now on the line and the Attorney General back in Washington dictated their strategy. He insisted the Hearsts should stupidly lie that they didn't have $4 mil and refuse to negotiate. He easily persuaded Reagan to back him up."

"Catherine must have been outraged."

"After I moved in with them she hated the way Randy and

I hung out drinking late into the night. One night, just before she moved out to the Claremont she came home and found both of us stoned. She blamed the disastrous ransom failure on Randy."

It's not easy spending your whole life as window dressing. What I say only matters if Randy happens to agree with me, if my view is convenient for him. I am seen as an ornament, a plaything, a selfish dimwit, and a nobody who happens to be married, at least for now, to the son of a megalomaniac. Now you understand why Patty was so eager to escape this house?

"Did Randy counter?"
"They started yelling."

After all I've given you, and our girls. None of you ever have to work.

At least prostitutes get paid for what they do. I have to give it up for free and then listen to your snoring because you're too vain to see a doctor. Maybe I need a rate card.

"Then she pointed a finger at me."

Randy, you listen to this guy, supposedly our soon to be son-in-law, because he has the key that opens any door: a penis. If you had listened to me, the woman who has put up with you for 35 years, none of this would have happened. The ransom would have been paid right away, just the way you pay your call girls, and Patty would be free. If you keep letting these junior G men from the FBI and all the nutty hostage consultants borrow your watch to tell you what time it is, you're not only going to lose Patty, you're going to lose me.

After taking a break to answer a call from one of his America First foundation board members Steve continued: "That was my last late night hangout with Randy. The following week Catherine consulted a divorce attorney and moved out."

"Why didn't she consider remarrying?"

"Their daughter Anne asked her about that. Catherine explained that after all the bad years with Randy she was no longer interested in doing daycare for another man.

"Randy remarried and moved to New York. Although he paid for Patty's very expensive lawyers, she never forgave him for the way he treated Catherine. Her mother collapsed and died in May 1993, right after swimming with dolphins in La Paz."

"Randy? "

"He died a year later in the arms of a 28-year-old geologist. He was planning another divorce to marry this young woman."

"Why are you telling me all this now?"

"They are both gone and I hope this will help you explain why Patty was not in a big hurry to return home."

"And, if they had ransomed her, what then?"

"That's one reason I called. When I was rewriting your book week after week, I thought there was a chance she'd eventually find a way to forgive me."

After committing publishing *interruptus* on our original manuscript, Steve was revealing critical details he withheld from our book and the one he eventually published after firing me.

"Steve, we were writing a good book. Why did you decide to pull out? I foolishly thought we were friends."

"Randy."

"You were showing Patty's father our manuscript."

For once Steve was silent.

"What! Why?", I pressed.

"I was trying to prevent an injunction blocking publication. Randy was worried about Catherine claiming I had leaked important details he shared with me about Patty. His lawyers warned this could become part of a disastrous divorce case that would cost him a ton. I did everything I could to reassure him. He was cool, but the lawyers freaked. They finally decided I had to dump you. I fought them but they insisted on retaining control of every word I published. It was awful. I hated hurting you and Margot."

"Why didn't you level with me instead of making me think you were a completely narcissistic, conniving asshole."

"He warned me that if I said a single word about anything of this to anyone, especially you, the whole marriage was off."

"Did he find the new publisher for your rewrite of our book?"

"Yes and that was how I was able to pay you off and repay the advance to Ballantine."

"You had no choice."

"The new publisher, a personal friend of Randy's who had been best man at his wedding, was very generous."

"Randy believed you were still destined to become his son-in-law."

"He believed our marriage would be a great success. I know it's hard to believe, but he saw me as a man who could make Patty actually realize her potential as a future leader of the Hearst Corporation. He thought Patty was a genius. He also loved the skunk I brought home. He liked my sense of humor."

"Could you have stopped being who you were if Patty had been ransomed?"

"Who knows? Then... I'm not sure. Possibly...with therapy."

"And medication."

"Not too sure about that either. The antipsychotics they were using then nearly wrecked me. I've got a great psychiatrist now at Langley Porter, UC San Francisco. The stuff I'm on now is wonderful. I'm a much better person. "

"What about that Wyntoon painting you were having appraised by Massey? How much did you sell it for?"

"Are we off the record?"

"Of course."

"As long as its between us I'll tell you the whole story."

Steve stepped over the sleeping dog, walked me downstairs and punched in the code on his safe in a cabinet below his fish tank. He began tearing up as he gently removed a linen bag and held the masterwork up as if it were a Torah.

"How much do you know about this work?"

"The appraisal was a little over $4 million."

"It's worth much more today. Do you know the story behind it?"

"Only that after Patty's grandfather died it wound up in a Wyntoon vault."

"Let me help you out. This particular painting was the work of a Tintoretto apprentice. Much of his work was done for Italian royalty. Demand was so heavy that he had to delegate. Of course no one was going to pay for work signed by an apprentice they had never heard of. He would add his touch and signature to the painting created by his team."

"I saw a Venice exhibition of his work. Didn't he hire women?"

"Yes and one of them, Elena Stromboli, had the extraordinary ability to match his work stroke for stroke. She worked seven days a week until one day the master suggested she take a week off. At a recital she fell in love with a violinist, Roberto Angelini. A wedding date was set and a crowd of 200 gathered at the cathedral. As the violins began to serenade the audience, Elena and her father waited by the church door for Roberto who never arrived. Heartbroken, she went home and began working on this painting."

Steve slipped the painting out of its embroidered bag to reveal a young man looking out a window at a church across the street. Waiting at the front door were a bride and her father.

"The story behind the painting, the one they still tell in this little village near Venice, is that every day Roberto would go to the window at the hour of his wedding and weep."

"What happened to Elena?"

"Furious that Tintoretto took credit for her work, she left the studio and began painting under her own name. Her paintings sold for a song. The impressive body of work she left behind was 'discovered' by collectors at the turn of the 20th century. When an art historian realized that she had left her initials on the back of each of her "Tintorettos," museums and the collectors discovered the real painter's identity.

"By the time Patty's grandfather bought the painting in 1929, some of her solo work created after she left Tintoretto's studio was beginning to appear in museums. Because she had toured Italy with a much beloved high school art teacher, Patty knew Stromboli's work and the story of her life. When she discovered this Stromboli 'Tintoretto' painting at Wyntoon, Patty remembered learning that Elena was featured in a number of exhibitions highlighting women painters of the Italian Renaissance."

"Great serendipity."

"She gave it to Massey who confirmed that this "Tintoretto" was actually Elena's work."

"Does the painting have a name?"

"Stromboli called it 'My Wedding Day.'"

"You knew it was worth $4 million before Patty was taken."

"Correct, and my idea was to use it to ransom Patty after family negotiations with the SLA fell through."

"You were too late."

"The FBI never stopped following me. Even if I found a way to get the painting to Patty's captors, it was too dangerous for them to sell it. They would have been arrested on the spot"

"Does Patty know all this?"

"I wrote offering to return it to her but she never replied."

"You're not going to sell it."

"It's my last link to our life together."

"The rugs, the other paintings at your apartment."

"I returned them to the family. Looking at them was too

painful. Now I want you to promise you won't tell anyone about this, not even your wife."

"Scout's honor."

As we walked back upstairs I asked Steve if he reconnected with any of the other women he'd been seeing in the months before the kidnapping.

Steve stood up and pointed out the window at a woman in his driveway slipping out of a red Tesla dual motor.

"I want you to meet Delilah," he said as she grabbed a bag of groceries from the trunk. "My wife's a social worker with Nevada County Community Mental Health and the mother of our four girls, I should say ladies. They now all have babes of their own."

"The Nabolom cinnamon twist lady?"

Steve nodded: "Thanks for coming, Roger. It's been great reconnecting after all these years. Good luck with your book. I think you may have the bestseller you deserve."

"I appreciate your honesty. It's been great reconnecting."

"If you catch up with Patty, do me a favor. Please tell her I can overnight the painting. All I need is her address."

Both of Steve's dogs chased me down the driveway as I headed back toward Nevada City. Rain pelted my car as I replayed our interview. Assuming he was telling the truth, Steve's insights were potentially a great boost for my book.

While I was grateful for Steve's *mea culpa*, I knew that none of what he told me mattered if I couldn't reach Patty Hearst. Although I wanted to believe Steve, I realized that his undercover work and his track record with me meant I needed to double check everything he told me. It was hard to believe that he killed off our book because he was being blackmailed by his fiancée's dad. By the time Randy supposedly threatened him, Patty's parents had lost control of her future. The chances of a reconciliation appeared to be zero.

More to the point, there was a fairly blatent subtext to Steve's chapter notes. Was he really trying to help me write a good book or just making sure that I didn't do damage to what was left of his reputation? Our new "friendship" was his creation and I suspected that key details were missing. After all this time I still didn't have a good sense of an ending.

The 5000

April 4, 2021, Oakland

Oakland

On a rainy spring morning I rode BART to the Lake Merritt station, walked past Children's Fairyland, where my kids had loved the puppet shows, and headed past Grand Lake to a doorway next to Fit-As-A-Fiddle gym. After punching in the door code I climbed the stairs to the second story landing. On the wall there was a blowup of a 1923 photo featuring a rabbi's son, Harry Houdini, escaping from a strait jacket while dangling from the *Tribune* Tower's 9th floor.

The office looked like the aftermath of a nuclear winter. As I walked past a row of empty cubicles, it was hard to believe this was all that remained of my beloved employer, the *Oakland Tribune*. Trading a paring knife for an ax, a series of MBA turn-around specialists from the UC Berkeley Haas business school had downsized the paper forcing most of my former colleagues to flee to public relations jobs promoting wet wipes, vaporware, marijuana home delivery and organic pet food.

Desks were piled high with a year's worth of reportorial fall-out. Coffee cups, plastic cutlery, last year's calendars, reporter's notebooks and family photos were layered in dust. Waste baskets reeked of French fries, and stale fortune cookies. A "Jerry Brown For President" poster hung on one of the cubicle walls.

This long rectangular floor was all that remained of the once proud *Oakland Tribune* owned by the "Senator from Formosa," Chiang Kai-Shek's best friend in our nation's capitol, William F. Knowland. Under the Gannett leadership of our nation's first African American big city daily publisher, Robert C. Maynard, the *Tribune* won the Pulitzer Prize for photography of the 1989 Loma Prieta earthquake. Among the casualties of that disaster was his editor's Oldsmobile convertible, buried under a ton of bricks.

During my time as the paper's last full-time travel editor in the late '80s, the staff labored together in the 21-story Tribune Tower, modeled after Venice's Basilica San Marcos. In 1995 the tower known for its neon-lit clock, sold for less than the price of a split level home in the Oakland hills—a paltry $300,000 including an adjacent five story building. Now merely the Oakland bureau of the *East Bay Times*, the paper that once had a staff of over 500, was down to just 20 reporters covering a city of 440,000. All that remained of my travel reporting from around the world were files of my clippings stored in the basement of the Oakland Library.

In the midst of the Covid-19 pandemic nineteen *Tribune* reporters had abandoned their offices to work at home. They struggled to work amidst the din of Zoom classes for their children and dogs needing to pee during phone interviews with the mayor, the police chief or the President of Clorox. In one awkward moment a reporter was interviewing Nancy Pelosi on Zoom as his wife strolled behind in a nightgown with her hair in curlers.

There was only one light on in the back of the office, the last man standing in the *Tribune* office, Harry Harris. He was also the *Tribune*'s institutional memory, the man who had actually been on the elevator when publisher Knowland famously turned to his Jewish city editor on a holiday eve and said: "Happy Thanksgiving or whatever you guys celebrate."

Harris had been there in 1983 when editor Maynard bought

the *Tribune* from Gannett in a $17 million deal that included just $800 of his own money and thus became the publisher as well. I joined the paper as a travel writer a year later. It was the greatest job I ever had. Both of us mourned in 1990 when 450 of our colleagues were fired on a single day by new owner Dean Singleton. And now, after 55 years of service to the *Tribune*, Harry reported solo like a distant war correspondent in Kabul, trying to meet multiple deadlines for the next day's front page. Some weeks he went to two, even three retirement parties at Bay Area papers. He kept working because of his uncertainty over the liquidity of the Newspaper Guild pension fund.

During his tenure as a police reporter for the *Tribune* and its successor, the *East Bay Times*, he had outlasted eight publishers, nine editors-in-chief, 11 managing editors, and 14 city editors. One hundred and ten county commissioners, eight mayors, 12 police chiefs, eight governors and 11 presidents had served during his newspaper career. The current owner, a 29-year-old hedge fund billionaire in New York, was buying up papers in fire sales coast to coast, including 13 owned by the Hearst family.

I had last seen Harry at his retirement party. Now he greeted me with the camaraderie of a fellow Vietnam vet who survived Ho Chi Minh's Tet Offensive. His workspace, piled high with his week's stories, was all that remained of the *Tribune* newsroom, where I had landed the greatest job in journalism, a passport to write about the world via planes, trains, cruise ships, automobiles and rickshaws. With the press room down, the paper was now printed in Fresno. I had covered the collapse of Soviet Communism, explored the Great Wall and the ruins of Pompeii and Herculaneum. It was my job to help readers plan the perfect Caribbean cruise, safely watch the erupting Kilauea volcano add real estate to the Big Island of Hawaii, figure out the best snorkeling sites in Bali and nail the best borscht in St. Petersburg.

Like an infantryman in a foxhole, Harry was prepared for anything fired his way from a sports editor trying to figure out how to score a couple of Oakland A's box seats for an old college roommate to an intern stranded because someone had stolen the battery from her company car. Of late he had been working overtime on stories about Joe Biden's mixed race vice-president, Oakland native Kamala Harris, born in the same Kaiser hospital on Broadway where my kids entered this world.

As I sat down next to his desk, Harry asked if I had any trouble finding the place.

"Not at all."

"I assume that means you have escaped Covid."

He responded to my quizzical look with his trademark grin.

"Anyone who has held on to their sense of smell has no trouble finding this place."

"You must be exhausted."

"Yesterday I hit a personal milestone covering my 5,000th Oakland murder."

"Does it get harder?"

"It doesn't get any easier. It's painful to write stories about the killing of a kid. The toughest part is talking to the families, the teachers, the friends. I cry a lot."

"You are a legend in crime reporting.

"I really miss the Knowland days, the Maynard days. They were so passionate about Oakland."

"I thought you hung it up at the San Simeon retirement party."

"I un-retired."

"How did that happen?"

"You remember my big present."

"Right, the family trip to Kauai."

"After we got back they all took a vote and decided I should return to work."

"But I thought the whole idea was to have more time with your family."

"No one asked if they wanted to have more time with me.

Turned out they had just posted a new opening. The guy they hired to replace me quit after a couple of weeks. He didn't realize that crime reporting meant you actually had to show up at East Oakland crime scenes in the middle of the night and interview the coroner. Say, how's that big book coming?"

"Great."

"Who is this publisher?"

"He's a polymath in Chicago, actor, director, graphic designer, composer, voice talent. We met in an acting class at Second City and he ended up being the production director on my first movie, *Waterwalk*."

"Did you tell him what happened to your first editor, the one that was going to bring the book out for the 25th anniversary of the kidnapping?"

"Uh?"

"How about the second editor and his publisher who had the book set for the 40th anniversary with a big party at the Claremont with all your old *Oakland Tribune* buddies on hand for a reunion? What a disappointment. I even rented a tux."

"Harry, let's not go there. None of those three untimely deaths had anything to do with..."

"...your prevaricating perfectionism?"

"Not every definitive story can be written in a single day."

"I'm really happy for you Roger. Congratulations, you've finally found a publisher who is going to live to see your book published. You know, young people are fascinated with the case. To me it's a little strange. People disappear around here all the time and editors aren't much interested."

"Patty was white."

"She was also very smart, sexy, and destined to be very rich. That's an unbeatable story. I am so glad she made it, unlike that poor Lindbergh baby. So sad."

"It was weird that the Hearsts tried to get the entire media to black out the story that first day, a big mistake. Can you believe the lead story page one that day in the *Examiner* was about a bunch of seals invading the boat docks at Pier 39? Why did you break the embargo and put the story out ahead of everyone else?"

"We're not in the business of extending professional courtesy to competitors censoring breaking news."

"And you won a Pulitzer for your coverage, if I remember correctly!"

"I did. You're right. The Hearsts were outraged. They were convinced I knew much more than I was reporting, that I could help them find and free Patty. Their reporters were constantly begging me for tips. The FBI tried bugging my phone. Fortunately a private eye, Hal Lipset, put a stop to that."

"Wasn't some producer talking to you about the film rights?"

"Turned out he was working for the Hearsts, hinting that he would pay a fortune if I would just leak where the Symbionese Liberation Army had stashed Patty."

"Harry, may I ask you something?"

"Anything."

"Why do you do this? Why are you here?"

"You mean why am I never going to quit?"

"Isn't there something else you'd rather be doing?"

"Roger, I'm not all that big on needlepoint and quilting. Casino drinks are all watered down. I never cared much for cross-country skiing. "

"I mean 5,000 murders, isn't that..."

Just then Harry glanced down at his computer screen.

"Actually as of three minutes ago it's 5,001."

"I should go."

"I'm on deadline, but before you leave there is something I want you to have."

Reaching behind his desk Harry pulled out an *Oakland Tribune* umbrella printed with breaking stories. Glancing out the window at sheets of rain coming in from the Bay he said: "I think you're going to need this. It just started raining and you never know when a pigeon is going to call your name."

Out on the sidewalk I stood under an awning and slowly raised the umbrella. Near the top was a three-column headline that read:

Tech Billionaire Found Shot In Tesla at Jack London Square

Harry Harris, Crime Beat

the end

Epilogue

June 2022

Garden, Michigan

After I finished Patty's story, my brave Chicago publisher James Sparling scheduled a small first run at his Carbondale, Illinois printer. We agreed on the title and, after several false starts, the cover designer came up with a winner.

"Don't worry, the first Harry Potter book started out with a run of just 500 copies," Sparling told me on a quick visit to my home in lakeshore Muskegon, Michigan. We were sitting at a picnic table in front of Tootsie's breakfast diner, the only one in my state with a free pinball machine in the vestibule.

"Freud's *Interpretations of Dreams* sold a little over 300 copies in its first six years. Not much happened until he went on tour in Buffalo, etc. It may take a little time but I know this book is the final word on Patty. Years from now people will consider it the definitive account. It's one of those journeys you can't stop thinking about it. My wife was positively smitten. She read it in one sitting on a plane to San Diego. It's the best thing you've ever written."

As we paid for our lemonades, James complemented Tootsie's waitress on their extensive alt-meat burger menu and then added to me, by way of an afterthought:

"Oh I'm thinking of sending Patty, the galleys as soon as they are finished."

As I started choking the waitress rushed over and grabbed me in the Heimlich Maneuver. Sparling quickly waved her away.

"He's fine."

"Let me get you some more water," she said, rushing back into the kitchen.

After catching my breath I tried reasoning with my publisher.

"Why would you want to do that? You're dealing with a $30 billion corporation here."

"I think there's an outside chance she'd give us a blurb"

"You mean, 'What a pile of shit—Patty Hearst.'?"

"Well, now, that would be perfect."

"Are you sure that's a good idea."

"Probably not."

"She'll probably toss it into recycling or use it for kindling."

"...which, since I'm going to send a pdf, would either get her a sticker on her trash can: 'unexpected item in the recycling' or blow up the fireplace."

"Smart ass."

A book is forever and finishing Patty's story decades later has been a highlight of my life. In many ways the legal tussle in Oakland so many years ago prevented me from publishing a book that would have raised more questions than it answered.

A great American story of empire and revolution would have hit the third rail of book publishing. That's often the problem with "tell all" books. They only tell you what a self-serving author wants you to hear.

Steve's personal goal, rekindling his love story with Patty, conflicted with our New York publisher's determination to create a compelling account of her first 19 years that presented multiple points of view. The further I delved into Steve's life the more I realized that their three years together was a prelude to a more important story. There was little in her pre-kidnapping world that explained the woman she had become. While she began moving out of her family home at 16, Patty remained estranged from the world of work. Except for a short time working at Capwell's Department Store she had never received a paycheck. Fighting alongside the Symbionese Liberation Army was her first real job.

The only way a Steve Weed book could realize its potential was to tell readers what they didn't already know. A successful narrative depended on delving into Patty's perplexing family and failure of the desultory ransom attempt. We also needed to explain why she decided to join the SLA and become a kidnapper. At the same time it was critical to pinpoint what persuaded her to spurn Steve publicly. Simply portraying her as a brainwashing victim sidestepped the rich vein of family history that made the Hearsts irresistible to audiences everywhere.

The family's back-story was nicely covered in *Citizen Kane*. The ultimate feel-good movie for the *schadenfreude* crowd, *Kane* mocked capitalism, politics, yellow journalism, imperialism and wannabe art collectors. It also established a decadent intellectual legacy for Patty's grandfather, the man who lived in sin with the unfairly ridiculed Marion Davies for more than three decades while residing in the cathedral of American capitalism. The woman the sexist Orson Welles parodied, represented by the dimwit Susan Alexander character in his movie, was a talented actress, as was Dorothy Comingore who played her on screen.

I was being paid well to make Steve a credible witness to an unexpected twist in this unique and unprecedented American saga. It was critical to prove that he had absolutely nothing to hide from a public inundated with conspiracy theories about his radical past. As Patty ripped him and her own family apart in her devastating *communiques*, his voice was submerged by the kind of one-sided black or white rhetoric which has increasingly become our favorite method of discourse. He had become a target for the media and it was my job to help him defend his role in the attempt to rescue the same woman trying to destroy his credibility.

I had left daily journalism behind on the theory that the only way to get to the truth was to find the time to talk to everyone. Now that I'd achieved my goal I was convinced that Mark Twain got it right when he said, "A lie is halfway around the world before the truth has got its boots on."

How ironic that a successful media empire was forced to publish front page lies in an attempt to save one of its heirs. In today's world of unverified, often libelous, at times homicidal social media it is harder to combat the kind of conspiracy theories at the heart and soul of radical militias like the Symbionese Liberation Army. Following the Hearst model, successful media empires, highlighted in shows like *Succession*, tell their audiences what they want to hear. Working *a-la-carte* they selectively target Mexicans, Asians, Jews, the elderly, socialists, women or anyone else that makes a convenient scapegoat. This was the genesis of the SLA, a gang committed to the belief that school superintendents deserve to die because they installed security metal detectors at the front door.

In her stream of consciousness communiques Patty made it clear that her plight was entirely someone else's fault. She did a good job of angrily shifting that blame to her own family and her fiancé. With her help, the Symbionese Liberation Army upstaged the Hearst family unable to find a path to rescue their loved one.

Over many years I wondered what would have happened to Steve and Patty if they had failed to answer the door for that nice woman feigning car trouble. Would they have finished their dinner and lived a good life with Steve becoming a professor at San Francisco State and Patty employed as curator at the Asian Art Museum? After many years I found it hard to envisage Patty and Steve living happily ever after.

A month after submitting this book to my Chicago publisher, I took a day off to catch up on errands. I was over at Ginman's

Tires waiting for a new set of radials for my Ford Fusion hybrid, when my phone flashed a call from a blocked number. Next came a text.

"Roger please pick up, these are not spam calls."

When the phone rang again I took the call.

"Roger please don't hang up. My boss..."

"Who are you?"

Five hours later I was finishing up a memorable pasty at a picnic table outside Lehto's on Route 2, just west of the Mackinac Bridge. A light rain began falling as a white minivan with a Yooper bumper sticker pulled up. The mysterious woman who'd called opened the passenger door and handed me a can of Vernors ginger ale.

"Va Va Voom."

"Easy password to remember, huh," said my contact after introducing herself as Amy DeJong. "Sorry to be so vague. So glad you could make it, thanks for trusting me."

With her chartreuse print dress, auburn hair pulled back into a ponytail and Ray-Bans, she could have easily passed for a college campus tour guide. I glanced down at Amy's sandals and congratulated her on a perfect set of rainbow colored toenails.

"That must have been a lot of work."

"My pedicurist at 'Toe-to-Toe' in Manistique is an artist who moved here from Greenwich Village after another $1,000 a month rent increase. She's the best."

As she drove along Lake Michigan's north shore, I sipped my Vernors, settled back and closed my eyes for a short break after the long drive to the Upper Peninsula. With its long sugar sand beaches and postcard perfect lighthouses, this roadway showcased everything I loved about living in a state surrounded by 3,600 miles of Great Lake frontage. Tourists like to call it a land time almost forgot, but in my eyes it remains the most memorable place on earth. Anyone who doesn't get the U.P. should turn back at the Mackinac Bridge tollbooth.

When I woke up from a nap, we were turning south onto the Garden Peninsula, a finger stretching down lake towards Wisconsin's Washington Island. Amy drove on through the hamlet of Garden, under a state of siege from recently installed wind turbines. Minutes later, she pulled up to a timbered lake house and parked. Gleefully squeezing my hand, as if she had just reeled in a Coho salmon, my new friend said:

"I want you to know I just finished your Michael Moore biography and watched your movie about the Air France plane that got lost mid-Atlantic. What fun. I've heard a lot about you. It's amazing that your company published that terrific Harry Potter Lexicon after the big legal battle with J.K. Rowling. It's so cool that you got to meet her in Manhattan federal court. The New York Times coverage was amazing. My niece loves that book."

"Can you tell me what this is all about?"

As Amy walked me toward the house, a door swung open and a woman, a decade younger than myself, stepped out and smiled. Even with her sunglasses on, I would have recognized her from a Cessna Caravan flying over the Upper Peninsula.

"Roger," said Amy, "I'd like to introduce you to my boss."

"Thanks for coming," said Patty Hearst with a hint of embarrassment. "I hope I was worth the wait."

The years had been kind to her, and judging from the pictures on the refrigerator she was now not only a proud mother but also a grandmother.

"After a tragic plane crash in Buffalo took my husband," she said, "I bought this place. He grew up here. The grandchildren love coming here from their Boston homes during the summer. The sailing is amazing. It's like Cape Cod without all the people. I am so glad you could make it."

Certain I was hungry, Amy served us macaroni and cheese with a kale salad, steamed broccoli and mint brownies. The women went for a good Bordeaux; I stuck with root beer. After finishing our meal we walked out into the garden and Patty told me she had just finished my book.

"Your publisher sent a pdf of it. He wants me to write a cover blurb."

"...and you got me all the way out here to tell me to my face that you're not?"

"Exactly, and now that we're done, Amy can drive you home."

We both laughed.

"I hope you won't be angry, but I understand your publisher has just put the book on hold."

"That's impossible. It's being printed right now."

"Let me explain."

"Hold on, Patty. David Pesonen, the lawyer who handled my case with Steve, died in Oregon four years ago. Now I have to go up against the entire Hearst Corporation in pro per unless I'm willing to be bought off."

"*Au contraire*. I just told your publisher there were some important details you left out."

"Such as?"

"We need to start going over your book. Can you stay for a few days? I've got a little cottage down by the water. Sound good?"

"You're not trying to kill my book."

Patty smiled, sat back and shook her head no.

"I'm a first amendment kind of girl."

"You want me to rewrite a kinder, gentler book?"

"Of course not. With luck, you might be able to sell a couple of thousand copies of what you've done. Maybe a few libraries will let you do a lecture in Sacramento or Inglewood. Is that what you want after all these years searching for the truth about me?"

"Don't forget the online edition and the audiobook. I've started producing movies. One of them, a mental health drama, has won seven festival best feature awards."

"You've written some nice books. Maybe I can help you make sure this one realizes its potential. Or would you rather see another one of your titles wind up on the remainder table?"

"You want to be my book doctor?"

"It's a good book and I love the title. Cover is not bad. It makes me look half decent. I want to talk to you about your ending."

"You want to fuck up my ending."

"I think I can help."

Over the next few hours Patty proceeded to dial back the years to my collaboration with Steve. Thanks to one of Steve's lawyers she had read a copy of the squelched book I originally wrote with him.

"It was a big help when I was putting together my own book. The draft of the one you tried to write with Steve triggered a lot of memories. Sorry I couldn't footnote it and give you credit for the work you did."

"There was no way I could copyright it," I said.

"That's what my lawyers told me."

"You took content from the book Steve killed," I persisted.

"It was much better than the one he wrote."

"So your dad, winner of the 'Freedom of The Press' award from the American Society of Newspaper Editors, and Steve's lawyers, joined forces to stop a good book and gave birth to two awful ones."

"Hold on. My parents were alive when I wrote my book. They were paying all my legal bills. I had to do the one they wanted," Patty added with a raised voice.

"Your mother wasn't doing well?"

"My mother had spent time at a psychiatric retreat. The drugs they were using at the time were primitive by today's standards. The book was seen as a good way to create a narrative she could live with, to convince her that none of what went wrong was her fault."

"You were trying to create a new reality for her by making things up."

"My dad's company lawyers had to vet every word after I got out of the joint. They wanted me to confirm everything I said in court on the San Francisco bank robbery case. My account of the Sacramento bank robbery helped get the Harrises arrested and convicted a second time decades later."

"After you were convicted on armed robbery, kidnapping, and assault charges you suddenly became a reliable narrator any book publisher could trust?"

"My sentence was commuted by another man from Michigan, President Gerald Ford. It didn't hurt that the publisher was owned by one of my dad's oldest friends."

"Do you think Steve believed you in those communiques from the safe house?"

"How could he? As a kid Steve was programmed to think life would always go his way. He was gifted, athletic, gorgeous - the kind of guy women battled over. He always believed people were lucky to know him."

"Is it true that you threw yourself at him?"

"Is that what he told you?"

"Everything was verbatim. I didn't change a word."

"And that's exactly why he fired you!" Patty jabbed at me.

"Huh?"

"Don't get me wrong, a lot of what he said in the book you wrote for him...

"The one he killed...," I tried to say.

"Right, a lot of that actually happened. Unfortunately he only remembered what he chose to remember. Everything else he conveniently forgot."

"A revisionist."

"Aren't we all retelling our stories to ourselves and others?" Patty observed. "We have to make sense of our actions and decisions. Our life was always about what Steve wanted and I went along. That was my marital job description."

Over the next several days Patty and I worked on the ending she had in mind at her tiled kitchen table.

"A great deal of what you've written is true. Unfortunately some of the people you really needed to talk to were unavailable for comment."

"Like Willie Wolfe."

"He's a key reason I called your publisher. His story is critical to your book. Without his perspective it would be impossible to explain why I decided to run with the SLA."

As we walked along the lakeshore, exploring some of the woodland trails below Fayette State Park's limestone cliffs, Patty filled in details of their short happy life together.

"Willie was a grad student at UC Santa Cruz, the last of DeFreeze's recruits to join the Symbionese Liberation Army."

"Did you know him before the kidnapping?"

"Only briefly. In December of 1973, after Steve had gone off on an east coast lecture tour to promote his latest book trashing American media empires, I drove down to Carmel and discovered the town was sold out. At the last minute I found a third story room in a guesthouse attic. Walking down to the beach, I heard a guitarist singing Beatles' covers on the porch of a small café."

"Who happened to be Willie Wolfe."

"He had come to town to care for a dear uncle recovering from a fall. We talked after he finished his set and then began a conversation that stretched out for several days."

"Did he know who you were?"

"I was pretty vague, as was he. It was one of those moments when we were both trying to make big decisions."

"You told him about Steve."

"He was very supportive of the marriage."

"Did that surprise you?"

"A little, especially after we made love several times on a featherbed in my tiny attic room."

"What was that like?"

"It made me realize what love could actually be."

"A step up from Steve."

"Don't quote me Roger...."

"I won't."

"Getting dressed after our first night together I knew I had to find a way out of my marriage with Steve. I finally understood why I was feeling suicidal about the wedding."

"Were you honest with Steve?"

"I tried. As always he tried to generalize by stupidly saying that everyone has doubts about matrimony."

"Comparing your doubts to others, rather than..."

"He wasn't listening. You know that song 'Jolene'?"

"Sure. Dolly Parton was worrying about another woman stealing away her husband."

"Not quite. In an interview she revealed that her inspiration for the song was another man she dearly loved."

"That must have been tough for her husband."

"In my case Willie was that other man."

"And at that point you were still single."

"Roger, I was stuck marrying someone I didn't want to marry. Sadly, Willie was on the edge of dropping out of college, divorcing his wife and joining a radical political group."

"Divorce?"

"He was pretty sure that he might not make it if he ran with these radicals. He didn't want his wife to worry about him. He felt she would be better off finding someone with a lower likelihood of getting killed. He told me those who do nothing are effectively casting their ballot for tyranny.

"One of my Berkeley political science professors had the same idea. He argued that there is no such thing as objectivity, that we all approach challenges based on what our brain already knows. Only when we are open to new ideas can we acquire the insight necessary to finally create a just and equitable world."

"The lovemaking must have been extraordinary."

"No one ever touched me the way Willie did. I didn't want to leave Carmel and suggested staying a few more days. He told me that was impossible."

"Of course the FBI already had him under surveillance," I said.

"Which ultimately turned out to be one of the reasons the Attorney General did not want my parents to meet the SLA's ransom demands. They suspected that it might have been an *arranged* kidnapping with my participation. I've spent a lot of time with the FBI after I was arrested and discovered that their real purpose is intimidation. They'll park the wrong way on your street to let all the neighbors know you're being watched. Willie was convinced they already had begun a file on me after our first night together."

"Was he the one who targeted you?"

"When the story of my engagement to Steve broke in the *Examiner*, he brought the paper to the SLA and made a perfect case for kidnapping me; not a violent kidnap, more of a consensual abduction. The guys wanted to go ahead, but all the women threatened to quit."

"He lost."

"Badly and he was certain that Emily Harris's plan to steal that incredible painting from our place would never work."

"There's a great black market for art."

"Willie argued that was far riskier than a kidnapping. Fencing a painting is dealing with a work of art and all that entailed and none of us in the SLA knew the first thing about the art market. They wanted media impact to promote their revolution. They believed that my enlistment would be a call to arms. They saw me as a modern day Joan of Arc who knew how to hit a target."

"Of course at that time there were far fewer sources of information than there are today."

"In every community a few newspapers, radio and television stations controlled the flow of information. Our family was a force in every market that mattered."

"And of course on the magazine racks Hearst was a powerhouse on style, sex, fashion, cooking, home design, parenting, you name it. From barbecuing to toilet training, your editors had all the answers."

"We set the table for the American agenda. Taking over a major city daily like the Examiner plus the family TV and radio station meant the SLA had a platform for their crazy ideas."

"Including the idea that you were a willing convert."

"That's where it gets tricky. Obviously I can't say that my own book and the movie it inspired were deliberately dishonest."

"I can."

"That's up to you."

"You're agnostic on all this?" I said to Patty.

"The answer to the question you've been asking all those years is I don't know who that young woman was, the one who helped rob the Hibernia Bank, and kidnapped that young guy in Inglewood. I've never met her. I stare into the mirror in the morning and I can't make out any trace of that woman, that outlaw."

"You could have been brainwashed."

"A lot of experts who seem to know a lot more about Patty Hearst than I do have agreed that I was a victim of the Stockholm Syndrome."

"That was pretty much the conclusion of the psychologist working for your defense in the bank robbery case."

"She could be right," Patty replied.

"Now you're going to tell me the trial narrative about being held in the closet for all those weeks was nonsense."

"Yes and no. For me and Willie it was the only place we could get away from the rest of the gang. We needed some privacy."

"You enlisted quickly."

"At that time I had no alternative; constantly fighting them to let me write my own communiques was exhausting. I threatened to go on a hunger strike. After many drafts I finally convinced them I knew exactly how to manipulate my father's company. They were so badly divided that I was eventually forced into the role of mediator, doing my best to make sure we didn't all get killed."

"You got along with all of them?"

"Even when they were fighting, everyone trusted me. That's more than I can say for Steve or my family. They believed I was trying to save their lives and launch a long overdue American revolution. None of them would have died if they had just listened to me. I insisted that fleeing to Los Angeles would be a disaster but they believed in their comrades' guarantee of safe passage. California hallucinating for sure.

"After Willie died in the shootout I had to run with the Harrises and, later on, Wendy Yoshimura. I didn't even have time to process his death properly. I kind of shut it out. It was impossible to plan anything. We did OK until the Harrises made the terrible mistake of returning to San Francisco after the Sacramento bank robbery."

On the last day of my surprise upper peninsula visit, we walked through the old company town of Fayette. The whitewashed quarry buildings faced a harbor framed by a limestone coastline. Windsurfers soared above the harbor as we approached a small marina where sailboats cruising the lakeshore were berthed for the day. This spot, one of the most beautiful waterfronts in the world, was a place I adored and visited often with my family. I had even shot part of my first film, *Waterwalk*, here. Patty and her family loved the place as much as I did.

"I think about the first Americans," she said, "the people who hunted these lands, fished these lakes and streams, helped the early explorers find their way. They were so resilient, creative and inspiring. They lived as equals. Women were treated with respect and dignity."

"Do you wish you'd had a chance to meet The Chief?"

"When I was 12 my parents took me to southern California to see grandfather's San Simeon. It was after hours and the public tours were over. They walked me into his bedroom suite and showed me the Della Robbia hanging above his bed.

"'Sometimes,' my dad told me, 'your grandfather would spend the whole day here in bed talking to his publishers across the country. He'd rise at dawn to begin calling editors on the east coast and work his way across the time zones. After finishing up talking with his San Francisco office, he'd phone Hollywood producers to talk over new story ideas. That was the Chief, always searching for a fresh drama that would excite audiences.' "

"Even if it wasn't true?" I probed.

"The dividing line between his newspapers and the fictional film projects he backed was paper thin."

"Give the public what you think they want and let them try and sort out the facts from the fairly tales later," I added helpfully.

"In many ways a newspaper resembles a novel or a movie. The test of any story is the creator's ability to make it believable."

"Did he ever stop working?"

"Sure. According to my dad just before dinner he would take his private elevator down to the pool, strip off his clothes and dive in naked."

"When I asked why, he said, 'Darling, sometimes emperors are uncomfortable wearing clothes.' "

As swans surfed the Lake Michigan whitecaps Patty gave me a thankful hug and said:

"Now that you know who we are do you think anyone will believe you?"

"I doubt it. Yet it all makes sense. People won't like that but I finally have an ending."

"Roger, I'm glad you never gave up on me. You're a very

brave man. Thank you for coming here, thank you for trusting me. It's been wonderful having a chance to meet you."

Back at Patty's house a few minutes later, her buddy Amy handed me a lunch tucked into a brown paper Jack's Fresh Market bag, and we jumped in her car for the return trip. My new friend, Patty, waved as we pulled out of the driveway and headed back to Highway 2.

"How did it go?" asked Amy as we drove past the whirring windmills casting their long shadows across the little town of Garden.

"She wasn't the Patty I expected."

"You were disappointed."

"I think I may have just fallen in love."

Later that afternoon, as I left St. Ignace and headed up the Mackinac Bridge incline cars slowed, then stopped behind a jackknifed trailer. Sailboats were racing across the straits linking Lake Michigan with Lake Huron as I helped myself to Amy's bag lunch, tuna on rye with a pickle. After popping open a fizzy can of Vernors and taking a swig I spotted a blue envelope with my name on it. Inside was a message.

"Roger, please give this note to your publisher when you get back to Muskegon. Hope it helps. Don't forget to send me an autographed copy."

The note turned out to be the highly-sought 'blurb' that my publisher had wished for. I read it for the first time on the cover proof he emailed over:

"Rapoport has written the book I wanted to write, but never could. He's right, my story is crazier than fact–only his wonderful fiction can do it justice. It's the perfect answer to all the questions."

–Patricia Campbell Hearst

Searching for Patty Hearst

Roger D Rapoport

JARNDYCE, ZENSOR & BUCHVERBOT

Attorneys at Law

April 1, 2023

Mr. Roger D Rapoport
2439 Brentwood St.
Muskegon, Michigan 49441
By Certified Letter and Federal Express

Dear Mr. Rapoport,

Our office is writing to you regarding the forthcoming publication of the book *Searching for Patty Hearst* on behalf of our client Mr. Steven Weed.

For quite some time Mr. Weed has voluntarily assisted you on the completion of this work. Despite his courteous requests you have refused to correct numerous factual errors or delete invented quotations attributed to him. You have also fabricated many events that never took place. Your attempt to disguise your personal attack on his reputation as fiction does not absolve you or your publisher Lexographic Press from the legal consequences of publishing this book. Our review of the chapters you have sent him for comment makes it clear that he now has no alternative other than to file for an injunction that will halt printing of this book and require the destruction of all copies of this manuscript. If you and your publisher proceed as planned this injunction will force all wholesalers and bookstores to destroy all copies of this book in their possession. In addition anyone who has actually purchased your book, including libraries, will be required to return all copies.

As you know Mr. Weed is a reasonable man and, as an act of good faith, he is willing to allow you to store two copies of the manuscript in the vault at our offices in Century City, Los Angeles, which you are welcome to inspect by appointment during weekday business hours excluding national holidays. After your passing your literary executor will enjoy the same privileges.

I am sure that on reflection you will find this a fair settlement of this matter, one that will spare you the enormous financial consequences of publishing this book and keep your reputation intact. Unless we hear from you by the close of business this Friday we will be forced to file for this injunction in court. I sincerely hope this won't be necessary.

Very Truly Yours,

Thomas Jarndyce Esq

Jarndyce, Zensor & Buchverbot
1437 Avenue of the Stars
Los Angeles, California 90067
Truth Social: @TJarndyce

lexographic press

May 4th, 2023

Dear Mr. Jarndyce,

Thanks for your thoughtful note.

Delighted to know that your client loved Roger Rapoport's novel. Can't wait to meet both of you in court when it is on the bestseller list.

In the meantime can we discuss visiting rights for the manuscript? I'm surely entitled to, at least, monthly visits. As a publisher I take the welfare of our texts very seriously.

My intern asks whether the book was permitted a phone call?

Sincerely,

James Sparling
Publisher
Hyde Park, Chicago
thread: @Lexopress

ACKNOWLEDGMENTS

I want to thank my wife and children for their many helpful suggestions. Every step of the way they have offered insights that helped me tell this story. I also appreciate the candor of so many people who helped me create this book. Their memories and generously shared documents were critical to my research. I also want to thank the many writers who have covered this story. Their articles, books and documentaries provided invaluable perspective. My editors at the *Oakland Tribune* generously gave me the time to interview Bill Harris for a three part series on the kidnapping. Harry Harris, still the reigning oracle of Oakland journalism, is a treasure and an inspiration. Thanks also to Henry Massie, whose final read was invaluable and to Yetta Goodman and Mary Bisbee Beek.

Writing this story has been a long journey spanning nearly half a century. Fortunately many key subjects who turned me down again and again finally decided to set the record straight for future generations. I will always be grateful to them for their courage and honesty.

Finally, I would like to thank my publisher, an unfailing champion of this project.

During the many years I worked on this legendary case close friends asked me why I kept coming back to it after my original book on Patty Hearst was canceled. Every time I considered letting go I received a letter, a call, an email, a text or a message that opened yet another opportunity. For me this has been the journey of a lifetime. I have made many new friends along the way. If you have additional insights to share please contact me at roger@pattyhearst.com and I will send you my confidential unlisted phone number. This website, pattyhearst.com, is also a great resource for journalists covering the 50th anniversary as well as scholars and students eager to fully understand the Hearst case.

I would be happy to arrange an interview at the undisclosed location of your choice. Until then, please support your local bookstore where I hope to meet every one of you on my upcoming author tour. For dates and locations visit pattyhearst.com/events

Roger D Rapoport, Muskegon, Michigan, May 4, 2023

About the author
Roger D. Rapoport is an award-winning author, filmmaker, and playwright. His work has appeared in *The Wall Street Journal, Wired, The Atlantic, Esquire, the Los Angeles Times, the San Francisco Chronicle*, and many other outlets. His films have shown at film festivals around the world. You can find out more about Roger and his work at rogerrapport.com

Also published by Lexographic Press
Angle of Attack: Air France 447 and the Future of Aviation Safety
Grounded: How to Solve the Aviation Crisis

Other books by Roger Rapoport
Is The Library Burning? (with Laurence J. Kirshbaum)
The Great American Bomb Machine
The Superdoctors
The California Catalog (with Margot Lind)
The Big Player (with Ken Uston)
California Dreaming: The Political Odyssey of Pat and Jerry Brown
Into the Sunlight: Life After the Iron Curtain
Hillsdale: Greek Tragedy in the American Heartland
Saving our Schools: The Case for Public Education (with Patrick Shannon, Ken and Yetta Goodman)
Citizen Moore: The Life and Times of an American Iconoclast
Crash Rio Paris

Travel Books
San Francisco 1990: A Bantam Travel Guide
I Should Have Stayed Home (series, seven books, editor)
Two to Twenty Two Days in California
Two to Twenty Two Days in the Rockies
Twenty Two Days in Asia (with Burl Willes)
Twenty Two Days Around the World (with Burl Willes)
Great Cities of Eastern Europe (editor)
The Getaway Guide to California
Walking Easy in the San Francisco Bay Area (with Wendy Logsdon)
Muskegon 365

Children's Books
The Wolf (with Paul Kratter)
The Rattler (with Paul Kratter)